CONFESSIONS OF
A GOOD ARAB

CONFESSIONS OF A GOOD ARAB

A NOVEL

YORAM KANIUK

Translated by Dalya Bilu

GEORGE BRAZILLER *New York*

Published in the United States in 1988 by George Braziller, Inc.

First published in Great Britain in 1987 by Peter Halban, Ltd.
Original Hebrew edition published in 1985 under the title
Aravi Tov

For information address the publisher:
George Braziller, Inc.
60 Madison Avenue
New York, NY 10010

Library of Congress Cataloging-in-Publication Data
Kaniuk, Yoram.
Confessions of a good Arab.
Translation of Aravi tov.
I. Title.
PJ5054.K326A8913   1988   892.4'36   88-16697
ISBN 0-8076-1210-3

AUG 1 9 1988

This translation has been made possible in part
by the Wheatland Foundation of New York.

Printed in the United States of America
First printing.

CONFESSIONS OF
A GOOD ARAB

Foreword

My name is not the name which appears on this book. I live in Paris, under a false name, haunted by longings for my country, perhaps my countries, which are one. Genealogical trees on both sides left me with the autumn leaves of Europe with which to cover my nakedness. In what follows I may be trying to pay a tax I owe myself, and a value added tax which those who want to settle accounts with me apparently think I owe them.

I am speaking of a tax of grief, not one of repentance, since I can hardly be blamed for being born who I am. I am an insignificant, if not accidental, victim; but in my room I live alone, and my mirror is not a reflection of objective principles. Perhaps what I'm really trying to talk about is a tax of love.

What follows was supposed to be a confession, a partial autobiography. After reading and rereading it I realised that if I sent it off it was liable to hurt people that I love. I rewrote my confession, I changed names and places (Hava, for example, was not the heroine of Koloniya), dates, personal histories, even a complex system of relationships in order to conceal the truth in such a way that the truth which I wanted to state would be accurate (but at the same time, and to the same extent, fictitious).

In the act of rewriting, for better or for worse, I wrote a story. A story was the last thing in the world I wanted to write, I wanted to weep and gnash my teeth, but what came out was a story. Accordingly, I shall be judged not only by what happened, but by the way in which I describe what happened. Which is a pity. The political message of this story too is simply a by-product of the truth I tried to set down, not desirable perhaps, but apparently necessary.

Many of those I loved are dead. Franz, my grandfather on the side of my mother Hava, used to say, you have to be close to God to be a little Job. Next to the soles of my shoes I search for the fear of God, his translators and interpreters have made him so cruel.

If they finally catch up with me and somebody decides, in spite of everything, to settle accounts with me, I'll laugh. I've come to the end of my tears, and of my fears too. I'm still in hiding not because I'm afraid of getting caught, but because I'm still trying to find an answer to the riddle of my life. If it wasn't my own neck I was putting into the noose and if it didn't hurt so much, this might have been quite a funny book, about as funny as the joke about the fastest runner in a ward of double amputees.

The only language I can write this book in is Hebrew, but the anger is bi-lingual. When I translate myself into myself I have to shoot at the mirror before it can shoot at me.

Yosef Sherara

1

After three years at art school in Jerusalem I decided to go back to Tel Aviv. Jerusalem suffocated me and the history which split me down the middle right after the city was united devoured me. The room in the old Yemenite quarter where I lived and where my mother Hava had lived too found me in the mornings wondering where I had lost myself when I lay down to sleep the night before. I wanted to paint the desert, draw up borders, maybe to rest. Dina, my girlfriend since the age of fifteen, had shown me the door long before. I followed her around, I hired a private eye who sent me reports on every poor fool who went up to her room to find the tears with which she had put an end to our love. I tormented her, I went to Acre to pick quarrels with Azouri, but mostly I sat around in my grandfather Franz's house and frightened Gertrude. My grandmother Käthe had been dead for years, and Gertrude who came to help out during her last days had stayed on to cook. After fifty years of stupor during which she had married, given birth to three fat daughters, and buried a husband whose name she couldn't remember, she fell passionately in love with the seventy-year-old scarecrow who was Franz and decided to crown herself his queen. I got in her way and she retaliated by boasting about the greatness of her sons-in-law – one of them was the greatest insect collector in the Haifa bay and also recited Shakespeare in ancient German at the local chess club, the second played the cymbals, and the third, a little Yemenite who reached his fat wife's navel, served tea to the clerks in City

3

Hall and in the summer worked as a lifeguard and blew his whistle until the waves went back where they came from, while his wife lay under an umbrella covered in sand, and once a dog had come and peed on her. Gertrude kept asking me why I didn't stay in Jerusalem, and I told her that the sacred stones and the sacred shit were waiting for her, not me.

After I went back to Tel Aviv my main occupation was getting up in the morning to wait for the night. Without Dina there wasn't any point in anything. I stood on the promenade at dusk and watched the perverts contemplating the women racing their pedigree dogs on the beach with sad indifference. One of them was selling holes to crawl into by the square metre. I was looking for someone to finance me to paint the desert red and that's how I arrived at Cafe Kassit. I didn't find any artists there, but I did find people sitting and staring at the street, and I sensed that they got up in the morning to do the same thing I was doing. Once I bought a galabiyeh and put it on and walked up and down the street telling people that my name was Messiah Ben David Rosenzweig. Rosenzweig was my mother's name and Messiah Ben David was the name of an actor I had once liked. During our daily telephone conversations Dina told me that I was making a fool of myself and she cried her purple tears. I told her that I would call myself Sherara, which was the name of Azouri's uncle, and she said, call yourself what you like. I was annoyed by the open options she was giving me. She said, calm down and then you can come back to me and I'll give you children. I cried because that was what I had dreamt of when we were younger and read poetry together and drank arak.

As I approached Kassit I started up my asthmatic cough which wasn't anything special but which had worked to my advantage before. The wind swept old newspapers and dry leaves along the pavement. I put a newspaper on my head and felt the rain falling on me, before it started falling on the others.

4

A few guys and a couple of girls sitting at one of the tables stared up at me. They looked as if they were looking because they didn't have anything better to do. One of them, with half-closed eyes and a balding head asked, Is it raining on you? I said, I'm the weather forecast. He didn't laugh, it was too much trouble for him to move his mouth. He said, you must be really screwed up, and I said, I'm looking for love, and he said, sit, you've found it.

I sat down and nobody said anything. After about half an hour the lights went on exactly opposite us, in the place where I thought Azouri was standing. I called the waiter and ordered a bottle of champagne for the whole table. Hezkel, the owner of the cafe, bowed to me over his huge belly, emerged for a moment from his normal state of slumber, and asked me, with a certain ostentation and perhaps with a tang of nostalgia for the days when people used to drink champagne in Kassit, if I wanted French champagne. I said yes. I allowed him to uncork the bottle and we all drank champagne out of tea glasses. I said that my name was Yosef, and they accepted it as if it were a suitable name for the occasion and there was no need for them to introduce themselves in return. I liked their attitude. The ritual anonymity enabled me to get into the picture and after an hour or so the rain which had fallen on me before began to come down on everyone and they looked at each other and one of them said, Yosef brought the rain to Kassit. I said, I didn't bring it. My time isn't your time.

One of the girls who was sitting with us, suddenly got up and went over to the counter. She sat on the cafe owner's sleeping knee and dialled a number on the phone. In his sleep he took a saucepan and put it at her feet. She began to cry and her tears fell into the saucepan. She replaced the receiver without saying a single word, stood up, and returned to the table. She said, the sonofabitch's wife answered me, she said I could go fuck myself. Rammy, the best-looking boy at the table, said gently,

5

don't worry Hedva. I liked the way he said it.

I wanted to paint the desert red, stick up a microphone in the middle of the desert and broadcast messages to the history in whose name everybody was speaking. I wanted to divide between the yellow-white desert and my red one, to build a new purple line, or green line, or red one. The whole country was chewing God then and they all had the answers in their mouths. I entered the Kassit crowd without anyone asking for my identity card. They accepted everyone and hated everything out of boredom. I phoned Dina and told her I had found friends after my own heart. Dina laughed sadly and said, sure! I said to her, I'm sitting here and bathing my eyes with dames. Their hatred's basic, Dina, each of them comes from a different loneliness, this isn't the generation that went to kindergarten and the boy scouts together. I got into a routine, every day from five to eight I sat there with them, hated with them, drank with them, and even had something to eat.

I asked them if they had seen a man drive past in a white Volvo which looked as if it had just come out of the laundry, park it, and stand opposite Kassit. They said no, and the minute they finished saying it Azouri appeared in his spotless white Volvo, drove slowly past the cafe and then stood opposite us in the doorway of a shop.

He stood there in his Mao shirt and elegant jacket and looked at me through his gold-rimmed spectacles. It was raining. He stood waiting in the rain. Perhaps they wanted to ask me who he was but they didn't waste their breath on words. They were so bored they seemed to have been born tired. Hedva asked if he always played classical music on the radio of his car and I said that's how he pulls the wool over everybody's eyes. Rammy was the first to react. I remember how he sipped the champagne the first time I came, slowly, with an interested expression on his face, looking at me out of the corner of his eyes. He was the only one who wanted to understand who I

6

was. In view of his tall slender good looks I realized that he was likely to bring a catastrophe down on my head, maybe because I had cast him in the role of an enemy from the word go. Hedva told me that he had woken up in the morning with a girl in his bed and hated himself. He doesn't even know her name, she said, and he's looking for love. I suppose it was then that the plan started taking shape in my mind. With bitterness she said, Rammy once fell in love with a prostitute because he was sick of fucking women without remembering their names. I knew that I had to bring him and Dina together.

And then the girl with the flower in her hair walked into Kassit, read the menu for an hour and ordered a glass of water, which she drank without hands. We all watched her and I said, she's got a mole on her back and that's the way she eats ice-cream too. In the steamy window I could see Azouri standing on the other side of Dizengoff Street. Rammy looked annoyed. He stood up and walked over to the girl and said something to her. She turned her head and looked at us with obscure hostility and Rammy came back and said with an almost spiteful satisfaction, she says she hasn't got a mole on her back and she doesn't know you from Adam. Nissan with the half-closed eyes said, when you were standing over there Yosef said that you had God on your back. I confessed I had indeed said that Rammy had God on his back, but this did nothing to soften him, he was waiting for an explanation. Nissan said, you're such a sweet liar Yosef, I could eat you up.

Two days later they were all on their way back to Kassit after taking in an afternoon show at the Paris cinema and they saw me standing at the counter of an ice-cream parlour with the same girl. I was holding her on a string and she was eating ice-cream without hands. When they came closer I showed them the mole on her back. After I dropped the blouse I had pulled up for their benefit they stared at me and they looked nervous. I shouted at her, Yallah! bugger off, and she started walking away backwards, with a terror on her face which she couldn't translate into words because the ice-cream was stuck in her mouth. Rammy ran after her and I started walking towards Kassit. I ordered a beer and when Rammy arrived and sat down, furious, Nissan pointed to me and said, he's for real, people, it's no trick. He's some kind of freak. Rammy growled into his fruit juice, she threw away the ice-cream and pretended to be a ballet dancer. Hedva said, perhaps she drinks water because she's in training. Poor Rammy whispered, she's only a human being, so she lied to me, so what, but how could you treat her like that? Hedva who was getting up to go and say nothing into the telephone while Hezkel put a bowl on the floor to catch her tears said, so what? Don't men torture me? I thought, I don't even remember where I met her and what I did with her, but it was clearer to me than ever that I needed to bring Rammy and Dina together. Afterwards, when I took her home, Hedva told me that Rammy's mother had jumped out of a window and killed herself in front of him, and then his father took his girlfriend and went away to America. Rammy had something to run away from and somewhere to run, looking for unhappy girls with flowers in their hair. Now he started on Azouri, he needed him to pick a fight with me. I knew that he was the only one there who gave a damn about me. He said, what the hell does he want? Why don't you look at him? And how did you know that she had a mole on her back? What's your story anyway? I said, man has infinite powers of endurance, and Rammy spilt what was left of his fruit juice onto his lap. Nissan finally managed to move his mouth enough to laugh and I said, let's forget the whole thing, I live in linear time, there's no past or future, time is like space, but I knew that I wasn't explaining properly.

Rammy was the sweetest guy I ever met. I already knew exactly how much suffering I was going to cause him. I wanted to warn him, just like Azouri wanted to warn me not to spend all my time hanging around in Kassit. I said to him, you're looking for love in the wrong places, Rammy, you were almost in love with that girl with the flower in her hair, until she started twirling like a ballerina. Rammy didn't understand my fear of Azouri. I knew I would never be able to tell him about the ancient blood fighting a desperate battle inside me. I wanted Dina to tell him about my two histories which both told the story of the same events from an opposite point of view, the events of which I was the victim. Neither the intelligence agencies nor the terrorist organisations really understood me. It wasn't in order to impress Rammy that I had known the girl with the flower in her hair in another dimension of time. And later on, after it was all over and the reporters came sniffing around Kassit, and everyone said that I had brought the rain to Kassit in order to make a big impression, Rammy, luckily for me, said nothing.

No, I couldn't go into all kinds of explanations. All I wanted was to belong, to insert myself in the gaps between their lonelinesses, to find a refuge in their tired rituals. I couldn't tell them about Franz or Azouri or Gertrude, I didn't want to have to answer their questions. My old longing to be Rammy awoke again, he was my idol long before I met him. Rammy, the hero of all Israeli storybooks, with the open, intelligent look on his face, the pain and the strength in his eyes. After I told Dina about the girl with the flower in her hair she said, how could you, Yosef, how could you behave like that! When she sat there and heard about Azouri and how I turned my back on him, she cried. She knew me only too well, she remembered all the insults, the time I fucked her uniform. She knew the anger that was in me and how much I needed to betray in order to be able to respect myself. She knew how much I would have given to be born Rammy.

She knew how I tormented Azouri when I stayed with him in Acre or met him at Franz's place, how I said to him, why don't you take your degrees off the walls and hang them on the sword your uncle inherited from Salah Addin, Azouri? You're playing a Jewish game Azouri! He was trying to get tenure at the university and I couldn't stand the humiliation of it – an Arab scholar, an international expert on the history of the Arab-Israeli conflict begging for tenure while civilised professors with glorious pasts in the struggle for human rights sat around arguing with him about seniority. They weren't interested in seniority. They saw an Arab and they couldn't swallow the fact that he was as learned as they were. But Azouri wasn't moved by anger or indignation. He was calm and deliberate. They have to suspect every Arab and they've got good reasons for doing so, he said. How well I knew that look, as cold as steel, when all the doors are shut in your face, when you're not Yosef Rosenzweig any more, but Yosef Sherara. I said to him, who asked you to be my father anyway? Why did you have to go and marry a lousy Jewess? How could I explain that to Rammy, or Hedva?

I remember what happened years ago, when I was living with Dina, trying to be Rammy. I went to Acre and sat opposite Azouri. We could see the sea through the window. The mulberry tree pushed its branches through the iron bars. The intoxicating scent of orange blossom was in the air and a ship was making its way across the bay to Haifa port. The Carmel hung in the window frame like a painting. I yelled at Azouri, you sat on the road to Jerusalem in the village of Koloniya, a Jewish armoured truck drove past, it had to slow down to take the curve and Hava was a sitting duck, you sat there at your ease and shot at her with your sub-machinegun. She was fair, you like them blond don't you? In the end Azouri cried. Azouri's got the biggest tears I've ever seen. When my mother Hava met him she was astonished at the size of his tears. I said to him then, you're sly like all the Arabs, acting like a moderate but out to get your pound of flesh, no matter what it costs.

10

Azouri cried and then he said in a gentle voice, wet with the tears that had gotten into his mouth, I.. Hava..how.. and I could see the blood bursting out of his forehead. He said, why do you always have to blame people Yosef, you've got no compassion, no love. You didn't get your extremism from me, or from Hava. I said to him, Azouri, I got it from the air, from the land that you're sitting on with its plundered olive trees and its longings for Salah Addin. I gave birth to myself, take your Arab hands off me! You mother murderer... and then he slapped me. We both cried. Because of his great love for my mother he couldn't answer my accusations. We wept into the night and drank vodka and afterwards coffee in tiny cups.

How far from Acre I am today. Paris is a beautiful city but not for me. The Luxembourg Gardens are in bloom, but for me the flowers are always dead. What wouldn't I give now to be sitting in Kassit and picking a fight with Rammy...

2

After I escaped from Israel I received a message: Rammy wanted to see me and I quote, 'anywhere you say in Europe.' He cared. Nissan and all the others had already sung their hearts out to the reporters who came sniffing around Kassit and they all said they knew from the beginning who I was and where I would end up. Hedva said to some reporter, how could he end up? All that anger, that impotence, the humiliation, the insults, the tough looks every time he had to show his identity card. Everyone in Kassit was suddenly an expert on Yosef, and only Rammy held his tongue. They came to him, they worked on him, but he didn't fall into their trap. Rammy of all people, after everything I had done to him. He didn't say anything about Azouri, and he didn't boast about his friendship with the man who had brought the rain to Kassit.

The humiliation of Rammy began when I phoned Dina and told her she had to come and meet the friends I had told her about. She spoke as always with utter mistrust. I knew she was going to come so I hired a car and drove to the Negev. I was looking for the right place to paint the desert red. After contemplating the desert spread out before me in all its savage splendour I stopped at a roadside bar. There were some giggling Danish girls there and a woman with a cross around her neck enthusing about Massada. I gave them the once-over and I knew which one I was going to end up with. This was the count-down and I had to sound convincing when I began to punish Dina and Rammy. I knew how Dina would walk into

12

Kassit and how she would order whisky and send it back to establish her status and ask Marcel for whisky without rocks and without any water in it either. I knew that the poet Goldman, who didn't even remember himself the last time anyone had read any of his poems, would say to Marcel, this young lady knows something about drinking, she's not playing games. Dina had power, she knew how to make an impression. She had already had poems published in magazines and she was beginning to get a reputation, she already had admirers and enemies and now she was making her first appearance on the cafe scene. None of them had ever seen her before. Rammy of course said that I was sure to come, I was probably just a little late, but Dina smiled at him and said, Yosef's never late, if he told me to come it means he's not coming himself! The moment Dina's lips touched the glass Rammy fell in love with her. Up to now everything was going according to plan.

She was my great love. At the age of seventeen she aborted the only child I was capable of having. Franz and Käthe's great-grandson was born dead, under local anaesthetic. I waited for her at the doctor's office and I took her home. Her mother said, Dina you look ill, and she said, it's nothing Mother, and lay down to rest.

She sipped the neat whisky exactly as I had expected her to and asked if Azouri ever came to Dizengoff Street. They asked, who's Azouri? and she said, a handsome man with gold-rimmed spectacles wearing a Mao shirt and an expensive jacket who drives a white Volvo. Hedva asked, the one who plays classical music on his radio? And Rammy said bitterly, yes, he used to come every day but he hasn't shown up for the last two days. Nissan said, Yosef always turned his back on him. Suddenly they began to take an interest, the general boredom was interrupted, Dina impressed them with her powerful female presence, her wide eyes, her flowing hair, her sharp face, the bitter-sweetness at the corners of her mouth. I

13

never knew whether Dina was beautiful or so perfectly and uniquely ugly that her contrasting colours, her soft, slender body and abundant hair, that suspicious smile of hers, the deep blue of her eyes, the violet shadows around them – all these things made men feel like children in her presence. Rammy said, who is this Azouri? And she burst into tears. She was crying because she was so sorry for Azouri. In her opinion Azouri was the most attractive man she had ever seen. She was always looking for the resemblance between us and the apple always fell too far from the tree. Rammy told me afterwards that what got him right from the start were her lips, her frightened eyes, the strength and mobility of her slowly moving hands, the soft huskiness of her voice. She and I would fight about our dead son. But the baby was a girl, she would say, as if she was a liberated woman and I were a primitive peasant. Her judgement of herself and her poetry was absolute. She never waited for praise or blame. She knew exactly what she was worth. Rammy couldn't grasp how much of a woman she had been already at the age of fifteen. I sit now in Paris and remember our walks, our picnics, the nights we spent in Azouri's house in Acre, the day we sailed on the bay and she took off her blouse in the soft rain and I painted her sweet breasts and the paper got wet and she took it from me and ate it. I said to her, you're the first girl in the world to eat her own tits and she said to me then, all that Arabs can think about is Jewish tits. And I remember how we were going home one night in the bus and there was a police inspection and they looked at my papers and took me away for questioning. She was mad and she wanted to get off the bus with me, but the policeman ordered her to stay on the bus. She yelled at him and one of the passengers cursed her in Yiddish and said, What's wrong, he's an Arab isn't he? Maybe you know exactly what he's got in his pockets? You want to die? They took me to the police station in Wadi Arra and this policeman hit me accidentally on purpose

14

and kicked me in the back and turned me around and punched me in the belly, all in this calm, almost casual way, and then he asked me, his lips were tight with fury but his voice was almost tender, maybe he was jealous, what I was doing with a Jewish girl. I said my name is Yosef Rosenzweig, and that's what's written on my identity card, and he said, yes I know, but both of us know the truth don't we? After that I went to the Ministry of the Interior and changed my name to Yosef Sherara, I had two identity cards and whenever I was eaten up with pain I would take the Arab one. Late that night Dina came to my room in Franz's house. I refused to open the door and she shouted in the passage and Franz came and opened the door. Dina came into my room and asked me to forgive her as if she had committed a crime, and suddenly I was sorry for her, for her love. Later Franz came in with a very sad expression on his face and said what's going on here, how can a policeman behave like that? He couldn't believe that anyone would humiliate his grandson so cruelly for nothing.

The first time they met in Kassit Rammy told her about his mother. That broke even Hedva up. Rammy didn't usually talk about himself. He was tough with the sadness of someone who has seen his mother smashed up on the pavement. Suddenly he felt that he had to tell her. They all began to talk freely, but Dina didn't give me away, she didn't tell them anything in spite of the curiosity they suddenly showed about me, but Rammy, who was completely bowled over by Dina, suddenly decided that he had to know who I really was, what my story was – he didn't understand that all he really wanted was to meet me on the most dangerous possible ground, our common love for Dina.

After a few hours of this Dina and Rammy got up and started walking in the direction of her flat on Nordau Street. Naturally, Dina, who had consumed several glasses of whisky, was feeling relaxed. She really wanted to be close to a good-looking

15

boy like Rammy. But she also thought that I was following them and she began to play the careless whore for my benefit. Rammy was hurt and he said, don't act like that, we're getting married. She grew serious, gave him an angry glare, with the bitterness of ten years of despairing love, and said, listen Rammy, nobody marries me, don't ever say that again. He was alarmed and said nothing. From the balcony of her flat they could see the park. Rammy could see the old woman across the road who sat on her balcony at night all dressed in black, hanging shrouds on the railings and listening to Verdi's Requiem. In the park below, young couples were looking for places to hide from the lamps, not all of which were broken. Dina brought a tray with olives and salted cheese, tomatoes, rolls and butter, onions and sardines. Because she thought I was waiting in the park below she put the last movement of Beethoven's Ninth on the gramophone and when she looked at Rammy and realized that she was going to go to bed with him she waited for me to phone her like a little girl who knows that she has to do her homework and nothing will save her.

My call came at the right moment, the old lady had already gone inside and closed the shutter, Rammy was as close as he could get to Dina. I asked her if she had enjoyed herself in Kassit and if Rammy was sitting close to her and she said yes, twice. I told her that I was with a religious Danish girl in a youth hostel next to a lousy bar in the desert and that she fucked without moving, and that she had the most transparent skin in the world, so transparent you could see Denmark through it. She said, have a good night and I said, I'm waiting downstairs, and she screamed, you're waiting inside my guts, and slammed the phone down. I wanted to ask her if she knew how unreligious Danes fucked because my Dane kept getting up to pray, but she didn't give me a chance. Rammy asked her who it was on the phone and she told him.

The next day I told Rammy everything that had happened

16

the night before. I told him that he was sick with the cancer of love. He said, she told me that you two were through. Rammy was really a noble character. He wanted to let me know that he had taken the trouble to find out that she was free before he went to bed with her. I told him, she won't be mine but she won't be anyone else's either. And poor Rammy knew exactly what I was talking about. He was in love but all the time I was there, sitting at the bottom of the bed. He asked Dina why she had told me and she said, look, he may have left here for good but I cried for a week when he left and there wasn't even a gap between the tears and he's still my only love, you can go to bed with me as much as you like, he'll always be there. After that she asked him why he told me and Rammy claimed that I got things out of him against his will and she laughed and said, look, I know him, it makes no difference if you tell him or not, he'll know anyway. I made trouble between them, I would phone Dina and tell her everything that Rammy had said and then I would phone Rammy and tell him that I had everything that went on between him and Dina at night written down, word for word. The more I humiliated him the greater his love grew. Dina said to him, it's because loving is against God, with me it is anyway, and going to bed with you – and you're a sweet guy and a great lover – is against Yosef, and he asked her, why does love have to be against someone and not for someone, and she laughed. He wanted her to love him a little and she was sorry for him. He couldn't stand her pity but he didn't have a choice. She was playing her own game on her own turf. And the game was fixed and Rammy knew it.

Dina was jealous even of the Dane whose name I couldn't remember. Her jealousy was the most absolute thing about her. Jealousy made her more attractive and Rammy began prowling around the house, looking for me in the park, trying to spot my private eye. Dina knew that I was spying on her but she wouldn't let me into the house. She wanted to save herself and she said, if you come back I'll go mad. You're not my boyfriend Yossie any more, you're Yosef Rosenzweig Sherara who wants to suck my blood. I'm not to blame for the divine love of Hava and Azouri, I'm not to blame that it fucked you up, I'm not to blame that Hava came to Käthe and told her she was pregnant with Azouri and Käthe went out of her mind and began to burn herself. All I am is a little girl who writes poems and wants to live because my mother was in Theresienstadt and came to Israel in an illegal immigrants' ship and met my father who managed somehow to get here before her, and now they're waiting for me to compensate them for all their agony. And what did I bring them? I brought them you, and you decided that you had to explain to them, every day, what it meant to be the Jew of the Jews, and how you were humiliated in the Jewish state, and after you left they would cry, they didn't know what to say, they felt for you, they were sorry, but they were full of an obscure dread, you're the *goy* they dream about in their nightmares Yosef, they didn't come here for you, they came here so that I would marry someone like Rammy, and you're not Rammy, you wanted to be Rammy once but who are you now? You've chosen to be the son of Azouri instead of the son of Hava....

Dina said to Rammy, listen little boy, I love him, and Rammy said to her, I'm patient, I can wait, you'll love me one day. When the Agencies found out about my 'freakishness' I blamed Rammy, but I knew myself that it wasn't Rammy who talked. I said to him, you'll be to blame if I don't have anyone left to hate in the end. And that sweet bastard smiled and grabbed me by the shoulders and hugged me. The secret I shared with Dina had already bound the three of us together. In order to make progress with Dina he would come to Franz's place in the afternoons, meet Gertrude's fat daughters who kept on buying themselves new dresses, look at the paintings, at the furniture that Käthe had brought from Berlin and listen to me explaining Dina's weak points to him. Why he agreed to this is beyond me, but Dina said that I don't understand anything about love because I think that love is a form of conquest. I said to her in my theatrical way, I'm not a lousy Zionist you know, and she said to me, Rammy at least knows why we're living in this lousy country and I prefer it that way because of my parents and what they went through, and I yelled at her over the phone, my mother Hava would have been fuel in Auschwitz or a lampshade if Azouri hadn't saved her and brought Franz and Käthe to Palestine, and Dina said, you're completely twisted Yosef.

No, it wasn't Rammy who told the Agencies about me, it wasn't Rammy who told them that I could see into the future. It must have been Nissan, who apparently worked for them, and who came to sit in Kassit for the sake of his soul, after or before beating up Arabs in the villages of the *triangle* – and my beloved Dina wasn't completely free of blame either, but I know that she didn't do it on purpose, even though I enjoyed pretending that she did, because I wasn't about to pass up an opportunity for blaming her for everything. I said to her, why don't you just shoot me like Azouri shot Hava, and she said, Yosef, you know that Azouri didn't shoot anyone. And she screamed at me too, you're an Arab in your guts, and then she came crawling and begged me to forgive her for what she had said. What actually happened was that two months after I began sitting in Kassit, in the middle of winter, a winter of terrible rains that year, they came to search Dina's flat because I had once lived there. She came home and found the Agencies going over her flat and she began to shout. One of them, who wasn't too bright, said, be careful who you go to bed with. She took the pot plant Azouri had given her for her birthday and hurled it at his head. But Bunim, the man I was later to work for, stepped in. He removed the tactless fellow from the scene, smiled at Dina with revolting fatherliness, and said, don't take any notice of him.

Bunim was old and tired, worn out with wars and troubles. He was a smooth talker and he liked using words like missive` instead of letter and quoting poetry and the Bible, after or before kicking Arabs in the pants or burning agents. He took advantage of the fact that he had been the captain of the ship that brought Dina's mother to Palestine and said, Just like your mother, a tigress. I remember your mother standing on the deck, thin as a stick, not trusting anyone. And Dina, who in any case had a hole in her heart because of the long and exhausting relationship with me, and who loved her parents who were simple people and only wanted one thing in life and that was a Jewish son-in-law and Jewish grandchildren after everything they had been through, fell for this corny line. Bunim knew how to tackle her, she wasn't an easy customer but he knew how to get what he wanted out of her. She said, yes it's true, he has this extra-temporal sense, and he's also torn enough to help you, he always wanted to be a good little boy and at school he wrote Zionist essays that made me want to throw up. Bunim stopped searching the flat and sat down and listened to her saying all the things he had already read in his reports from Nissan, and he knew that I would fall into his trap.

The day I was told to present myself at the Agencies Dina went to Kassit to sit with my friends. She knew exactly where I was, Bunim had taken the trouble to let her know. Dina was proud but she wasn't conceited. She knew she had lost this round, and she asked herself if there had been an element of revenge in the things she had said to Bunim. She wondered if deep in her heart she believed that even I, her lover and Hava's son, was still an Arab who under all his skins wanted to kill her. She was nervous and jumpy. Rammy's love was beginning to make her restless. She said to the people sitting there, When I come here he doesn't come, but you're all his prisoners as much as I am. They wanted to see Dina, whose reputation as a poet was beginning to rise with dizzying speed on the literary stock exchange, as Rammy's girl. Rammy was their blue-eyed boy. The obscure affair between Dina and myself was something dark which they didn't want to recognise, even though they sensed its existence, it was the movie they didn't want to pay to see. Rammy was one of them and I was an outsider, they could feel my strangeness without knowing exactly what it was. Nissan probably knew more, but he knew how to keep his mouth shut too, or else he was just too tired to open it. And then Dina took out her knife and cut. She told them they were playing a cynical game, that every one of them had given me a loan without getting it back, and what's more they all knew they would never get their money back and they said nothing. So why did you keep quiet, she said, why didn't you say anything? If Rammy or Nissan had owed all of you money, wouldn't you have talked about it? Wouldn't you have discussed it out loud? They were taken aback. They all remembered the money I had taken from them. And they also remembered that after I had visited them all kinds of little things had disappeared, at Nissan's it was a key holder, all kinds of trivial trinkets and souvenirs, but especially war mementoes. And she, hating herself for saying it, said it aloud, And what about the petty thefts? He steals war souvenirs from you, doesn't he? It was Dina who said 'war souvenirs', putting her finger on the totem that united all those suckers into one camp on the other side of the moon from me. She was upset and nervous and sad, in her mind's eye she saw me sitting opposite Bunim and she was sorry for herself instead of being sorry for me. She looked at Rammy and Rammy looked at her, he loved her with every one of the eyelashes he fluttered at her. The shell of self-righteous tolerance cracked. They became talkative, she told me afterwards with a smile, information about loans and thefts flowed freely. Dina knew how to work on their black consciences. Look what he's doing to Rammy! Rammy buried his face in his hands, they felt insulted for him, and they looked at her in

21

astonishment. She was no longer a poetess playing bored games with a bunch of professional cynics, she threw all her cards down on the table. They felt uncomfortable, all their suspicions came to a head. Nissan said through half-shut eyes, we all know what's behind it, don't we?

Dina told me afterwards that at that moment exactly Goldman the poet began to recite the menu aloud to his ex-wife in a hasidic chant and Hezkel joined in in his sleep, and she was already regretting what she had done, she felt like a traitor, but I didn't believe her. She raised her glass of whisky and said, let's change the subject, your silence is only the other side of his stealing. She didn't explain, she said, let's drink to Yosef, laughing because she couldn't find the right tears for that moment, which she said was like spitting at something sacred. And all those shmucks, the only friends I ever had, except for that time in Haifa when I hung around with Arab intellectuals and lived with Laila and Kassem, all those shmucks raised their glasses, one of them a beer, Hedva her grapefruit juice, Nissan his whisky, and they said, to Yosef! and thought with repulsive glee about my little thefts, they wanted to understand why they hadn't spoken about them out loud but most of all they were happy that I had been caught red-handed. And Dina added, to the little thief, to my little prince, and Rammy grew sad and said, he's not a thief, Dina, you know he's not a thief. His gentle rebuke caught her by the throat, unguarded by the armour I had been forcing her to wear since the age of fifteen. Her glass was arrested midway between the table and her mouth. She fixed him with her haunted eyes that had a thousand years of sadness imprisoned in them, and to me she said afterwards that what she suddenly thought of was an elegant old Pole kissing the hand of a prostitute in Yarkon Street, not that she had ever seen any elegant old Poles kissing the hands of prostitutes in Yarkon Street, but Dina was always fishing images out of realities she never knew in order to annex

22

territories she had never been in and queen it over them. Rammy saw her sad eyes and thought, she's counting my mother's blood on the pavement. They all became poets to the sound of the poet Goldman singing the menu to the woman who had once been his wife and whom he continued to feed every day at six o'clock in Kassit. Nissan said, what are you trying to do, Dina? Circumcise a Coca-Cola bottle?

The state of her soul was up for sale but there were no buyers. Rammy couldn't find the right currency. She looked at Rammy and she almost betrayed me, she almost fell into his arms but he didn't seize the moment, he didn't understand that she was ripe for the plucking. His delicacy, his gentleness, his strength, his conscience made him a thousand times more beautiful and he wasn't ugly even without them. Rammy was a very attractive man, perhaps the most attractive around, but he wasn't quick enough, he didn't grasp the changes in the mood of his capricious queen quickly enough. Instead of pushing his advantage he suddenly turned into a philosopher and said, poor Yosef, he probably has to steal from himself and we just happen to be around, and these words destroyed the moment for her. Dina hated that kind of explanation, she drank her whisky and she forgot the moment when she had almost fallen into the hungry hole in her heart. She too suddenly saw Rammy in the light that I had always seen him in: the good-looking, kind-hearted Israeli, an officer in the commandoes, an outstanding soldier, protesting against every injustice but always doing what he was told in the end, searching his soul while he shot from the hip. How often I've thought about these killers with their pure souls, how many times in my life I've wanted to be Rammy, even on the other side, Azouri's side, when I was in Haifa trying to be their Arab, I wanted to be an Arab Rammy, a Rammy toeing the line with a rebellious expression on his face, defending the motherland and suffering pangs of conscience, loving his enemies but killing them with the most sophisticated means available, believing in a dream which no one had translated correctly for him. Rammy could be the way he was because people loved him, because they wanted him to be Rammy, they cherished and nourished the Rammy in him. When I wanted to be Rammy they brought proof to show me why I wasn't. My revenge was Dina. Rammy would never be able to stop her from being mine.

Rammy didn't understand why she kept changing her mind, first wanting to see him and then not wanting to see him. Tormenting him and then kissing him. Saying in a moment of tenderness that she loved him and later denying it, asking in surprise, so what if I said so? I'm not responsible for everything I say in the middle of a fuck. Rammy, who didn't see everything in black and white like most of them, remained facing Dina with blood on his lips. One days she said to them, Yosef fights alone, without friends, he's not like you, he's always alone, you're all heroes like Rammy with comrades-in-arms and group spirit and a mother who washes and irons your uniforms for wars and for demonstrations against wars, and hundreds of people to tell you how cute you are. Yosef hasn't got anybody to tell him how cute he is. He's got no backing. The opposite side of his war is himself. Nissan understood what she was talking about but Hedva thought immediately about herself and her lover and his wife and started crying. Nissan said, he's fighting on both sides of the barricades. And Dina looked at Nissan. She didn't want to give me away yet or Nissan either. She said, the true battlefield is in the heart, Nissan, and besides, you'd better remember that everyone here has got something to hide, we've all got our dark sides and Hedva isn't the only one with a side that says nothing into the telephone. Nissan was frightened, he didn't want his bohemian cover blown. Dina said angrily, in this country everyone thinks he's got a monopoly on justice, God makes them all into saints and the land takes them to its bosom and spits blood. The war is hopeless because nobody knows how to win it, and nobody wants to lose honourably. Nissan lost control and said, the only thing that's stopping us from winning is all kinds of defeatists, smooth talkers and professional bleeding hearts. There is a solution, all you have to do is stop thinking in terms of justice and start thinking in terms of necessity. Dina smiled at him. We all know those speeches off by heart already, Nissan, she said, and we're not impressed. Besides, I've got your number and one day I'll hang it on a tree opposite Kassit for everyone to see. Rammy said angrily to Nissan, you're mad, you're a war maniac, you see Arabs on sticks as if they were lollipops, you don't even understand what's at stake in the war that Dina's talking about. Nissan smiled with his half-shut eyes and said, ask Yosef, he knows exactly what I'm talking about, Dina only provides the subtitles to the movie.

3

Bunim sat facing me in the room to which a sullen-faced woman had brought me. He contemplated me with a kindly expression on his face but beyond it I could sense the dry, tired anger flowing straight from his soul, the deliberate, fanatical anger of a weary soldier. It wasn't the fact that I was an Arab that bothered him. He was too intelligent to divide the world into good and bad. It was the fact that I was Franz's grandson that got his goat. Because of the humiliation which this caused him he wanted me to bring the rain a lot further than to Kassit. On the wall was a photograph of a young boy in a frame that wasn't exactly black but more of a dull steely grey, as if it were not grief which had moved Bunim to place it there but a grim desire to force everyone to their knees before this charming and pathetic figure. Later I learnt from Dina that it was a picture of his only son. My history was catalogued in a thick file which lay in front of him. He asked me the year of Franz and Käthe's arrival in the country. I told him the year and the month. He smiled with his mouth but not with his eyes. Afterwards he told Dina that when they had arrived in the country he had been the commander of Haifa port responsible for defending it against attack from the direction of Acre. Acre was a code word for Azouri. What he really wanted Dina to tell me was that he had already had Azouri in the sights of his gun then. I understood him. I too knew how to beat Azouri with that stick. Bunim's hostility towards me was so profound that I had never experienced anything like it, even on the faces of the

26

policemen and soldiers who have searched me on buses or broken into my house when I was living in Haifa. They were only doing their jobs, but he really had his heart in it. He killed and crushed people out of principles which were so full of words like *justice* and *morality* that you could smell God sitting between the lines furrowing his face. If Azouri had had a real God, a God of his own, I would have called on him to help me, but Azouri was a poor excuse for an Arab, as I lost no opportunity of telling him. When Hava and Azouri went to France to bring me up far away from the 'tragedy', it was Azouri who was homesick for Israel, not Hava.

For Bunim the real, deep treachery was that I was Franz's grandson. If I had been an ordinary Arab he would have had no problems fitting me in between his morality and a bullet from his gun. A year ago when I decided to escape from the country and I went to Dina to ask her to help me she stared at me with a glazed look in her eyes and I saw her squirm, rebelling against me, against Bunim, for me, for Bunim. For a moment she didn't know which side to help, which justice had the greater claim on her. I know that look. I took pity on her and escaped without her help. She was glad enough to accept my excuse that I didn't want to get her into trouble, but perhaps if she had seen the look on her face when I came like a hunted man to ask for her help she wouldn't have let herself off the hook so easily.

The truth is that I really could paint. Not important paintings, but I could paint. Only, something always stopped me, whenever I achieved something I had to smash it, run amok, look for something to take revenge on. The restlessness that led me in the end to Bunim was like a conditioned reflex, and when Bunim looked for the roots of the offence I caused him by the mere fact of my Jewish blood, he knew exactly what he was looking for. Dina understood, but none of the others could have known that Azouri and Hava didn't meet at Abu Cristo's in Acre by chance, and Azouri could have been my father even

27

before he met Hava, my mother on Franz's side. He could have been my mother's father, because Azouri and my grandfather Franz began their story in the year that Bunim was born.

The story of Franz, Käthe and Azouri began in the year 1917, two years after Franz, a young man of twenty-two, after three years at medical school in Göttingen, had decided to abandon his studies and enlist in the Kaiser's army. He not only enlisted, he became an officer and fought so bravely that he was awarded the Iron Cross. All this was quite unusual for a Jewish boy in those days, but Franz's sister had already converted to Christianity, at home they celebrated Hanukkah with a Hanukkah lamp in the shape of a Christmas tree, nobody opened any doors in their house for the Prophet Elijah, and the Bible seemed dry as dust to the young Franz, who was tall, fair, polite and reserved. His grades at medical school were so high that his teachers predicted a great future for him even before he graduated, and when his grandfather tried to drag him to the synagogue on the Day of Atonement he looked at him with polite indifference and wondered what he was doing in their family. Franz's sister celebrated his enlistment, his father was unconcerned, perhaps a little sad, his mother was upset, but Franz felt that he owed it to his country, he had always had a sense of order, honour and duty. After the war, when the defeat became known, Franz's sister Hilda killed herself, and the day he came home he was welcomed by a dead sister and alien funeral rites. Hilda committed suicide for his sake too, to mitigate the disgrace, to make the defeat his defeat too, not only the German nation's, and dilute it with real blood, blood flowing from the depths of the history she hated with all her heart. His father wasn't unduly disturbed by his daughter's hostility to his forefathers. He was a German, a small businessman, a member of the Mosaic faith, who wasn't too enthusiastic about being a Jew. In fact, he wasn't particularly enthusiastic about anything. He was his wife's husband and his

28

children's father and he wanted no more than to be the connecting link which would lead them from the decaying old world into which he had unwillingly been born to a different world, free, clear and new. He refused to give his children a sense of belonging to anything except their immediate surroundings. Franz was thus born without a real past. He borrowed what he could from others. He was intelligent enough to realise that he was a Jew but he never attached any importance to this fact except as a handicap of sorts which might, in certain circumstances, even be used to his advantage. Because he was a lieutenant in the army who had been decorated on the Western Front and also taught cannon ranging for a time according to a method which he had developed himself and with which he had achieved impressive results, he was considered a brilliant young man and his officers too forgot that he wasn't exactly the normal type of Junker that they were used to. For them he was as much of a Prussian as they were, because in war men became what they were intended to be by God, not by hysterical women – in the words of the drunken captain who sent Franz with a group of German officers to Palestine to help the Turks.

He arrived in Palestine in 1917, was unmoved by the charms of the mysterious East, and tried to defend himself against the fierce Turkish officers who kissed him savagely and bit his lips in their enthusiasm. They would sit on balconies greedily devouring charred meat while barefoot musicians tied to ropes played below, and threw them pieces of bread which they swallowed as they played. Everything seemed strange and hostile to him, the Turks weren't interested in hearing about his method of cannon ranging, they wanted to fight and win with cruel heroism. German girls from the Germany colony of Wilhelma arrived at the Fast hotel in Jerusalem where Franz was billeted. Their parents sent them with barrels of wine and Franz's friends danced with the German girls who were

29

looking for husbands with their mouths open in fixed smiles because their mothers had told them not to stop smiling. But Franz did not want to dance with the buxom girls with their dreamy eyes and bovine faces, he was beginning to feel a kind of loneliness whose nature he did not understand and his ties to his friends weakened, except for one Turkish officer who had studied in Vienna before the war and who was fond of saying, this Orient stinks like a rotten egg. They walked along the walls of the ancient Kings of Israel and Franz, who in his despair had begun to search for the glories of the past, found a country eaten up by decay, built like a badly planned ruin, people dressed in rags, hunger and death, typhus and whippings, trees chopped down to fuel the trains to transport the barefoot soldiers and cannons which did not require any ranging. Horses carried soldiers with orders to places that did not exist on the map, and Franz felt that he had landed up in another century in which he found no grace or beauty. The Jews he met looked like scarecrows planted in a foreign soil. They spoke broken German and tried to cling to him but he felt no closeness to them. They spoke passionately of a future whose nature he did not understand, rode on horses or sat wretchedly in front of empty shops, and like a pack of hungry dogs they fell on the stones of the Western Wall and chewed them. Franz searched for some kind of beauty to cling to. His Turkish friend took him to visit wealthy Arabs whose large houses were at least richly carpeted and where good food was eaten. Men dressed in dark suits discussed the future of the world with a solemnity which was rather pompous but not lacking in discrimination. The wealth and luxury in these homes made Franz feel sad, he asked himself what he had in common with these people and he began to think about his grandfather and his prophet Elijah, perhaps he would find the enormous beard of the prophet spread over the Carmel where he was buried, perhaps it would provide him with some sort of answer to the emptiness he felt inside him. He was tired of pursuing military distinctions, all he wanted to do was to rest until it was all over, go home and finish his medical studies and begin work as a doctor.

He arrived in Haifa, which was then a little village on the slopes of the Carmel mountain, in order to build a second line of defences, or perhaps to bring greetings to the Prophet Elijah from his grandfather, about whom he only now, in the light of his revulsion from both the Arabs and the Jews, began to think rationally, a quality he was accustomed to attributing to himself with a certain sense of satisfaction, if not arrogance. His grandfather began to acquire the right proportions in his mind: a man who had brought with him to his father's Berlin the thousand years he had spent with his forefathers in the East, preserving something which could on no account have come from here. Franz remained indifferent to Palestine (until he came there again as a refugee) due to the fact that although he knew little of Jewish history he realised that the rupture between what had happened here two thousand years ago and what was happening to his grandfather in Berlin today was too deep and final to be healed. All that was left of the glorious kings of Israel and Judea were Arabs dreaming of Greater Syria, manufacturing silkworms from silk and going to Damascus to buy their curtains, people capable of producing nothing but a wilderness. In the total desolation and decay he saw all around him lay the answer to the lack of all practical initiative and the idle dreams. Franz was alarmed by the dreams of the Jews he met. His grandfather, he thought, would never have dreamt such dreams. His grandfather was praying to a city that was finished, a Jerusalem of ruins and the Fast Hotel. The Jewish melancholia of Palestine was full of a despair which he was neither able nor willing to understand. And thus he arrived at the Carmel in the footsteps of a group of nuns in black habits singing a song full of sorrow and

31

compassion as they walked over the rocks with lighted candles in their hands, and he came to the cave of the Prophet Elijah where aged Jews with wild beards welcomed him like a long-lost son. Franz stood there feeling somewhat embarrassed, searching for the memory of his grandfather, thinking, my grandfather lights candles and opens the door on Passover night for a ghost enshrined in this dark hole and preserved by these pathetic and repulsive old men, and he fled to the enchanting garden he had seen on his way up the mountain. It was an enormous garden spreading from the middle reaches of the Carmel to the sea below. Franz had never seen such an exquisite garden. The trees were planted in circles within squares, the garden looked like an enchanted arabesque, dexterously weaving circles into squares with marvellous precision and noble grace. The labyrinthine gravel paths, the candles burning there, the variegated blooms captured his heart. He stood at the gate and saw through a luxuriant growth of foliage and creepers a great house embellished with arches and domes.

He entered the great iron gate and met abu-al-Misk ibn Kafur Sherara, who was sitting in an inner courtyard with Franz's Turkish friend who said, allow me to present Rosenzweig Franz, and Kafur nodded his head. He was wearing a silk suit and holding a sword which he claimed had once belonged to Salah Addin, and he was surrounded by a number of elegant ladies smelling of perfume and drinking the blood of the vine out of tall goblets. They looked at Franz in the dusky light and afterwards they laid romantic traps for him from which he fled. Abu-al-Misk Kafur was looking for allies in his future war for Greater Syria and he therefore supported Turkey, while not forgetting to send out signals to the Germans and offer them assistance when required, for which he was handsomely rewarded. Franz, who could see the Turkish officers in their filthy underpants going in and out of the rooms leading off the vast courtyard, was captivated by the beauty of the place and he began to speak about cannons and the second front which might be opened, centred on the Carmel. But no one was seriously interested in a second front, they all thought that they could still win on the first, horses came galloping up the mountain, and Franz drank cold grapejuice and ate roast chicken served by a giant Sudanese eunuch who wore a white kaftan and looked like an extra in a German opera. He spoke to Kafur who never got up from his chair and who was the fattest man he had ever seen in his life. He touched the sword on his knees as if the fabled heroes of the ancient Orient would soon ride again and the victory of the Ummayads were at hand.

Haifa was a very small town in those days, almost a village. A few eccentrics lived on the Carmel in turreted mansions and waited, each in his own corner, for a different Messiah. The gardener who had planted the magical garden came from the German Colony which abutted Wadi Nisnas, where Arabs lived side by side with a few Jews. On the other side of the bay lay Acre. On a clear night you could see Tyre. The gardener, who spoke only to the trees and refused to answer the questions of human beings, had designed the garden in such a manner that three times a day the scents of hundreds of trees and flowers merged in a symphony of many-coloured smells. In the labyrinthine garden with its neatly pruned trees Franz saw a silver path winding down to the sea. The beach was fenced and there were a number of hexagonal structures made of painted reeds standing on it, cutting Kafur's sea off from the shore curving towards the bay. The orchestrated garden looked like a fragrant arabesque to Franz as he parted from his Turkish friend and began to walk down the silver path to the sea, feeling the beard of his grandfather's prophet slipping through his fingers. He thought of the cruel, bored faces of the women in the inner court, about the beauty hidden here by the fat man whose dreams of the return of the Ummayad and

Abbasid caliphs did not, apparently, contradict the crosses stuck up on the fence and the cross suspended between the folds of fat hanging from his neck. Kafur spoke angrily about the cunning Jews buying up every hectare of land, and Franz did not reply. Abu-al-Misk Kafur was named after a tenth century Ethiopian, a diseased slave who ruled the land and lived in Acre, searching for the caliphs of Ummya and Abbas among the rocks of the countryside which was less desolate then that it was now. He made the earth quake for six months in order to defeat his enemies and to punish the rebellious Egyptians he stopped the waters of the Nile from overflowing their banks for a whole year and brought famine to the land. Franz descended the path with the fragments of legends buzzing about in his head. Between the prophet Elijah and the Ethiopian Kafur he preferred his strict teacher of anatomy who spoke with cold contempt of German romanticism and said to him before he left for Palestine, don't come back bewitched by the magic of the Orient, everything there is dead, finished off in the great night which came down like a curtain over Asia for a thousand years. Franz had despaired of the Turks, he no longer cared about the fate of the second front. If they wanted to defend the Carmel it was up to them, if not he had done what he could.

Dina likes this part of the story. She says, you bear an ancient seed in your blood, Yosef. Perhaps she gets so excited about the ancient seed because she's a poetess. Franz says it's all nonsense, all those stories about the blood flowing in our veins is one big lie. Azouri says, you have nothing but what you can prove. My uncle Kafur was a miserable dreamer who lost everything because no dream can ever bring about a reality which will equal it. That's the trouble with the Zionists too. I think about Azouri and about Kafur as I sit opposite Bunim. Bunim wants me to operate against Azouri's brothers. This is his sweet revenge. He loathes me so much that if I fail they'll write *burnt* across my file and find a dirty way of selling me to their enemies. If I'm hanged in some Arab country for what will be called 'crimes against the Arab nation' Bunim will tell the reporters 'off the record' that a 'so-called agent' was hanged, and add that no such agent ever existed. Arabs are the favourite material of the Agencies, their hatred is a drug that keeps them going. The whole question of blood makes me wonder, what do I really bear in my blood, and who the hell cares anyway? And nevertheless I know that everything that has happened to me in my life was determined by Franz's descent to the seashore that day in abu-al-Misk Kafur's house. I say to Dina, blood or no blood I know that I existed long before I came into this world. In order to be born who I am I had to programme myself, lay my plans in another dimension of time and space so that Hava and Azouri could finally bring the catastrophe down on my head. And that's why Franz was already full of some aspect of my future being on his way down to the sea. And Dina notes down words which will later become part of an elegy for a betrayed artist.

At the bottom of the path, next to the sea, Franz met Azouri. Azouri was then a boy of thirteen. He was writing in the wet sand. Franz approached him. The sight of the boy so weakened him that he sat down on the sand and got wet the uniform which had previously made an impression on the women of the house with their cruel and murmerous desires. In the darkening light of the late afternoon the grey eyes of Kafur's brother's son shone like rare precious stones. Hundreds of years of ancient chivalry and glory married the beauty of the cold northern lakes which the crusaders had brought with them nine hundred years before to the blazing yellow desert in the eyes and face of Azouri, my father who according to Dina is so much better-looking than I am.

35

4

It was a rare moment of oblivion. Franz looked at the boy who was tall for his age, dressed in a suit and tie, saw him scratching in the sand and froze. Something which had been hidden inside Franz all his life suddenly flowered and opened up wide in astonishment to the boy who was Azouri. At that moment, dazzled by the beauty of the boy, Franz could, if only the boy had been a young woman, have fallen in love, married, had children, and died. A whole lifetime flew past in a second. Azouri explained that he was calculating the exact time of the sunset according to the moment at which the sunrays touched the crests of the trees above. A woman looked black against the glaring white of the sand. The sea shimmered. A fishing boat materialized in the dazzling light as if it had emerged from the sea and carved the moment into a junction of marble and blindness, turning it into a work of art which Franz and Azouri would never be able to recreate. They sat and wrote equations in the sand, and Franz marvelled at the speed with which the boy grasped their precise and abstract magic. Azouri looked at Franz's uniform, at his handsome face, his blue eyes and his short cropped hair, and he saw him as the polar opposite of the violent men with their big moustaches who surrounded him and wanted to make him into the jewel in their crown. All Kafur's women lusted after the boy and Kafur would laugh in his chair and say, he's mine, not yours, he belongs to the kingdom and the glory, not to a bunch of women. They swallowed his insults in silence. Kafur fed people because he

36

wanted to see them fawn. He was a shrewd, intelligent man and he didn't trust anyone. He was so sly and so suspicious that he didn't even trust himself. The colours of the rapidly sinking sun seemed to Franz and Azouri like a brilliantly painted trap into which they were about to disappear. Franz took out his watch and peeped. The boy was right. Azouri's calculations were amazingly accurate. The moment the sun began to sink the garden, for the third time that day, began to exude its symphony of intoxicating scents. What happened between Franz and Azouri? Dina says to me, admit that it was love. Yes, I say, but what kind of love? I know that it was only through Käthe, whom Franz met six years later, that the love the man and the boy felt for each other in that painful, golden sunset hour was consummated. Why painful? Did they embrace? In a rare moment of confession Franz once told me that he sat there, looking at the boy and surrendered, according to him, to the most wonderful feeling he had ever had in his life, as if he were seeing himself give birth to his own father. How could a boy like Azouri make you think he was your father? I asked him, and he said, he bewitched me, as if the word *bewitched* were more than just a word. Azouri said that Franz looked at him and he looked at Franz and they both knew in the terrible closeness they felt for each other that two pieces of an ancient coin had suddenly been welded, but there was no market where it could still be used to buy anything. Perhaps you could have sold it to a coin collector, I said but he said, no, not to a coin collector either.

What remains is therefore my own irrational theory, I was there, in potential. I had to be born in order to spoil the stereotypes that made things so simple for Bunim and Nissan, and also to understand them with the part of me that comes under the stereotype of 'holocaust survivor'. Not that Franz was actually a holocaust survivor, he got out before it happened, but his humiliation when they expelled him from the hospital, the Judaism they forced on him in the shape of the yellow star, were enough to make him into a refugee. I needed that meeting to be born, I said to Dina, so that I could come into the world and hurt all of you. I wasn't responsible for the defeat of Franz's pure reason as he sat there dazzled by the beauty of the boy, wanting to embráce him and unable to embrace him, I knew that one day Käthe would stand between them as the impassable barrier to their embraces. That's all very picturesque, said Dina, but it's not realistic. In that case, I said to her, how do you account for the fact that I brought the rain to Kassit? And she said, there must be some logical explanation for that which you simply refuse to explain. When it suits you you're a sentimental Arab and when it suits you you're a clever disillusioned Jew. Dina, I said to her, there are a lot of silly sentimental Jews and a lot of shrewd clever Arabs, you yourself are falling into the trap set for you by your parents and your teachers, and perhaps above all by the historical necessity which that Marxist when it suits him, Azouri, talks about; the necessity which you refuse to accept, the history which is the only history you possess. You suffer with me because you're in love with someone you think wants to kill your unborn babies, and she said but Yosef, I got pregnant by you and it was you who made me kill the unborn baby, and I said yes, but you agreed willingly, another mother, pregnant by a different father, wouldn't have agreed so easily, and poor Dina cried.

No, I can't really understand the overpowering effect of Azouri's beauty on Franz, try as I might to bridge the gaps in the minimal amount of information I possess. They sat very close to each other, and then they went back and had supper in the inner court with the women who were already giving Franz looks of loathing and contempt. Kafur was no longer sure that he had a Jew-killer in his hands. Azouri was the first to address Franz as a Jew. He said to him, don't take what my uncle says about the Jews to heart, he's got a big mouth but he'll never shoot at you. Franz was astonished at the word 'you'. The revelation of his Jewishness, which he had never hidden but which he had not admitted either, astounded him coming from the mouth of a young boy who had met very few Jews in his life and who might have been expected to take Franz for what he seemed, a young German officer. But Azouri was never taken in by external appearances. He himself always wears a Mao shirt made of a rough material and over it an expensive jacket. He buys the jackets specially in Paris, so you can see how important it is for him, even today, to keep up appearances. Dina says that Azouri is the most attractive man she's ever met. She says it to get at me and also to explain Hava's love for Azouri as inevitable. He was so handsome that she fell. Dina doesn't understand that Hava, to her dying day, didn't even realise what a good-looking man Azouri was. She was blind to beauty, in her eyes the world was colourless, the thing she loved in Azouri was precisely what startled Franz, his profoundly intelligent grasp of who was what and when, and also his ritualism, the fact that he was capable of standing opposite Kassit for a month without giving up, accepting my denial of him without bearing a grudge. Azouri had a gift for smelling out the truth about things and people. Whether Judaism is a nation, or a religion, or a tradition or a fate, it seems to have a smell. Azouri grew up in the labyrinthine garden of smells which came together three times a day in intoxicating olfactory blows. He said to Franz, I know that you're afraid, but my uncle is a braggart who understands nothing, a big talker who does favours to barbaric Turks and gets presents in return, and one day he'll swell to such a size in that chair of his that he'll burst like a balloon. Franz said, it's rather uncomfortable to be a Jew facing the sword of Salah Addin, and Azouri said, that sword is aimed against the whole world, the poor Jews looking for land here are only first in the firing line because they're so weak. Franz remembered these words later on, when I came and cried to him about the way I was treated when I came up against the law and the mean, cruel Jews, and he said, perhaps Azouri was wrong about those poor Jews, he didn't realise how quickly they would forget what it feels like to be a powerless minority.

I am still trying to capture the moments of falling in love. I would like to describe them in their nakedness. A man meets a boy. A low, sweet murmur escapes from their hearts and turns into a song. The song transfixes them in the garden, offers them up as a sacrifice on the neatly trimmed trees, the intoxicating waves of smell. The women look at Franz like some kind of pervert, they all see the unashamed yearning with which the two of them gaze at each other. Later on Käthe appears bringing balm for the wound which opened up inside them when they realised that their love would never be consummated. And the yearning remained forever unfulfilled. Their love was bodiless, they missed the opportunity for what might have been a simple but a different story, they waited for Käthe to arrive. And so I missed the chance to be the first boy in history to be born to a twenty-year-old man and a thirteen-year-old lad. They were incapable of realising something which was too big for them. I don't understand relations between men any better than Franz and Azouri understood them, but I can imagine that what happened to them was the same as what happened to Dina and me. Our love was so powerful that we had to destroy it. If I had been able to go on seeing her everything would have been fine, but she couldn't let me come to her, she couldn't let anyone else take my place, and so what was left was a sweet and terrible dread, an eternal yearning like the yearning the Jews feel for their Messiah who will never come in the flesh, because he is the essence of expectation.

And then Franz left Haifa. He went to Jaffa, to the Turks.

40

The battle on the Yarkon began. Then he went north. A telegram summoned him back. He rode to Haifa, Azouri was waiting for him. They sat on the beach in silence. They sat there for ten hours side by side saying nothing. The love that was flowing in them suffocated them with its power and they chose to silence it. General Allenby conquered Jerusalem, the great and final battle began. Franz was sunk in gloom. Kafur sat in his chair as usual but there was a look of defeat in his eyes. His Turks fought their lost battle bravely, neighing horses rode up to the huge house with bloodstained soldiers on their backs. They went upstairs to make love to Kafur's women with shouts and cracks of their whips, there was a smell of blood in the air, dying soldiers made their way painfully north. Kafur swallowed more and more roast chickens and slept in his chair at night. The Sudanese servant ran away, blood began flowing from the trees. The day that Franz left Haifa the garden began to disintegrate, rotten cracks, previously hidden, gaped in the house which began to die, and the Jews bought up hectare after hectare of land (and what they didn't buy then they took in '48, says Azouri). Abu-al-Misk Kafur courted the land speculators and made deals with them. His heart filled with a dry hatred, the kind I know on the lips of Bunim, Kafur saw the houses going up on the ruins of his garden and he ground his teeth and hid his gold. Now he was already dreaming of Palestine instead of Greater Syria.

I fell into Bunim's hands so easily because in the meeting between Franz and Azouri a certain attitude was adopted, all their lives withdrawn, frustrated lovers have been trying to prevent me from shooting the imaginary gun bequeathed me by abu-al-Misk Kafur, or perhaps Franz's grandfather who lit candles and opened doors for the prophet Elijah. Bunim knew how much I wanted to be Rammy and how much I was actually the descendant of abu-al-Misk ibn Kafur Sherara. Hava was wounded, it's true, but not by Azouri. However much I wanted to blame him, my aim was never accurate enough. My life was to be the story of the failure of their love, their battles would be fought on my body or in my soul. Bunim who knew this said to me, we know a lot but one thing isn't clear. How on earth did your grandfather, the respectable lung surgeon, come to meet that Arab boy Azouri, who wrote all that dangerous rubbish about the history of the Jews and Arabs in Palestine? I said to Bunim, Azouri is an international expert on the history of the Jewish-Arab conflict, he wrote the truth, which is why both the Jews and the Arabs hate him so much. But however much they hate him they can't shake his reputation. You know it and I know it. How did they meet? I made them meet in an enchanted garden that you destroyed with your own hands, like you destroyed everything that was beautiful in this country, you're afraid of your own shadows, whatever you don't destroy you can't believe exists. Bunim laughed. He said, we made the desert bloom, we drained the swamps in a country rotting with neglect and decay. I said to him, you took a wild desert studded with little sapphires and you built a Warsaw made of cardboard, and afterwards a Berlin made of plywood. Bunim said, what do you mean 'you'? And what are you? I said to him, are you asking me? If I were one of you, you wouldn't have had to recruit me in order to try to destroy me. Bunim smiled a tired smile, I might almost say, a romantic smile, and said, you have too dark a picture of our services, Yosef, and I said to him, try being on the other side of your services for a change, and then come back and talk to me. The connection between Franz and Azouri really got his goat, as if without it everything would have been different. And this was perhaps the source of my strength, since it was also the source of his deepest doubts.

5

I can sit here on a bench in the Luxembourg Gardens with the neat flower beds opposite me and pretend to myself that I'm strolling through the garden of abu-al-Misk Kafur. From the garden I never saw except in ruins I come into the world via my mother Hava's womb. I sit in Uzi's office, one of Bunim's assistants. An ageless woman is sitting there knitting socks for her soldier son in Sinai. For a moment she puts down her knitting and listens to the radio. A doctor called Rafaeli is giving a talk about piles. Outside the sun is shining, a fine winter day. I tell her what I see and she goes to the typewriter and mechanically types things about a mountain range, Kuneitra, snow beginning to fall, a tank stuck in the mud, an unidentified plane trying to locate a column of tanks, next to it a squadron of helicopters manoeuvring themselves right into a cloud sitting on the point of a mountain. At the foot of the mountain a large, well-fenced village, a herd of cattle, an officer wearing a coat with a violent green fur lining putting a group of men through an exercise in crossing fortifications, a tank with a battering apparatus attached to it, perhaps a folding bridge, a truck loaded with missiles, I try to identify the type of missile, the helicopters disappear into the distance, and I see a mobile radar station suddenly advancing towards a small village not far from the big village.

I don't ask any questions but later on Bunim tells me that I described an exercise which took place next to the separation of forces' lines on the Golan Heights. Our agreement was for me to 'see' and report what I saw. And they could do what they liked with what I told them. I didn't tell them about friends and family. If Azouri decides to join George Habash's organisation tomorrow, that's his business. Bunim says, yes, yes, but what if that officer is a relation of Azouri's? He wants to torment me but I don't react. I'm a good Arab, a good Arab speaks when spoken to, I say to Bunim, and the knitting woman laughs. Franz says that I'm the most Jewish Israeli he knows, weaving silken threads of survival, like his grandfather, an expert at the ancient Jewish strategy which is being forgotten over here. Franz says that I possess the sense of irony that the Jews in Palestine have lost. Bunim says I'm a good Arab because I've got a Jewish sense of humour, when something hurts me I know how to laugh with my mouth shut.

I go backwards in time. Between keeping tabs on Rammy and Dina and working for Bunim I burn in the fire of my memories. Looking into the past I find Franz returning from Palestine to the last battles on the eastern front and afterwards going home to Berlin, where his sister Hilda, unable to bear the disgrace of the defeat, has killed herself. In the difficult years after the war Franz completed his studies. His father was lucky and didn't lose much. Franz, who had come home full of bitter thoughts, absorbed himself in his work, he began specialising in lung diseases almost by chance, invented a method of sucking foreign bodies out of the lungs and gained a reputation for himself. The famous Professor Maier made him his assistant, he operated on the rich and on old generals returning from the war with damaged lungs. Sometimes he sat in cafes and looked at the other people, he never went to parties or nightclubs, he had a few friends and there was a woman he saw for a while, his mother was waiting for grandchildren, her daughter lay in a Christian cemetery and her husband, Franz's father, had a stroke and died. At the funeral the cantor sang *El Malei Rachamim* and women his mother had known for years

44

stood looking in astonishment at the bearded, grotesque old Jew. Franz looked into the open grave. A few years before this Walter Rathenau, who had recently been appointed Minister of Foreign Affairs, had remarked that the Jews were an Asiatic tribe on the soil of Prussia. Franz contemplated the Asiatic funeral rites and went away feeling demeaned. He was worried about his mother, who was suffering from cancer, and he took her to have a series of tests. It was impossible to save her, he knew that within two or three years she would be dead. Franz could smell the loneliness lying in wait for him. His father and his sister were dead and now his mother was going to die too. He was appointed resident surgeon at a new hospital which had just been opened in the west of the city. By now he was driving his own car and he rented a new house for his mother which he furnished with ostentatious elegance, as if he were building her tomb. Azouri wrote long and detailed letters and Franz asked him again and again to come and study in Berlin, promising to foot the bill for his tuition because abu-al-Misk Kafur's fortune was beginning to slip through his fingers and what he hadn't hidden away he was afraid to touch. Azouri wrote that there was no longer a private beach, the house had fallen into ruins, he was living with his parents in Acre, his uncle came to visit, he had been obliged to sell his sword to an antique dealer.

Franz's mother begun to hang up pictures of babies on the walls. Franz developed new instruments for drawing liquids from the lungs. He went often to the opera, the streets were full of cripples, inflation was raging but he hardly felt it. His sick mother took care of his needs, things began to settle down, the cafes were full, Franz saw visions of the Carmel and the beautiful boy writing on the wet sand, young actresses slept in his bed at night and in the morning he took them for drives in his car. His mother's impending death caused him pain such as he had never felt before.

Käthe arrived from Hamburg to visit her brother, a wealthy hypochondriac who spoke to her admiringly of Franz, although Franz said that he read too many medical books and was liable to die of a heart attack because of a printing error. Käthe who had been born with cardiac arrest was not afraid of anything. Her closeness to death was absolute, she was always bumping into moving objects, such as cars, horses and carts, and was a frequent patient in the intensive care departments of hospitals, where doctors would save her from death and hope that some of her noble and indifferent beauty would rub off on them. After a month in Berlin old ladies with stiff necks and lined faces began inviting her to garden parties. It was summer and the old ladies, most of whom were widows whose husbands had died of overwork and worries about war and inflation, were planning their grandchildren. Käthe Salomon, a young lady from one of the richest families in Germany, was in great demand.

Franz's mother perceived Käthe's fundamental gloom, her longing for death, at a party given by friends. She took her aside and spoke to her, but nobody thought anything of it. Franz Rosenzweig was not one of Käthe's suitors, he did not spend his nights fluttering from nightclub to nightclub, and none of the women took him into account as a future husband for Käthe Salomon, a family which had been milking the soil of Germany for three hundred years. The words 'milking the soil of Germany' are the words of one of the duennas, who were all very German but belonged to a generation which remembered things the young people had forgotten. Franz's mother took Käthe by the arm and led her to the verandah, where she stood her in the light of the lamp. Käthe said to her, you must be Mrs Rosenzweig, my brother speaks of your son as if he were a poet. Franz's mother smiled. Käthe's looks pleased her, and perhaps also frightened her: Käthe had a noble brow, soft brown eyes, dark gold hair, and her cheeks were so sunken that she looked consumptive, but Franz's mother knew that she was not ill but in the grip of the same dread as her daughter Hilda, who had dreamt of being a nun and could not accept the pain of humiliation and defeat. Käthe said, don't tell me that you too are hunting for a daughter-in-law here? She spoke neither angrily nor contemptuously, but in a calm, matter of fact tone. Franz's mother said honestly, why don't you come and see us? Franz will be glad to meet you, I know this sounds silly, but I think you will find him interesting. He's so lonely, he works so hard, he fought in the war and came back sad and full of nightmares. He possesses the best pair of hands in Berlin and his future is assured. Then she lowered her eyes and said in a voice that was almost a whisper, I don't need the Salomon dowry, we are wealthy people in our own right, neither I nor Franz have any need of your lands, your businesses, your factories and banks, we have plenty of money of our own and we live well, perhaps far more than well. If you were a poor orphan I wouldn't be speaking to you any differently.

Franz's mother invited Käthe to dinner and prepared Franz's favourite dishes, which she imagined from her impression of her that Käthe would like too. Franz was taciturn and drank a little wine, he realised that his mother was trying to marry him off and he understood that she wanted him to provide her with a grandson before she died. As soon as Käthe came into the room he froze, she resembled Azouri so closely that she might have been his sister. He looked into her eyes and pondered the elusive laws of nature when he discovered them to be full of the same haunted mystery which he had seen in the eyes of Azouri, and which I was later to find in the eyes, different in colour but similar in shape, of Dina. During their conversation Franz realised how frightened Käthe was, how ill at ease she was in her body, and he thought of his disembodied love for Azouri. Franz understood that Käthe was playing with death because nothing she had encountered in her life so far, neither the country nannies nor the summer vacations nor the huge paintings hanging in the vast halls of her parents' mansion, portraits of people invented by artists in order to give the family a past it never had, none of these things had given Käthe a reason for living. Her panic touched his heart, his pity for her attached itself to the mirror-image of Azouri which she wore on her face. Miniature galaxies of stars died in her fearful eyes, as they had in the eyes of his sister Hilda. He understood his mother's reasons for bringing Käthe to dinner. The grandchildren would stay in the family.

When I write about Käthe I tremble. She was a woman we all loved. Franz loved her, Azouri loved her, Hava and I loved her, everyone who knew Käthe loved her. She was our dream girl. When Hava came to tell her that she was pregnant, perhaps she was avenging herself on her mother not only for what had happened between her and Azouri, but also for the love we had all given her so abundantly.

The inexplicable bond between Käthe and Franz, a bond which lasted to her dying day, had already come into being by the time dessert was served, a lemon mousse flavoured with curaçao. Franz said little, Käthe looked at the little painting by Paul Klee which Franz had acquired a few weeks before; they sat in the salon and drank coffee served by the giggling maid who had imbibed too much of the curaçao before pouring it into the pudding. Outside the long, silvery northern night descended, the glimmering lamps splashed the trees with a golden light, and Käthe said, if you cut me open with your scalpel you'll find dust. Franz said that he would take her to the opera to see Don Giovanni, and she said, if you have already bought tomorrow you will have to pay for it with the day after too, and he said, the day after tomorrow we will go to visit my sister Hilda's grave. Käthe was not upset, she liked the idea of being introduced to Franz's dead sister. That moment, the moment when Franz spoke the sentence so at odds with his sober and respectable appearance, was the moment when Franz's mother could stand up, say that she was not feeling well, and faint. Franz looked at his mother, caught her in his arms, and said to Käthe, now that my mother feels the future is safe she can begin to die.

Azouri said sadly to me, you understand, she gave herself to him that first night, he fell in love with her because she resembled me. But in the cosmic design she belonged to me and he knew it. He wouldn't have taken her from me. I told Azouri that he was a bastard and he said that I didn't know what he was talking about because I lived in a permissive time which understood nothing about true love, then there were rules of behaviour, there were manners, Franz broke the rules, and I said to him that the one who had broken the rules was Käthe.

In honour of their wedding celebration Franz brought his mother home from hospital. A number of his old comrades-in-arms came to the wedding in uniform and sang songs, in which Franz too joined this time, unlike that former time in the Hotel Fast in Jerusalem. Käthe wore a white dress and the officers, who were already beginning to grow old, saluted her. After a few weeks she began to long for Azouri, about whom Franz would tell her, almost ritualistically, every evening when he came home from the hospital. Sometimes I think that all Franz really wanted was to prepare Käthe for Azouri's arrival in Berlin, and that in order to make sure that their love would be consummated this time, consummated as it had to be consummated, he had to marry her first. Franz sometimes wondered if Hava was really his daughter, or if perhaps she was Azouri's daughter, but deep in his heart he knew that Käthe had never gone to bed with Azouri and that Hava was his daughter. For reasons which are inexplicable to me, Franz would have been a happier and more contented man, and not the little Job who buried all the people he loved most, if Hava had been Azouri's daughter.

Käthe's femininity, Azouri said to me, was a certain kind of death. She was infected by the smell of the war which Franz bore within him, and it may well have been this smell which was the original source of the bond between them. When she spoke of the knife which would reveal dust when he cut her, she saw the staring eyes of the dead which Franz had seen in the war. In bed she would hear Franz groan in his restless, horror-haunted sleep, and then she would smile, not wickedly but for the happiness which wiped out the body which she never once desired. If I were a cynic I would tell Bunim, who never stopped cross-examining me about my personal life, that Käthe went to bed with the blood which was the only side of the one-sided justice he was always saying really interested him. Bunim was the most cynical blood merchant I ever knew, he started out with an idealistic belief in justice and ended up by infecting younger men like Rammy, without their even being aware of it, with an idealistic belief in the necessity of bending justice for the sake of realising an ideal.

In Palestine things had changed. When Azouri arrived in Berlin he no longer came from that enchanted garden from which Franz had set out. The British had enthroned kings in Egypt, Iraq and Transjordan. The Sheriff of Mecca played the game of dividing the East. The French and the English were locked in the trap of their intrigues, and the Arabs were beginning to see the future in different terms. Azouri had completed his studies in Haifa, travelled around the country a bit, visited Beirut where his elder brother was already going to college and studied for a year in Italy before coming to Berlin. If I were Bunim I would say in the word he's so fond of using that the East had sent Azouri to Berlin like a missive. Käthe's longings came to an end when Azouri came into the room. Azouri looked at his mirror-image and fell in love with her on the spot, and Franz looked at Azouri and was glad. Käthe

50

looked at Azouri and said to herself, he will have to love me through someone else, and she laughed to herself because she knew that from the beginning Franz had loved Azouri through her. Franz once said to her, we use the word love too freely, Käthe, Azouri never loved you, he desired you but he loved me.

They were walking then on the beach, it was a late autumn day, there were a few children playing on the sand, and Käthe said, you can be very cruel. Underneath all that polite reserve you're a cruel man, Franz, and he said to her, think about what happened, about all those years when Azouri courted you, touched you in corners, waited for you in the street. You evaded him but you wanted him, he fought me but he spent all day waiting to talk to me about you at night. He studied Judaism to know the enemy. I was a German then and so were you, Azouri waited for you with Jewish patience, he bided his time, he saw in you what I had seen, the exact feminine image of himself. Why were we such fools, why did we let that madness devour us? And Käthe said, perhaps we had no choice, Franz. Your mother wanted me, she held Hava in her arms a few days before she died. We paid the price in full, Franz, I've been ill for years. Azouri has taken our only daughter Hava from us, and who knows what will become of our only grandson Yosef growing up divided against himself? Sometimes I think it was all a mistake but mistakes like that don't just happen, someone has a black sense of humour. I curse the day that you brought Azouri home, Franz.

Franz said, but for Azouri we would never have escaped, but for Azouri we would have landed up in Auschwitz. Käthe said, an Arab had to come to Berlin from Acre for Franz and Käthe to understand that Dr Herzl wasn't the clown my father ridiculed when he got a letter from him asking him to support the idea of a Jewish state. My father laughed all night long, I thought he would have a seizure and die. My father accepted

51

you because he had no choice, when we went to Hamburg he welcomed you as if he were glad to meet his son-in-law, but when we brought Azouri to visit them my mother cried but my father sat with him in his study and found a man after his own heart, perhaps he wanted Azouri more than he wanted you. How easy it is to fall into his net, that grey-eyed Oriental prince who looks like a mediaeval knight trapped by the rays of death. I have nightmares, Franz, I live them, I have devils inside me who were born and died on the day I was born with cardiac arrest, I returned to the death I came from and then I was returned to the life which I never wanted, which was never meant for me. No, Franz, you should never have brought Azouri home.

6

I said to Dina, abstinence smells of perverted sex, and she said, you leave Rammy alone, he's the most decent man I've ever met. I told her I was jealous and she laughed and said, you're not jealous of anyone, the one who's jealous is me.

I'll never forget the night that Rammy came to see me. I was living in Franz's house then, Gertrude had gone to visit her daughter in Kiryat Bialik and Franz was sitting in his room. The tree in the garden had grown, its branches touched the balcony on the third floor of the handsome Bauhaus building which could have done with a new coat of paint. Rammy spoke about Dina and how I was waiting inside her with a knife. He asked me why I didn't leave them alone, why I didn't give them a break. I love her, he said to me, I work hard, I only go to Kassit once or twice a week now, I'm studying at night, I want to build a life for me and Dina, her parents are growing old, bad memories are coming back to haunt them, you're waiting for them in the corners of their souls, they can feel you, they're afraid that as long as you're around Dina will never get over you. Her last book of poems was acclaimed, she was on television, they're proud of her, people are talking about her, writing articles about her. There's a lot of gossip, people ask all kinds of questions, I say nothing, she says nothing, everyone wants to know if we're really a couple or not, and the truth is I don't know myself.

I didn't answer. I'll never give Dina up. She's my anchor in a reality that wants to spew me out. I've got rights too, and that's

53

something that Rammy, for all his conscience and humanity, can't grasp.

Azouri once said to me, Käthe didn't love me, I can tell you that in all honesty. She may have wanted me, my body, what she thought of as the other side of herself, but she never dared. I tormented her, I couldn't help myself. I did well in my studies, Franz helped me, he opened doors for me, and then the same doors slammed shut in his face and he himself was no longer welcome in the homes into which he had introduced me. After the 1929 riots in Palestine people began to see me as an ally in the hatred seething below the surface over which Franz and Käthe walked so blindly. I let off steam in cafes, in bars, I travelled from town to town, I studied for a year in Cologne, I went to visit friends in Paris, I was restless, Käthe disturbed me, Franz disturbed me, I wanted her and she wanted me but she didn't love me. She let me burn with desire for her, Franz would smell my hands on her dresses and choke with love, we were three tormented creatures, lovers, enemies, call it what you like. They were singing the old songs again in the beercellars and I have to admit, it excited me. I was a Marxist, I have made a thorough study of the German communists, but they were too slow, they were spineless idealists – under their very noses a different Germany was growing. The real culture was being celebrated not in the concert halls Franz was so fond of frequenting, but in what I heard in the universities, in the wild all-night parties, in the forests, at the meetings where people brandished ancient spears with a gleam in their eyes that frightened me but at the same time fascinated me. Perhaps I had to revenge myself on them and I didn't know how, I drifted with the stream and I didn't drift with the stream, it was easy to vacillate then, left-wing cabarets existed side by side with all the old words that would later close the doors in Franz's face, I could smell fire but I didn't want to warn them yet. Hava was born and when she was born Franz was busy

54

operating on some foreign Prime Minister, and I stood over Käthe and she showed Hava to me and Franz's mother kissed her. When Hava grew up I would take her on my knees and read Wilhelm Bosch to her and Franz would look at us and think, all the time he would think, whose daughter is she? And Käthe called her Greta, she had two names. Käthe garlanded her fair hair with flowers and dressed her up as a Tyrolean peasant girl, and one day someone took her picture in the street and it appeared on the cover of a magazine with the caption 'The racial purity and beauty of our children which will wipe out the memory of the treachery.' I showed the magazine to Käthe and she laughed, but Franz didn't laugh and he said, we should sue them, and I said to him, you haven't got a chance, Franz. Rathenau had been assassinated long before then, I could feel the thinness of the ice on which Franz and Käthe were skating, the layer of culture of which they and the other Jews like them were the finest jewel. Under that layer of ice the earth was shaking and they never even heard it. They thought that Hitler was a clown. I knew what the young girls I met at parties and in bars thought about him, they were madly in love with him. My party was weak and split, arguing about Trotsky and Plehanov while right next to them a new country was growing up and gathering strength, waiting to redeem itself. Hava was already two years old, then three, and four, a beautiful child who was blind to beauty, clinging to the mother whose lips were still and cold as ice when she kissed her. One day Franz walked into his lecture hall in the medical school and found himself caricatured on the blackboard, impaled on a spit with a lot of pigs surrounding him, and the word *Jude* coming out of the backside of one of the pigs. Who drew this, he asked them and the students stared at him in silent solidarity. He went to fetch the dean who stood there helpless and embarrassed, the children were already marching in the streets with armbands on their sleeves. Franz wanted somebody to tell him who had drawn the picture on the blackboard, he came home in a rage and I said to him, but you know who drew it Franz, and he said, no, I don't. I laughed, yes I laughed, and I said, they all drew it, there's no place for you here any more. And then, as my attempts to seduce Käthe met with the same humiliating failure and I saw her passion and her shame, dreaming perhaps that Franz would die so that she could make love to me once and then die herself, I began to try to influence her to leave the country. I forced her to see what was happening and I made her afraid. You're Jews Käthe, I said to her, and your life here is coming to an end. It was strange to hear me talking then. Even the Zionists were saying that things would probably get bad but it wouldn't be so terrible, there was no need to panic. I said to Käthe, take Greta and go to Palestine, and Franz said, if I go anywhere it will be America, they'll take me there, they need surgeons like me. And it was Käthe, Käthe of all people, who said you'll come with me to Palestine, to the rocks and the ruins, to the Carmel you told me about, only there will we be able to lick our wounds in peace. She had begun to smell the fire. And Franz refused. For two years I argued with him, and Hava stood there and heard the shouts, she saw me trying to embrace her mother, she saw me trying to save two stubborn Jews, and she cried, and one day Käthe burnt her dresses and packed everything up in crates. Franz was fired from his job at the medical school and his students walked behind him in a row and sang obscene songs. He marched like a soldier, like a man, he remembered his youth as a German officer and put on his uniform and went to a rally of his old regiment in a forest. No one spoke to him, they simply didn't see him. They stood round a campfire singing, and then someone who had fought with him said, why are you walking around with an iron cross you bought in a shop and everybody laughed, and someone else shouted, he didn't buy it in a shop, Franz was a good soldier, but nobody took any notice, they threw beer bottles at him and started walking away. Two drunk soldiers he had once watched dancing in the Fast Hotel knocked him to the ground and urinated on him, and he still believed that it would all blow over, he kept on going to the hospital where nobody spoke to him until he was fired from there too, and then I decided to leave Germany and I said to them, I'm going back to Palestine, and I went. I'll never forget that last night. We wanted to huddle together, to cling to each other like children, Franz read poems and we wept and drank wine, Hava fell asleep in the room, everything was already packed because Käthe was already waiting for the fire, and we danced among the boxes and the crates. It was a party, wild and sad, and in the middle of it all the maid came in and announced that she couldn't go on working for them any more because it was against the law. We were like a family, for the first time in years we forgot the tension, we forgot my lust for Käthe and hers for me. The Salomon family laughed over the phone and said, there's nothing to worry about, it will all blow over, and they bought themselves a little more dubious honour with a lot more money. I want to tell you, Yosef, I know very well what it meant to be a Jew then, but I also knew what it felt like to be a friend of the murderers who vandalised the front of Franz's house and burnt his car. I flirted with them and they said, Azouri understands us, he knows what the Jews are like, he's an expert on the Jews, a friend of Haj Amin el Husseini, whose picture was in all the papers then because he too was prepared to burn the Jews at the stake, and he wasn't a German but an aristocratic Arab like me. And who saved Franz and Käthe in the end? An Arab, the nephew of abu-al-Misk ibn Kafur Sherara who had dreamt all his life of an Arab empire under the protection of the Turks and who was already dreaming of a Palestine under the protection of Germany...

Käthe who had spent all her life drifting through a crystal palace in a nightmare learnt to be practical because of the smell of the fire. On that last night, after the dancing was over, she put her hand to her throat and said, I need to feel something and what I feel is death. I don't love you, Azouri. And Franz said, she wants you, and Käthe said, Franz wants you, not me, and Azouri said, we all want each other, Käthe, that's what's so terrible.

Azouri said to me, Käthe was death's dream girl, she played us against one another, we loved each other and what happened to our love? I said to him, you're still waiting for the revolution, for Jewish-Arab brotherhood in the land of Israel, you still believe, against all logic, you're a romantic Azouri, an incurable romantic, but one thing nobody can take away from you, you saved your own worst enemies...And Azouri, who saw the image of my mother Hava in me for a moment, an image which never left him, and whose longings for her were the sweetest thing I ever saw in my life, said to me, Yosef, how did we get into this mess? Why did Hava have to die that way? Why didn't I take Kafur's sword and stick it into my heart as soon as Franz went back to Germany to search for Käthe whose daughter Hava had to destroy her because of all the pain locked up inside her? And I said, you're talking like an Arab, Azouri, sticking swords in your heart and dreaming in technicolour, you haven't learnt a thing, you never left your uncle's Haifa, you're a noble man but you're lost, Azouri.

7

Rammy and Dina together are a Zionist story. A mother lying smashed up on the pavement on the one hand and refugee parents who arrived in the country as illegal immigrants on the other. When Dina asked not to be made a corporal in the army they told her it was out of the question, and she became a corporal. When she ran away from the camp she was punished and the punishment was to stand next to the flag all day long. To Rammy all this was a joke. As I told him more than once he had killed my relations in wars which he called just wars. I detest just wars because the minute you define them as 'just' you necessarily imply that the other side is unjust. But when I wanted to be Rammy and enlist in the army, when everyone thought my name was Yosef Rosenzweig (which was the name on my identity card), I believed in just wars and identified with them totally, so totally that I hated myself. When I went to work for Bunim I was already a professional traitor.

There was a time when in order to heal my wounds I played on both sides of my blood. Käthe's history against Azouri's history. I wanted to find a foothold. I studied the history of the town I didn't dare live in as if through that history I would be able to take part in a just war against Rammy and Nissan and even Franz. The two opposite histories of the Jewish-Arab conflict strengthened my hand against Bunim too, who had no history at all. He said to me, I have no history, Yosef, I make history, and I felt sorry for the man who must have had some reason for killing his roots and becoming an expert in the art of just revenge.

Daher al-Amar, the bedouin sheik of Acre and Ahmad al-Jazzar, the 'Butcher', who succeeded him and lived up to the reputation implied by his name, symbolized Acre for me, as the town from where Alexander Yannai was repulsed, the town the ancient Hebrews never managed to capture, which stood firm against the roots which Franz, who had already begun to search for the past in broken potsherds, spoke of with emotion in rare moments of weakness. I read everything I could lay my hands on about Acre. About crusader Acre defeated after two hundred years when, in the words of the chronicler, 'the Latin Kingdom came to an end and night descended on Asia...' About Jazzar's Acre where nuns cut off their noses to avoid being raped and were cruelly massacred for their pains. About the visitors to the town, who included Maimonides and Rabbi Moses Haim Luzzatto, all the famous generals from Alexander the Great and Julius Caesar to the Great Napoleon who was defeated at the gates of the town which I wanted to conquer or die in. About the streets canopied in silk, the great fortresses crowning the surrounding hills, the port from which the silks and the perfumes set sail for Europe, and the idea of the European universities, in Oxford and Cambridge and Paris, and the idea of the Prussian Kingdom which was conceived by the Teutonic Knights in Acre and Jerusalem. I discovered the memoirs of an Englishwoman who wrote about the sensuality of Acre, and the Venetian glass which originated there. The combination of Daher who married a different woman every week and Jazzar who built an exquisite mosque, cut off heads and noses and threw his slaughtered wives into the sewers, went to my head like a long visit to the perfume market in the Old City of Jerusalem. But then I thought about the history of the Salomon family, the history of the Jews in Germany before it became Germany, and the more I thought about it the more I realised how deep their roots were in the soil from which Käthe was later expelled. And I thought that perhaps I was trying to recreate Kafur's garden, seeking the symphony of smells which Franz and Azouri had told me about in the synthesis I was trying to brew out of my two histories. Unfortunately however the dark side of this brew was already clear to me from an early age, the product and the victim of two histories which were in conflict in the here and now, in a country where my people were always at war against my people, my people against my country, my state against my people. In the last analysis Azouri was born into a history which saw the 1948 war as a British-Jewish bloodbath, and when my mother Hava was wounded in the desperate attempt to save Jerusalem from the British command's Arab Legion, Azouri's brothers were rebelling against the robbing of the land from its rightful owners. What the Jews call the 'disturbances' of 1936 – the year that Franz, Käthe and Hava arrived in Palestine – is referred to by the Arabs as the 'Great Revolt'. When Bunim stood like a shield between the Haifa port and the bullets coming from the other side of the bay as the last Jews of Acre escaped to Haifa, the Arabs of Palestine went on a general strike which was intended to stop Franz from coming here.

In Acre, where my mother and father were later to meet, a great kingdom once came to an end with a magnificent flourish. In 1948 a few Jewish shells put an end to the Turkish rule that had lasted for hundreds of years when the Israel Defence Forces conquered the city which Napoleon had failed to conquer with a single three-inch-mortar. An English princess called Charlotte once sat opposite the bay which Azouri can see from his window, the sea which I can feel coursing through me, trying to counteract the three hundred years of the history of the Salomon family I have written records of, and I'm not talking now about the two thousand years I have no records of except for words about fires and persecutions, but about the

61

three hundred years the Salomon family had behind them in Germany when they marched to Theresienstadt and afterwards to Auschwitz, and they rebuked the soldier who was beating them with the words, you're making a terrible mistake, Hitler must be informed, he would never allow us to be treated like this. It was here in Acre, my father's city, when we were on a school excursion in the tenth grade, that I saw Dina standing next to the breakwater. We were fifteen years old, I stood next to her and told her about Azouri, I told her everything, we held hands, she said in her wonderful husky whisper, why did you wait till now? Evening fell, we saw the sun setting, the sky on fire, behind us were the crowded alleys full of Arabs, and an elegantly dressed man came up to us and said, look, there's Haifa, and laughed as if we didn't know, and looked at the fishes gleaming in the water with a sad expression on his face as if we had robbed him of something which belonged to him. I wanted to say to him, I have a title deed to this place as long as your arm, but he had eyes only for Dina, for her legs paddling in the water, in the sea which her mother had seen on the night she arrived on a little ship under the command of Bunim and was put down in secret on the shore of Nahariya, and she too saw Acre where Daher and Jazzar had ruled and hundreds of nuns had cut off their noses and been raped anyway and the blood ran in the alleys. Dina let me embrace her and perhaps no one has ever embraced her like that again, although she claims that Rammy is a great lover, and ever since then I have been in her body like a cancer and she in mine.

8

They left Germany in 1936. The decisive battle took place against the Salomons. They turned up in a state of hysteria, Käthe's mother's eyes were red with tears and spite, she could hardly control her rage. She said, how do you think you're going to live there? Käthe is not used to a harsh climate, and Franz, for whom Azouri's departure was like a lover's command, said, we've made up our minds. He was adamant and he turned his battle into Käthe's battle, and Käthe's father shouted, you're taking our little girl to a godforsaken wilderness when she's been used to civilization all her life. He paced up and down the room gesticulating with heavy anxiety. Hava stood in a corner of the room and looked at her grandfather who said, for three hundred years that place has been a bloodbath, and what about the Turks! Franz said that there were no Turks left there any more, and he remembered the way they kissed each other on the mouth and bit each others' lips. He missed Azouri, he felt as if he had already parted from the Salomons years before.

After they had gone home with their tails between their legs Käthe said, I've had a lot of wine to drink, I'm feeling gay, I don't know what I'm saying, and this is the chance to tell you what I feel, this is a new beginning. When I was a child I was afraid to look at my body and I didn't even have one to look at, no body was possible, not for me or anyone else. And then you came along. I love your soul, Franz, and I love your eyes, but your haven't got a body. Once when you were sleeping I lifted up the sheet and I looked at you and I wept. I've never loved anyone else. How was Hava born? I let you be the lover of my soul. You reached me through a body that was silent and will always be silent. There was only one man who did have a body, but I never loved him. Now he wants us to leave this place, but we won't go to him.

No one came to say goodbye to them. Their crates accompanied them and were loaded onto the ship in a port overcome by gloom and full of people rushing about in a frenzy which was in sharp contrast to the calm which had suddenly descended on Käthe. Franz said sadly, referring to his friends and his wife's family, perhaps they were right not to come and see us off.

The voyage passed quietly. From time to time they went up to walk on the deck. When Franz and Käthe sailed to Palestine Jews could still take their property with them and they were like wealthy travellers in a world gone mad, in the ballroom people danced the foxtrot. Hava held a teddybear to protect her in her arms. She didn't let go of it for a minute. In Haifa Franz's friend Moshe, who had arrived a few years before them, was waiting to welcome them. He took care of the papers and certificates for them and after a few hours in the port, opposite the Carmel which Käthe refused to look at, Franz stood at the gate and tried to bore a hole into the past, to see the mountain through the hundreds of houses which had been built on it in the meantime. A city had grown up around the little town he remembered. He tried to think of Azouri on that distant twilight but people told him to hurry up and officials asked questions and Käthe sent them all to him and he signed papers. When they left the port they didn't know that Azouri was sitting in his house on the opposite side of the bay, in Acre, writing his articles, pursuing his research, active in Party affairs. From the direction of Acre people were shooting at the traffic on the roads, they were shooting at the port of Haifa and Bunim was

64

defending it. Bunim also made sure that no one would throw stones at them on their way to Tel Aviv. In the evening the Rosenzweigs arrived at the Käthe-Dan hotel on the Tel Aviv sea shore. Käthe went out to the balcony and said, we're bastards aren't we? Running away like that and leaving everyone behind us? Later on Franz remembered these words, but at the moment they sounded false and wrong in Käthe's mouth and he didn't want to pursue the subject with her. Suddenly he missed his mother. He had left her behind together with his father and his sister, and he was no longer certain that the world he had left behind would ever be returned to him. This is how people feel when their ship is sinking, he thought.

Moshe was the secretary of the new symphony orchestra and Franz went to listen to a rehearsal. He came back to the hotel and found Käthe and Hava sitting on the balcony eating ice-cream. He said, they're playing Schubert. It's funny, but I don't remember ever having visited Tel Aviv when I was here all those years ago. What a small, white town it is. Käthe smiled. It was a moment that was detached from everything. Azouri was already out of the picture. Longing for Berlin had not yet taken hold of them. They were living in a seam between the times. In the street the children laughed at Hava because she looked so different in her strange clothes, her pale skin and fair hair. They tried to be friendly, they said, you must have brought stamps, bring us your stamps and we'll swap them for sabras. She didn't know what sabras were, she didn't understand what they were saying. Her mind tried to absorb the words streaming into her head, disjointed syllables stuck there like screams. Her native intelligence warned her not to behave like her mother. She went down to the sea and hard rubber balls hit her. When she swam in the sea they jumped on her but their violence was a form of courtship, and she was a little girl who understood their bodies, their air of vitality, their mischief celebrating itself, and she learned quickly to calculate her moves, to act stuck-up, keep her distance and put them in their places. Perhaps this was a decisive moment in her life. She said, there's something frightening about them, and later on, when she grew up, she knew that these children had aroused her longings for something which they had never had, the past which her parents had given her to pack in her suitcases. Compared to her they were the children of a huge blank. Everything here was coming into being, without a past, and they were celebrating its birth. Hava knew even then that only the cunning of time and the patina of the past were capable of turning their savage shouts into whispers.

After two weeks in the hotel they rented an apartment and paid a contractor to build them a new house on the sea shore, an apartment house in the Bauhaus style. After they had been in the country for a year Käthe's sister arrived with her husband. But they had only come to Palestine because they were given certificates by mistake, they were looking for a way of reaching America. They hid from the sun and waited. Käthe said to herself, how strange that Azouri has been forgotten, that Franz never mentions him. And I too never think of him.

The truth is that Franz made enquiries. He tried to find Azouri but was told that in these troubled times nobody went to Acre and the inhabitants of Acre did not come to Tel Aviv. Franz went to Jaffa. The Arabs thought that he was a German doctor from the Catholic hospital and Franz saw them aiming their guns at the Jews in Yarkon Street. The whole thing looked ridiculous to him, a war that was being fought over a few square metres at the end of which stood a building which he was told was going to be an Opera house.

Hava went to school, she learnt Hebrew quickly. Käthe learnt to say a few words, Franz worked hard at his Hebrew but he spoke it badly and he said, I'm like a child, it's hard to be an old child. He was given a job at the Hadassah hospital, and within a short time he was the chief surgeon in the chest and lung department. The first operation he performed was on a man who had been shot in the lung on the Tel Aviv beach, close to the building of the National Opera. Käthe became pregnant. Who knows, she said, perhaps the air here makes wicked women pregnant, and she went to supervise the final stages of the building of their new house. Moshe took her to a chamber concert in the museum. Franz was respected, but he remained foreign in his aloofness and severity. He was teaching himself to build more than a house. After years of fighting Käthe to give him a son he now felt that he was giving birth to his son in his mother's womb. In other words, with a certain sense of belonging. In order to put down roots he began to dig in the garden. He found potsherds, which he was told might be ancient. He began to search for antiquities and on Saturdays he went to the beach at Apollonia and took Hava with him. He dug in the sand with his hands and found ancient glass vessels, and he wanted with all his heart and soul to feel that he belonged to something ancient and remote, to the place from which his forefathers had been expelled. The idea that he belonged to two thousand years of exile, the exile which Hava was beginning to learn about at school, was still foreign to him.

Although the new country bored and frightened Käthe she learned to keep out of the sun and began to feel a serenity she had never felt before. They moved to their new house and Käthe was already seven months pregnant. She sat on the balcony and looked at the caravans of Arabs passing not far from their house on their way to Jaffa with sacks of gravel loaded on their camels' backs. Women in short trousers came and planted a little garden with a goldfish pond in front of the house. The furniture from their seven rooms in Berlin was squeezed into the four rooms of their apartment in the new house. Hava's friends came and looked with awed expressions at the Klee and the other paintings on the walls, the Lieberman, the delicate drawing by Dürer, the lovely Nolde. And

67

Hava knew how to take their awe and harness it to her schemes for capturing the children from Jaffa who came to spoil the tender new plants in the garden. She sat watching with amusement when they undressed a little Arab and when one of them said, let's roast him on a campfire, she said, yes, burn his nails, and then she was sorry and she knew that she was to blame, first she let them look at the paintings and then she sent them to torture children who looked to her as if they were hungry for love, not that she knew what love was but their eyes spat a strange fire at her. She tried not to think about them and in her dreams a dim memory of Azouri stirred. She asked Franz if he knew where the man who used to read her Wilhelm Bosch was and Franz said angrily, I don't know, he's gone away, but he didn't tell her where he had gone.

The maid Yona did all the shopping, cooked, and looked after Käthe. She complained about the furniture and said that Käthe had brought cobwebs with her from Berlin. The house was like an overcrowded museum, and Yona said, what has all this got to do with me? but she didn't leave, she stayed with them for many years, until she grew old.

Franz bought a little Morris car and drove to Haifa to visit his friend Herman who had also come to Palestine and obtained an appointment in a hospital in Haifa as head of the orthopaedic department. After a long conversation and a walk on the slopes of the Carmel, where the traces of abu-al-Misk Kafur's great house were still visible – decaying remnants, the rubble of a demolished building and a ruined garden whose trees had been chopped down and replaced by new houses spilling down the slope towards the sea – he took his car and drove in the direction of Acre.

Outside Haifa two young men stopped him at an improvised roadblock. He knew that they had pistols in their pockets but they looked innocent enough. They told him not to go to Acre and he said, I'll go wherever I like. They tried to frighten him but he refused to be intimidated because in the last two years in Berlin he had seen what hatred could do, even though he didn't think that he really understood it even now, he had seen them breaking his neighbour's bones, he remembered how he had tried to help her and been pushed aside with contempt, although at that time they didn't even suspect him of being Jewish. Afterwards he had worn the yellow star which Azouri had sat and sewn onto his coat for him. The insult of his students' laughter still reverberated in his head, they had called him a Jewish pig, but they were too busy to take any notice of his irony. He paid no attention to the arrogance of Bunim and his friends who tried to stop him, he saw people bleeding, perhaps in need of a doctor, he didn't think that they would shoot at him, and he drove on.

In Acre his arrival passed unnoticed. No one was expecting a Jewish doctor. He spoke German and asked for Azouri. A little boy hung onto the car and guided him through the winding alleys. The sight he saw then was perhaps the biggest surprise in a lifetime of surprises. In a dim alley, with the sunlight filtering through a long tunnel made by the roofs of the houses which looked like the crenellations of an ancient castle, stood a group of little boys in brown uniforms with a man wearing a brown suit and black boots, a swastika on his armband, putting them through a kind of military drill. They held sticks instead of guns. The man was abu-al-Misk ibn Kafur Sherara. Franz recognised him from a distance. His great stomach had no chair to support it now. There was no Sudanese servant to stand above him and serve him cold drinks. He raised his arm in a salute and twenty barefoot children shouted 'Heil Hitler!' in a funny accent. Franz stood there mesmerised, as if he were watching a violent but utterly ludicrous movie. He didn't want abu-al-Misk to see him, Azouri was nowhere to be seen, the children shouted 'Heil Hitler!' and the alley echoed with their shouts. Abu-al-Misk Kafur looked at them despairingly, they

69

were his last hope of reviving the Caliphate of the Umayyads, the swastika was crooked, not properly sewn on, the uniform was a cheap imitation, the boots were torn, Franz felt sorry for the ludicrous little Fuehrer and slipped into a side alley. A little boy led him up a flight of stairs, a woman in a green dress and veil opened the door halfway and said, Azouri isn't here. She asked him who he was and he replied, I am a priest from the church in Kfar Yassif, and she said, he's at the Party offices. She said the word 'Party' with a kind of disgust and an accusation which included him as well. A priest from Kfar Yassif indeed! She knew all the priests around, her eyes said, and he wasn't one of them. Franz asked when Azouri would be back and she said, I don't know, perhaps he's gone to Tarshiha, and then she gave him a sad stare, perhaps the sight of abu-al-Misk Kafur in the window behind her and the shouts reaching them from the alley aroused her anger, perhaps her love. Go away, she said, I know where you really come from, go quickly, they'll kill you, and she shut the door. Franz thought, what does she know? Who does she think I am? But he went quickly down the stairs and returned to his car. Children began running after him. He drove fast. A British policeman stopped him next to the huge prison which made him think of a monster and asked him what he was doing there. Men dressed in white were cleaning the main street and dropping the rubbish into white baskets. The street was spotlessly clean. The policeman accompanied him in his car all the way to the exit from the town. He said, crazy country, bang bang all day long, in broken, sympathetic German. Franz smiled and drove away. When he came to the road block they took him to a little house on the edge of Kiryat Haim. Bunim sat facing him, a fatter younger Bunim than the one I knew. They tried to make him tell them what he was doing in Acre. He heard the suspicion in their voices, he smelled their fear and he wondered why everything was so full of fear in the place where Azouri had told him he

70

would have nothing to fear any more. He said to them, in Berlin I was afraid, here you make me laugh, I am Franz Rosenzweig, the lung surgeon, I went to look for an old friend, he wasn't home. They stared at him and Bunim said, from now on look for your friends in safer places uncle, and Franz stared at him in surprise, Jews who played with hatred as if it were a tennis ball were something new in his experience. Bunim's eyes were already weary of all the wars he was still to fight, and there was a kind of hostility to strangers in them too, Jews and others, who got in his way in his single-handed fight against abu-al-Misk Kafur, who probably had no idea of how ridiculous he looked directing his pathetic army of street urchins in the alleyway in Acre. When Franz came home Käthe asked him how things had gone and he said, Haifa has grown and abu-al-Misk's garden is ruined, and what I once saw there no longer exists. She knew that he was talking about Azouri but she said nothing. The sun dazzled her eyes and only her furniture gave her a feeling of security. Gradually the shooting died down, the fighting stopped, and people began to speak of the impending world war. Franz went to a concert with Moshe in order to calm down and remember abu-al-Misk as he had once been, when the great house was still standing in the enchanted garden, when he was a young German officer and Bunim was a hungry child begging in the street.

Years later when I sat opposite Bunim in his office he paged through my file and said, what was your Jewish grandfather really doing in Acre in the middle of the disturbances? Selling secrets perhaps? I laughed. I told Bunim that he knew very well that Franz had not gone to Acre to sell secrets. Bunim looked disappointed. He would have liked to get at me even from Franz's side. I said to him, so you think Franz spied for money do you? Not like me for an ideal. Bunim wanted to slap my face but he restrained himself. I wasn't burnt yet and he could still use me. Franz didn't go looking for Azouri again, he said to

Käthe, we could have met in a different reality, here a meeting with Azouri would have different, dangerous implications, we'd better forget him. She smiled. She thought about Azouri so often that she had already forgotten just who it was that she was thinking about. She answered Franz, he must have plenty of problems of his own, why should he worry about us?

The war broke out on the day that Käthe gave birth. Uri was born twisted and without a hand. He couldn't breathe properly and they attached him to a respirator. Käthe touched him and Franz thought about the Arab children shouting 'Heil Hitler!' He won't be a Bunim against those children, he thought, and wondered why such a thought should have come into his head. Two months after he was born Uri died. When he died Käthe put on a white dress and went outside. She bought a bunch of flowers and she wouldn't let go of them. Her face which had been rigid and panic-stricken for two months opened up into a kind of dark vitality, as if she were touching the other side of Uri in her soul, her son who had been taken from her before she had a chance to love him.

At the funeral she refused to cry. Her mourning had taken place long before, when she had gotten it into her head that Uri was Azouri's son. She knew that if Azouri ever gave her a son one of them would have to die, and she was glad that it wasn't Azouri. Franz began to fear for Käthe's sanity. If he had been born eight hundred years before he would have thought that she had been bewitched by a devil. Käthe's sister looked around her in astonishment. So many friends from Berlin had come to the funeral that only the glare of the sun seemed foreign. Hava stood and looked at her dead brother, but she did not approach the edge of the grave. The cantor sang *El Malei Rachamim* and Franz stood alone, a little apart from the others. It was not so much pain that he felt as a kind of futility as he looked at this first and only root that he could have planted in his new country. Käthe had failed him, he didn't know why, perhaps it was a curse, he said to his friend Moshe that night as they walked down the dark, deserted streets, fragrant with orange blossom, and a shiver ran down his spine.

Hava left her primary school and started her secondary school. She had friends who hid biscuits and tea in a cave on the sea shore. They said that if the Germans came from El Alamein they would take their stand in their sea-shore Massada. They told Hava about Massada and she found an old revolver which Franz had brought back from the war and took it to the cave. They aimed it at the sea and sang songs around the campfire they lit in the cave. Hava loved those nights, the boys were full of a fierce lust, drunk with the discovery of their new bodies, and she sat squashed between them, she didn't let them kiss her but she liked the feel of their bodies pressing against her. She knew that none of them would possess her because they lacked the true smell of her strangeness and her dreams. Tel Aviv was bombed, Yona bought sardines and sugar, everyone was hoarding and Yona hoarded for Käthe who went to the flea market from time to time to buy more furniture. She always wore white and she fed the pigeons on the roof. Opposite them lived a man who had been looking at the sea for four years through a telescope. He was guarding the town, but the town didn't know. Käthe knew and she sent him five tins of sardines, and he thanked her in a note which he let down from his window on a string. Hava took the note to her mother, who read it and said, perhaps I shouldn't leave the house any more, perhaps it's too dangerous to go out. Franz said to Hava, your mother is ill and she doesn't know how ill she is. Hava said, she's fragile. She understood her mother's panic. Franz could rely on his daughter.

The war went on for four years. Hava went to the same school and played in the same playground. The house began to change, the goldfish disappeared, the water in the pond grew murky. The garden ran wild and nobody pruned the bushes for years. Tel Aviv grew up around them, Franz and Moshe went to the desert to search for potsherds, Käthe went with them and then she came home and sat for three days next to Uri's grave, scratching her life history in German on the little tombstone with a compass she had taken from Hava's school satchel. The cemetery guard called the police but the policeman who came in short trousers knew Frau Professor Rosenzweig, whose husband had operated on his mother, and he said to the guard, don't worry, nothing terrible is going to happen, she's not even wearing a hat, and he laughed. The guard went to pray and then he went to summon Franz. No one could move Käthe from the grave. They gave her an injection but still they couldn't move her. Hava said, don't behave like a lunatic, mother, and Käthe said, my life is over, I've done what I had to do, you and Franz will be better off without me. Hava embraced her mother but she did not feel love for her. Perhaps the love she felt was too great for her to contain. She tried to feel sorry for her but Franz said, the last thing we should do is pity her, Hava, it wouldn't be fair towards her. After three days she came home and Yona cooked her cauliflower soup. A pigeon flew into the room by mistake and in its attempts to get out broke a crystal vase. Neither Yona nor Käthe moved. There was something horrifying in the desperate attempts of the bird to escape from the room. When it finally flew away Käthe said, I hope it wasn't wounded by the crystal, and Yona said, that was awfully frightening.

Cobwebs began to grow on Käthe, who was full of a gay desperation, and to bind her with sticky threads to her furniture. One day her sister went out and walked with half-closed eyes in the direction of Dizengoff Street and was run over. Käthe did not go to the funeral. She let Franz stand there and measure out the doses of death. An old woman who had arrived on an illegal immigrants' ship sat in their house and told them in a whisper about what had happened to Käthe's parents. She told them how Käthe's father had shouted on the train to Theresienstadt, Hitler must be informed, and how Käthe's mother had wordlessly tried to support her husband. Käthe imagined her father in the ghetto, and afterwards, when he left the ghetto, marching alone, in a torn coat but full of pride, holding himself apart from the others, leaving his wife who had died of hunger behind him. He walked all by himself, said the woman spitefully, he was too stuck-up to talk to anybody, he said, I have nothing to say except to the authorities, and he stepped onto the train. Käthe sat opposite the woman embroidering a tablecloth, she took a pair of scissors and cut the cloth to shreds and threw them into the garden. The woman thought that they would give her a cup of coffee at least, but Franz was sunk in reflection and Käthe thought, she's not getting any coffee from me, and she said aloud, I don't serve coffee here. The woman left in anger, kissing the *mezzuza* on her way out.

Franz's love for Käthe grew stronger over the years, he collected information diligently about people who had died three thousand years ago and tried to forget the haughty and ridiculous figure of his father-in-law going to his death in Auschwitz because he did not want to stay in the ghetto with stinking Jews who ate rotten potato peels. Franz thought that the deeper he penetrated into the past of his new country the freer Hava would be from the devils haunting her mother and from his own dreams of Azouri, and abu-al-Misk and brown uniforms in Acre. If he had kept his ears open then, if he had wanted to hear them, he might have heard the cries of 'Heil' from the little village of Soumail too, a little village on the outskirts of Tel Aviv where they sold birdseed for pigeons and delicious *halva*, and whose inhabitants would soon be chased off their land and their houses torn down to make way for the new street of Ibn Gabirol which stands there today.

75

9

I translated these chapters into French and gave them to a woman I know to read. An extraordinary woman who lives in the Rue Madame surrounded by young admirers whom she cons into thinking that she is some kind of combination between Stalin and an old Jewish God with *mezzuzas* and phylacteries. I go to her sometimes when I need a woman to put out the fires burning inside me. She said to me, Yosef, you write like a Jew but all you really are is an Arab refugee in Paris. I told her that I write what I remember and I remember what I know from what I have heard and discovered by investigating the past. They all spoke to me, Azouri and Franz and Hava, all of them, I was a Jew and I'm still a Jew, I write with their pain but with an extra pain too. She said, there is no extra pain, it's either one or the other, you have to measure the size and the strength of the opposing pains and decide between them. I said to her, but you can combine both pains, and she laughed and said, somebody had to win, you or you. As if the very fact of my being in Paris today isn't proof that in the final battle I was defeated on both my sides. I'm the most defeated person in the whole of my accursed family, a family which succeeded in fading slowly into oblivion so that I would remain as a memorial to all those whose offspring I was. Hava's grandfather is no more foreign to me than abu-al-Misk Kafur, both of them anachronistic attempts to act out obsolete dreams on a terrifying turf where the game was fixed.

When the War of Independence, or what Azouri prefers to

call the war of '48, broke out, Franz was already a different man to the one who had arrived in Palestine a decade before. The look he had seen on the face of the old woman who came to beat Käthe with the stick of her pathetic, ludicrously aristocratic old father haunted him. And the spectacle of abu-al-Misk ibn Kafur Sherara in his brown uniform and boots did nothing to exorcise it. Her eyes bored deep into his heart, the hospital filled up with refugees who had hardly any lungs or bodies left. All that held them together was their suffering, a suffering which Franz had escaped. He sensed an accusation in their looks and voices, he began to feel that he had experienced their sufferings himself. He even said to Käthe, we should all be circumcised again. She stroked his head. The sicker she became, the further she drifted from reality into the dim regions of memory with its vague imagined shapes, the more dependent she became on Franz. She no longer measured his body as a barrier separating her from death, she let death slip away from her into her parents. They had already died for her and she thought of them without pity or love but with the feeling that they had taken her with them and that the end of her suffering was near.

She even grew to like lying next to Franz in bed and feeling him close to her. They had learnt to love each other like people tired of a long war. Hava observed them uncomprehendingly. She was trying to find a foothold in the new reality, but she did not know how to behave in it, she had no identity of her own and she did not know what identity to adopt. I know Hava only from the stories about her. The Hava I spent my childhood with was a mother, not a woman. If I loved her I loved her against Azouri, who later killed her, but for me her death too was the result of a plot hatched by many people, Azouri was only the executioner, a butcher like the Arab Jazzar. I know that Hava wanted to be part of the great moment that was coming into being. Underground movements sprang up, there was a feeling of faith in the air, the dead were waiting in their mass graves in Europe, their representatives were arriving in dribs and drabs on the illegal immigrant ships. Hava stood on the Tel Aviv beach when the refugees of the Patria landed, she saw their pale faces, their haunted eyes, later she joined the Hagana and went to study in Jerusalem.

Much later, years later, Azouri said, it isn't true that I didn't try to contact Franz and Käthe. I tried but it was difficult. Once I phoned, but the line was engaged. When Azouri said this Franz burst out laughing. Of all the things he might have expected Azouri to say, this sentence was the last. But precisely because of its absurdity Franz decided to adopt it and he said to Käthe, you see, Azouri has been trying to find us for fifteen years, he phoned but the line was engaged. I wonder who was talking all that time, maybe it was Yona.

Franz knew that Azouri was trying to capture something which no longer existed. The years had slipped out of his hands because it was impossible to translate their love into the new reality, where Azouri was already a member of an oppressed people. It was only in Germany that he could have sensed Franz's approaching doom before Franz sensed it himself. Now Franz was part of the success story of those pathetic scarecrows Azouri himself had mocked in 1917, and whose grandchildren had brought a catastrophe down on his head. Azouri said, out of the strong we must bring forth sweetness, which was a reference to Samson and the honey in the carcass of the lion, but Franz who was weak on biblical studies did not recognize the quotation and he thought, how affected Azouri has become, what a peculiar way of putting things...

Azouri said to Franz, you're very well preserved and Franz said to him, you look as if the years have passed you by, you seem to have jumped straight from the age of twenty-nine to the age of forty-five without collecting a wrinkle on the way.

Azouri looked at Käthe and he realised how much time had passed. She hardly knew who he was any more.

In Jerusalem Hava lived in the Old Yemenite quarter in a little house where I myself was later to live when I was an art student at Bezalel. She was a quiet girl, she studied at the university on Mount Scopus, her friends said she had the gentlest hands in town. Hava's beauty was so quiet and delicate that it revealed itself only to eyes which looked long and searchingly. She was neither happy nor sad, during the day she studied and at night she wove her dreams. She met a boy called Hanoch, I don't know his surname, when I tried to find out more about him I came up against a stone wall, even Bunim refused to tell me who he was or where he was buried. Hanoch moved in with her and built her a four poster bed like the ones they saw in the movies on Saturday nights. Sometimes Franz would come and take them out to eat in restaurants. The town became grim and tough, barbed wire fences went up around the British buildings, there was a feeling of unavoidable catastrophe in the air, people were already seeing Messiahs on the rooftops, when the sun set it vanished never to return, some people tried to bring the Messiahs down from the rooftops and others cursed all false Messiahs and their prophets. In Hava's neighbourhood the pious Orthodox Jews vowed to die rather than allow the blasphemous Zionists to take over the country. Franz was afraid of Jerusalem. Hava and Hanoch took him for walks to picturesque places and he examined the little jars in the Rockefeller museum with the magnifying glass he kept in his pocket. Every morning from Mount Scopus Hava saw the desert I would later want to paint red; in the harsh light of the midday sun it grew white and glaring filled with ancient knights galloping on horses and she was afraid. She worried about Hanoch who went on secret missions in the night, and somehow she sensed that if anything happened to him she would not be able to go on thinking about him. Hava was afraid that her

79

relationship with her mother prevented her from loving anyone, her life with Hanoch was the product of her need to know someone intimately. One day when she herself was already accompanying armed convoys, she came home covered in mud and found a man in a leather jacket and a balaclava helmet waiting for her. He told her that Hanoch had been killed in the Galilee and she looked at him and felt empty. She looked out over the rooftops at the Valley of the Cross, she saw the white towers of the monastery shining in the rays of the setting sun, there were grey clouds massing round the mountains on the other side of the valley, and she felt as if something had been amputated inside her, as if she was cut off from herself and not only from the gentle and handsome young man with whom she had spent a whole year of her life. The moment she was notified of his death he was wiped out of her mind. She did not go to his funeral, his brother came to see her and she said, let him belong to your parents, I only had a small part of him, we didn't talk much, he hardly knew me, I didn't know him, we were looking for warmth, not love, we found a secret that couldn't be cracked. The brother lost his temper and burnt his brother's blanket. The smoke came out of the chimney on the roof. Hava said, you want to find your brother but you won't find him here. The brother cried, and she could find no pity for him in her heart. His parents phoned Franz and he asked her at least to pay them a condolence call. Hava said out of the question, on no account will I go to see Hanoch's parents. And when they phoned again she took the phone and said to his mother, I never knew a boy called Hanoch. Franz went into another room and wept and Käthe began sticking strips of adhesive tape to the windows. A new war was coming, and Käthe thought about the old woman who had come to tell her about her parents and who looked like a slaughtered chicken.

Hava said to Franz, perhaps I had a boyfriend once, father, but I don't remember him. And years later, when I sat facing

80

Bunim in his office he said to me, what a wicked woman your mother was, betraying the memory of her lover. I stared at him and I said, so now my mother's a traitor too is she? Would you like me to go round to the schools and tell the kids that Hava the heroine of Koloniya they read about in their text books was a wicked traitor who married an Arab and wiped out the memory of her boyfriend Hanoch, that blue-eyed boy, that spoilt darling, that poor hypocritical Rammy who was killed when the explosives he was going to kill Arabs with blew up and killed him by mistake? And Bunim smiled sourly, but he couldn't keep the imploring note out of his voice when he said, you can do what you like Yosef, but you'll be sorry if you associate your mother's name with Azouri. I said to him, Azouri is a thousand times more of a Jew than you are, Bunim, you don't even know what being Jewish means, you're a fanatic, a monk, a grim grey bureaucrat who carries out orders, what have you got in common with the old lady who went to see *Ben Hur* with her grandson and she began to cry and her grandson said why are you crying, bubba, and she said, look at those lions eating the poor Jews, and he said to her, they aren't Jews, bubba, they're Christians, and she stopped crying, and a few minutes later she started crying again and he said, what is it now, bubba, and she said, look at that poor lion over there, he's not eating at all, and Bunim said, that's really funny, you Arabs are already telling Jewish jokes, and I said to him, what do you mean 'you Arabs'? Aren't I Hava's son? And he said, on Azouri's side. And I said to him, you know what, from now on I'll always say Hava, my mother on Azouri's side, you're a sonofabitch, Bunim, you're a sonofabitch and you know it.

Käthe's brother-in-law left for America at last. Käthe said to him, I bury the dead, my child-bearing days are over.

If you see Azouri in America tell him that his daughter lost her lover and she doesn't even remember who he was. Here everybody dies, where did he send us, that Arab? The town was full of people with nightmares and Käthe couldn't stand hearing their groans at night any more. She didn't listen to the radio either with its endless lists of people searching for their lost relations. She didn't even hear about Hava's heroic battle.

Hava was driving in an armed convoy to Jerusalem. When they approached the village of Koloniya the shooting began. The commander decided to carry on. The road was narrow and winding and the village spilled down to the road and bestrode it, an ancient Roman village which had undergone a thousand metamorphoses. Before it was destroyed it was the biggest and one of the most beautiful Arab villages in the country, or so Azouri said, with a sadness which was rather restrained for him. Hava was sitting at the right-hand window, with the driver between her and the village. The driver was hit and the truck began rolling down the hill. Hava pushed the dead driver out and pressed the pedal of the brake down as hard as she could with her foot until the truck ground to a halt. It stopped opposite the two-storied house from which most of the shots seemed to have been fired. Hava searched desperately for the driver's ammunition, the boy sitting at the back of the truck had taken her gun and apparently was dead too. No shots had been fired from behind the wall of sandbags at the back of the truck. She found a revolver but she didn't know how to load it or how to release the safety catch, it was a heavy old-fashioned Mauser. She found a handgrenade and climbed up to the sandbags, and then they shot at her. She didn't seem to care. She didn't think about what she was doing and she didn't have the proper training to know what she was supposed to do anyway. Somehow she succeeded in releasing the safety catch, she remembered that you had to wait a minute, and then with all her strength she hurled the grenade at the house. The grenade fell inside the window and she heard shouting. It exploded and she saw a man falling out of the window. Behind her in the convoy was an armoured car full of dynamite, it was hit by armour-penetrating bullets and it exploded. Hava was left alone on the road. The truck behind the armoured car was approaching quickly, but suddenly it stopped with a screeching of brakes. On her right, between the trees, she could see the Jewish village of Motza. There were supposed to be soldiers there but they weren't there. She stood there like a fool, said Azouri, like the heroine of a patriotic movie, and looked for another grenade. She found one in the dead soldier's pocket and she threw it. And then she saw a man in a hat and a brown suit aiming a submachine gun at her. She wanted to climb down but she couldn't make her legs work. The man was the only one left in the house. In the distance, from some other house, more shots were fired, but they missed her. She looked straight at the man aiming his gun at her, like a dancer moving through the steps of a ritual, he slowly perfected his aim, his eyes were so close that she could see the yellow flecks in them, the flush spreading over his cheeks, he was taking his time and she gazed at him without moving. It was a kind of ritual execution, she said later to Azouri, passionate and restrained. The barrel of the gun moved slowly over my body; he postured and pranced, he moved to and fro, the hatred radiating from him so violent that it had to be controlled, his face a mask. Hava found another grenade in the dead soldier's outflung hand, hidden bleeding between the sandbags, she looked at the dancing man, suddenly he laughed out loud, she laughed back at him, soldiers started running towards her from the direction of the second truck which had finally ground to a halt. Hava threw the grenade at the exact moment that the broadly smiling man fired a round of machinegun bullets at her. She felt a pain, she bent down to take hold of the pain, and she was almost sucked up into the hole opening inside her, but then she straightened up taking off her shirt and with the same movement waved it in the air. The upper half of her body was naked, perhaps for the first time in her life her breasts were bare to the

83

light of day, and at the same moment the man exploded in front of her eyes. The grenade she had thrown hit a pile of TNT, the man in the brown suit flew into the air and his blood spurted towards her. The Arabs in the neighbouring houses fled. The explosion was deafening, and Hava said afterwards, I saw his bullets flying towards me, I saw a spark, I felt a pain but before the pain I saw an arrow of death flying towards me, the blood gushed from my legs and hips, the pain was so bad, I felt my body like a red flag waving at the man who wanted so badly to touch me with his bullets. Someone jumped up and took Hava down from the back of the truck and half naked she was placed in the cabin of the other truck. Despite the pain she remembered to look for her shirt but she couldn't find it; someone gave her a shirt, she put it on and then she fainted. Hava said to Azouri, I'm sorry about that village, all the beautiful houses were destroyed. And then they chased all the people away. They destroyed the houses one after the other. The man looked at me, I saw his face, he was waiting for his death, perhaps he was looking forward to it. And perhaps I was too. Hava never forgot to say that the man shot her as if he were enacting a ritual, and she never forgot to add the word 'fascinating' either. The fascinating ritual of death.

10

I can understand Hava, my mother on Azouri's side. I can understand her attitude to ritual. Rituals are like form when it turns into content, they shield us from reality. When I sat with Azouri and accused him of shooting Hava at Koloniya he was obliged to tell me again and again what he knew that I already knew very well – that he had not fought in the 1948 war at all. Perhaps his need to repeat this over and over again instead of giving me a slap in the face was connected to a certain sense of guilt which stemmed precisely from the fact that he had not fired a shot. Azouri arrived in Palestine a year before Franz and Käthe. He heard of their arrival and he tried to phone and the line was engaged. This was true enough but it doesn't explain the fact that he never tried again. When he arrived in the country he tried to get a job at the university and he was turned down. This hurt him. He got a job teaching at a Christian high school, a man with five degrees. From time to time he published a scientific article in British, French or American journals. After some years, a year after the end of the Second World War, to be precise, he went to France and taught at the Sorbonne for six months. They say that he had a woman there, a woman who was married to another man. Did he love her? I never asked him and he never told me. He came back to Acre and spent his time between his house in Acre and an apartment in Haifa. He was active in the Party out of some need to belong, to be part of something bigger than he was, but I know that Azouri was as much of a Marxist as I was a Turkish

85

monarchist. He published a florid love story in Hebrew, under a pseudonym, and it sold thousands of copies. When he showed it to me years later, I laughed. I said what I had already found on many occasions to say to him before, you're the last of the romantics, Azouri. In this nonsensical novel he describes a man in love with a little girl, watching her as she grows up in a mansion in Jerusalem, a poor man living in a slum, haunting her house, throwing her a flower from time to time, gradually insinuating himself into her thoughts, her fantasies, her desires. A handsome man. The girl grows up like a princess. Men court her and she rejects them. In the morning she finds herself naked, curled up like a foetus next to her bed. Her parents, alarmed by her lust, beat her and send her to a convent school, where she marches in crocodile, her hands behind her back, with all the other black and white uniformed girls, while he stands watching her from his hiding place in the shadows. Although she never sees him, she knows that he exists. She runs away from the convent, she says to her parents, I can't stand the waxen smell of the nuns any more, their decaying bodies inside their long, stinking dresses. They send her to a school in Switzerland. He arrives in Switzerland. She senses his presence there. They smell each other.

I laughed and said to Azouri that he was a sly bastard. Azouri understood that I was hinting at something he had not intended at all, at least not when he wrote it, and he said what I wanted him to say, he said that he and Hava had indeed sensed each other long before they met. And he didn't have to shove it down my throat either, I had guessed as much. As someone gifted with a certain freakishness whose highest morality was betrayal, first through Bunim and later through the Organisations, I knew that I had aimed Azouri and Hava against one another. Azouri wasn't the only one who wrote idiotic stories in his head.

Azouri did not fight, he occupied himself with Party affairs.

He spoke of Arab-Jewish brotherhood but believed in no more than he saw with his own eyes. Young women from the Jewish sector mingled with the tough men who then formed the nucleus of the Party. There were dreams and there were meetings and when the '48 war broke out Azouri stayed in Acre. His father went to Kfar Yassif and joined Fawzi al-Kaukji's 'Liberation Army' for a while. He may have fired a shot or two, taken part in a skirmish or two but that was all. The family as a whole were not great fighters, like many others they shouted and denounced the Jews, but they didn't shoot. Azouri was an admired figure in the town and nobody held his refusal to fight against him. He seemed destined for greater things. Only his dying uncle, clinging to the tatters of his dreams of glory, set forth to do battle at the age of sixty-seven and came home to die of a broken heart after the rout of Kaukji's men at Mishmar Ha-emek. Azouri sat at home. He said to his father, when the war's over let me know who won, and he didn't even listen to the radio. Perhaps he imagined Franz sitting somewhere not too far away and thinking of him, operating perhaps on lungs punctured by Arab bullets. He even imagined him patrolling the streets at night and shouting 'Switch off the lights!' but he never imagined that within a space of time which only Käthe knew how to measure Franz himself, haunted by the eyes of the refugees then arriving in their tens of thousands in whose faces he saw a twisted mirror image of himself, would turn into a soldier fighting a great war on the land of Israel to save the Jews who could have been Franz if Azouri hadn't saved him – the Jews who did not arrive on the refugee ships because they lay buried in the lands which Franz had left behind him.

When Azouri emerged from the rain of bullets and shells from the single mortar with which the Jews conquered Acre, the movement of populations began. First they chased the Arabs to the shore. Two days later they brought Jews from

Haifa, who had just arrived on a refugee ship, and they gave them their houses. The Arabs began returning to the villages they had fled to wait for the victory their leaders had promised them within two or three days. The Jews marched them to the Lebanese border and ordered them to cross. It was chaos. Every Jewish commander decided on his own policy. A Catholic priest was brutally beaten but he did not desert his flock. A Khadi from the el-Jazzar mosque came out to defend his people. A refugee Rabbi hid his face in shame. Azouri doesn't go into detail about this period, he sticks to the documented facts. When I, the son of Hava and Azouri on their own sides, try to understand exactly what happened in Acre I realise how I grew up unwittingly into two opposing stories. Each side blamed the other. The Arabs stood on the shore. They went to Tyre and came back. Many did not come back. One of Azouri's brothers went to his brother in Beirut who helped him to reach Amman. Another brother escaped and opened a shop for electrical appliances next to the King's palace, when Abdulla was assassinated in Jerusalem he was standing not far away. Azouri kept his head. He re-established the local Party branch firmly on the foundations of Arab-Jewish brotherhood because he realised that both nations were doomed to live or die together. The Jewish military government persecuted him precisely because of his moderation. He was placed under house arrest. No one told him exactly what he was accused of. A Jewish woman from Haifa who was in love with him came to Acre and stayed in his house, but he never went to bed with her, he says. Before this she had been his brother's girlfriend, his third brother who ran away and waited for her to join him in Cyprus. She didn't want to go, she had faith, she pasted up posters and she was arrested. She sent his brother, who had gone to Beirut, letters by indirect routes. I needn't go into all the details, the story of the conquest and oppression may be far from simple but the facts are well known. Later, in order to make Azouri feel better, Hava would say that she was sorry about the destruction of the beautiful village of Koloniya. But by then he had already begun to understand the destroyers and he said, in a war for life or death, where each side is persuaded of its own justice, destruction is inevitable. We should have persuaded our leaders to accept the UN partition plan and we didn't do it, refugees bleeding from their wounds wanted a state of their own, and it had to be at my expense because my own people didn't have the sense to grasp the historical moment, they didn't understand that they were being offered independence, they wanted the whole cake and they were left with nothing.

Azouri was not a faint-hearted Jew-lover, as the people in Beirut were to say later in the venomous barbs they directed at him for his great work on the history of the Jewish-Arab conflict in Palestine. Of all the books I have ever read on the subject Azouri's is the most accurate, the most objective, even Bunim uses it against me sometimes. No one is prepared to accept it as fact, but Azouri didn't lie, he wrote a work of methodical research. Once he said painfully to me, when Hava was sitting on my knee in Berlin and I was reading her Wilhelm Bosch, I hated her. She was the barrier between me and Franz and Käthe. I couldn't fight them but she was an easy target, as she herself has often said that she was a sitting duck for the man in Koloniya when he shot her and made her into your national heroine. I laughed because he said 'your', and I said to him, I'm the son of Azouri on the side of abu-al-Misk ibn Kafur Sherara, and he said, no, you're not. You're a stranger everywhere, to me, to him, to Hava. You belong to yourself alone. You've read the story I wrote under a false name. Am I really an incurable romantic? I'm a man of science, a cautious investigator, it's hard for me to believe that I ever wrote such rubbish only because, as you say, I've always remained a sentimental Arab at heart. I was looking for a possible reality, perhaps not necessary, but basic. In this one we're punished. They took away my uncle's land in Kfar Yassif. Land is the Arab's bread. He lives for it and on it. He has no motherland but his land. You took his sky too. You put a Jewish God there with a national anthem like Hatikva. I said to him, not *you* took, *they* took. And then I asked him, so how did you love Hava? And he said, like fire. And I said to him, only an Arab would say 'like fire' and he laughed. He said, they insulted and humiliated me. They confined me to Acre and put me under house arrest. I wrote. Once I phoned Käthe and Franz. Käthe answered the phone but I didn't say anything. There wasn't anything to say. We were three intelligent people, Yosef, two Jews and an Arab. We knew it was forbidden to look for what had been lost there. I wrote, they wanted me to be on the local council, the military governor tried to fraternise with me and bend me at the same time. There were Jews living in my uncle's house, in the houses of my cousins who were sitting in refugee camps in Lebanon. The Jews uprooted the lemon trees to fuel their stoves in the terrible winter of 1949. I understood what my brothers did not understand, where they had come from, what suffering lay behind them. I knew that this was no reason to exile me, to insult me, to turn me out of my home, but I also knew that the old laws were gone for ever. There were new laws, and I'm not talking about government legislation or the decrees of military governors, I'm talking about a kind of wish to console the inconsolable, to understand the pain of the walking dead who were cutting down my lemon trees in Acre. Azouri said to me, I didn't want the need I felt to defend Acre, to defend my sky and my historical earth, after you had already taken the beautiful houses and orchards, Kafur's garden and sea, the land in the Galilee, I didn't want what I did here in Acre to be directed against Franz and Käthe. I wanted to protect Acre for the sake of my grandchildren. How could I have known that if I ever had a grandchild it would be a dead foetus aborted by a Jewish girl called Dina from the boiling seed spilt by my half-Jewish son.

This was the crudest and bluntest thing I ever heard from Azouri. He was angry then because of Laila, the Arab actress I lived with for a few months in Haifa when I was an Arab nationalist who had come to Azouri's communism as a way out, a misconception of the true rules of the game, a surrender to a remote and foreign regime. Azouri said to me, you won't solve the Arab-Jewish problem in bed with Dina or with Laila either. I told him that Laila lay in bed next to me in a pitiful room in Haifa with pictures of Che Guevara and a little Palestinian flag on the wall and books in Arabic which she never read and books in Hebrew which she read when there was nobody there, and she said to me, you're a savage, Yosef, a savage. Once I had a Jewish boyfriend who brought me flowers, he covered me in flowers and my parents nearly killed me, and I was ashamed, I felt degraded. And suddenly she said to me, you know what, you act like an Arab, and I hit her. All the years I had spent acting the Jewish child in school: Yosef Rosenzweig, Yossie, grandson of Franz, honorary member of the international association of lung surgeons, son of Hava, a national heroine in schools for the study of death and just wars. I yelled at Laila and the more I yelled at her the more she understood that I was the Arab she wanted to love but couldn't, growing up in this country had distorted her, Arabs weren't people to her, they were a national identity. Her Arab friends had let her down. After sleeping with all the left-wing Jewish girls in Haifa they married the girls their parents chose for them, and Laila, the liberated woman, the only Arab woman around who lived openly with men, who wasn't afraid, who refused to give in to her parents and family, who never went to pray, who refused to accept her nationality as a mark of Cain, Laila sought the brotherhood of man in bed with me and cast me in the role of the Arab who beat her. Laila wept and said, go away, you stink like a peasant, and in the middle of the night I went to the nearest telephone booth and I phoned Dina and I said to her, come back to me, leave everything and come back to me, and she cried and banged the phone down. I walked all the way to Acre, I walked the whole night and I was stopped by some policemen who insulted me, one of them hit me, but I didn't care, I arrived at Azouri's and it was then that he said those harsh, angry words to me. He dreamed of human relations and came up against Jews who weren't like Franz and Käthe, they were fanatics. He got in their way, he was shit, he was Arab filth, which is something he hadn't taken into account when he went to Käthe in Berlin and told her that he smelled fire and she had to leave to save herself and Franz and little Hava. And don't forget, he said to me, this was long before the holocaust, it was only a question of human rights then, the Nuremburg laws were harsh but we live here under laws no less harsh, there were no concentration camps and gas chambers then. It wasn't because of what happened later that I took Franz and Käthe away from Germany and brought them here, that was unimaginable then.

Azouri had his reservations about Laila (he didn't say so, but I knew him), she was too Arab, he wanted me to go back to Dina. With Dina, he thought, I would have a better chance. I told him about her parents. I told him what a catastrophe it would be for them if we ever got married. And he pitied Dina's parents and translated the pity to Franz and Käthe. But I'm talking about things that happened much later on. First came the humiliation and the insults, the plunder, the man who stood on Acre beach for two days and two nights and never fired a shot, and Israeli soldiers pushed him into the water and wanted him to go back to some Arab past in the sea. You don't forget things like that, said Azouri, and then he added, you know what, I've already forgotten it. What I haven't forgotten is my mother. In '48 she was fifty years old. A beautiful woman, but no longer young. My father went to Kfar Yassif and maybe he fired a few shots, brought the guerillas a bit of olive oil and flour, a few *pittoth* and cheese. And then he came home and hid in my brother's house, the one who escaped to Beirut. His wife sat at home. A traditional Arab home, said Azouri.

And what was my father? A man with a little education, a minor clerk in the British mandate. My mother was a beautiful woman and she was burning with hate. I left Acre and went to Haifa, the Jews conquered Haifa and the Arabs stood there hanging their heads and watching their beloved homes being destroyed. I went back to Acre but my mother was no longer there. You understand how a son feels, and I'm an Arab Yosef, an Arab son of an Arab, when he hears that his mother has run off to Tunisia with an officer from Kaukji's army, that army of arrogant braggarts and murderers and not progressive freedom fighters. Every now and then my clever, sober father would come out with these empty slogans and I must admit that it gave me a kick to hear them coming out of his mouth. My mother was rejuvenated, he said, she cried her eyes out and she ran away to Tunis in a fishing boat with an officer in Kaukji's army, from Iraq I think but I'm not sure. In any case I came home to an empty house. My mother didn't know how to write, my father came home and found that his wife was a refugee in Tunisia, gone off with a moustachioed hero who had killed three Jews next to Afula. I cried for him but he didn't cry. He was a strong man, not like his brother abu-al-Misk. A realistic man, close to the land, not a big talker. Later on he re-married a woman he brought from one of the villages near Acre. At that time he was working as an interpreter for the military government. In the meantime my brothers had scattered, the house was almost empty. I had apartments in Haifa and Acre and I had to stand in a queue at the military government offices to get a travel permit to go from Acre to Haifa and back again. My father was in charge, sometimes he was ashamed to look me in

93

the eyes. I wasn't angry with him, his wife was nagging him, she began to despise him. She wanted him to take a knife and go and avenge himself on the wife who had betrayed him. It maddened her that he wasn't angrier, that he didn't kill her or kill himself, that he helped me to obtain travel permits from the Jews. She became more and more trapped in the hatred boiling inside her.

In bed she offered my father a cold body, she never smiled, she cooked the meals and withdrew into herself. One day she killed herself in her room. We were sitting in the kitchen, first we heard her cry, Go and stick a knife in her! But my father never stuck a knife in anyone, he was an Arab manqué, torn from what he had grown up on without arriving anywhere else. I too, Yosef, he and I, we are mutations from which you were saved. You inherited your anger from my parents' parents, not from me, not from my father. She killed herself before our eyes in order to punish us but we weren't punished. I have to weep for her heroism. Like Hava, she was a brave fighter in a lost cause. She walked into the room and my father said, look, there's blood coming out of her mouth, but how does the blood get to her legs when she's already slit her throat?

Afterwards I buried him too. And your mother too. You're all I've got left and you're sticking the knife into me that my father never stuck into his faithless wife or into himself either. His second wife was preoccupied with thoughts of Arab honour too, she had somewhere to come from when she walked into the room where my father refused to stick a knife into himself or anyone else and sat in front of the window starting at the bay. And you sit here now, you come from Hava's side not mine, from Hava's side on Franz's side, stay there, Yosef, it's for your own good. I said to Azouri, how could you? You came back here in '48, you saw what they were doing to you, humiliating you, taking your land away from you, how could you keep quiet, how could you stay so calm? They took everything away from you, they banished your family, they destroyed your father, they made you into a Jews' Arab, how could you? And he looked at me without saying a word and I added, they're foreign conquerors, like the crusaders, self-righteous hypocrites, and they'll end up like the crusaders too. And Azouri said, no, I think you're mistaken Yosef, you'll stay here but we'll stay here too, that's the tragedy... When I went to work for Bunim I took abu-al-Misk Kafur's sword with me, the sword which had once belonged to Salah Addin, to take the revenge that Azouri's father had not taken. The truth is that I was never very accurate. My 'freakishness' worked sometimes. I was often wrong. But here and there I gave Bunim things that helped him. The sword worked against me, not for me, even when I brought the rain to Kassit, I didn't bring it all the way, close but not right up to the door. And thus I could sometimes bring a certain smile to Bunim's dead lips. And may God have mercy on the little children who go to play such absurd and desperate games on the turf of a man like Bunim.

11

One day Dina got up at nine o'clock in the morning and drank a cup of coffee. She put her ear to the wall and heard me breathing on the other side (I wasn't there, of course) and the cup fell to the floor and she heard it scream. The figure of Hava, my mother on my grandfather Franz's side, emerged from the wall. Dina sat down and wrote a poem. At one-thirty she finished writing the final version of the poem and she felt hungry. Rammy phoned and she agreed to go and have lunch with him. She read him the poem and he asked who the woman was and she said, Azouri's Hava, and he said, we learned about her in school. Dina tried to laugh but her mouth was full of dead babies and she couldn't laugh, and when she ate she felt as if she was chewing me. She said to Rammy, I feel as if this wine is Yosef's blood. He tried to make her feel sorry for him but she had no pity to spare. I was sitting then in Bunim's office and trying to focus on something that had already happened or was about to happen but I couldn't see clearly. The whole thing lacked a certain reality and Bunim didn't like abstract things. I told him about painting the desert red, and the idea sounded so far-fetched to him that he didn't even tell me I shouldn't do it. Rammy said to Dina, I've organised a crop-spraying plane for Yosef, a friend of mine will take it up and the paint company will provide the paint. Dina said, Yosef will never be an artist, he isn't capable of feeling the seriousness of the child he once was in an adult way, his innocence is the innocence of an avenger, not of a child. But Rammy didn't understand what she

96

meant. She took her poem to the editor of a literary supplement and at five-thirty in the afternoon the editor told her the poem would appear in the week-end supplement in ten days' time. She went home and felt empty. Rammy tried to lie down next to her and she pushed him away. He asked why, and she said, please go now, it's useless, I belong to him and he isn't capable of loving me in the way I want him to. She tried to get in touch with me through the walls of Bunim's office but she was right and I knew it. Who did I ever love? When did I know how to love? Rammy knows how to love, he deserves to be loved. Dina was paralysed. In the evening in Kassit Nissan would say to her, with hidden mockery, where's Yosef? Why doesn't he come any more? and she would say, he's busy on something important at the moment. Hedva was still running to the telephone to say nothing and weep into the saucepan Hezkel put on the floor to catch her tears. I wanted to go back to Kassit. Dina's poem was published and everyone admired it. Even her enemies admitted it was a breakthrough. Only Dina was ashamed. I phoned and she said to me, come and make love to me Yosef, take me and do what you like to me only free me from this suffocation.

I went. Rammy was sitting in the passage sticking stamps in Dina's stamp album. Everyone who knew her stuck stamps in Dina's stamp album for her. I told him to get lost. He turned to me with a look of surprise on his face. The only question he found to ask me was, how did you get in? I told him that I had always had a key to Dina's apartment. I paid a third of the rent too, and he said, still? And I said, you fool, for ever, I paid the key money and if you take the trouble to inquire you'll find out that this flat is registered in the name of Rosenzweig. Then Dina called out, Rammy, be a good boy and go away. He went into her room and she gave him a look so cold it froze even me standing at the door. She said, leave us alone today, it's got nothing to do with you or with you and me, I need Yosef here

97

today. Rammy said, but you said he wasn't going to come here any more, and she said, it's only temporary, I'm suffering, Rammy, I'm full of grief, I'm burning, now go. I helped Rammy pack his things. I even pitied him. Dina's hands were shaking. She said, I wrote a poem about your mother. Then she got undressed and lay on the bed and switched on the light so I would see how great she was. I lay down next to her, as close as possible, and I entered her. She looked at my chest, she stroked it, she touched my throat taut above her. Her eyes were veiled, panic-stricken; I thought about Gertrude twisting Franz around her little finger and her three fat daughters who would soon be my aunts. I touched her lightly, and suddenly I felt the closeness that was a kind of emptiness that only she knew how to fill me with, and I began searching for all the days and nights that I had left inside her ever since she was fifteen years old, bleeding in the laundry room on the roof of Franz's house. She said, poor Rammy is waiting outside. I asked her how long I would have to go on humiliating him like this and she said that in the end he would get her, he would liberate her from me and she wouldn't love me any more. I said to her, you'll always love me, Dina, and she laughed, sometimes she had a sad, bitter laugh, full of innocent cunning, and she hugged me tightly. I tried to think what love was, who Azouri was in relation to Hava, my mother on Azouri's side. Dina's body was the sea in which I caught my poisoned fish. I said to her, you're a beautiful woman, Laila, but she didn't fall into my trap, she said, you don't know anyone called Laila, Rammy. Actually I was thinking not of Laila but of my mother, there were devils in the room, the devils Dina made her poems of, and one of them was my mother, she was jealous of her, Azouri loved my mother, not her, my mother was dead and she understood my mother's death better than I did.

I remember that night because it will stay with me forever, like everything else about Dina, whose marriage to Rammy didn't work out and who is sitting alone in her flat today trying to write poems in our private codes, thinking that perhaps one day we'll be able to tell everyone to go to hell and allow ourselves to be carried away on a wave of sentimentality, to rebel against our firm resolutions never to meet again, sitting there alone and searching for a way back. Once I said to her, Dina, death was the only way out for Hava and she knew it.

The next day Rammy came to see me. I told him all about my night with Dina. She's available again, Rammy, I said to him, you can think what you like but go back there because she needs you. At the end of the night, I said to him, we came to blows, she threw books at me and I treated her like dirt, I can't help it, if you stay you'll keep on bumping into me because the truth is that I'm crazy about you Rammy, but we can't be friends, something will always keep us apart, I don't know what it is, not the Arab in me, not the patriotic little Israeli in you, but something deeper, Dina, maybe it's Dina, her devils, her poems, she wants to be Hava and you don't even know who Hava was even though you learnt about her in school, I can't explain, it's connected to an old story about Haifa, and the First World War, and Germany, to Käthe trapped in a web of death, to Franz, to so much holy shit.

*   *   *

Hava lay in hospital for five months. At the same time Käthe set her watch at half past four and broke the spring. She said, the time is half past four, on the first of June 1936. Her time stopped the moment they stepped off the ship at Haifa port. Franz asked her why she needed to wear a watch at all, and she said that it was necessary. The hands on her watch never moved until they fell off. Käthe visited her wounded daughter and she began to call her Greta again. Franz brought Herman, the orthopaedic surgeon from Haifa to see her, and much love was devoted to the healing of her leg and hip. She was wounded in the gall bladder too, and when her leg and hip were healed the doctors told Franz that there was no knowing how long she would last. Franz went to see her every day and Käthe said to him, you don't have to go every day Franz, she'll die without you too. By now she could hardly identify the objects which had once injured her, and her daughter Greta's death seemed to dematerialise in front of her.

Hava was discharged from the hospital and outside there was already a Jewish State. Franz operated on wounded lungs and looked after his daughter. After a few months Hava returned to Jerusalem and resumed her studies in the new temporary premises in the Terra Sancta monastery. She graduated with a master's degree in education and psychology. A friend of Hanoch's, who wanted to get closer to her, taught her how to overcome her limp. Franz sent her to Haifa to Herman who operated on her again and lengthened her leg a little. Franz went down to the beach with her in the mornings and they swam and she did exercises for her leg. Time on Käthe's watch stayed still.

*   *   *

They visited the Jazzar mosque, the old prison, walked along the walls and arrived at Abu Cristo's restaurant. Hava and the other girl in their party wanted to use the toilet, and the boys waited impatiently, they wanted to see the big caravanserai before dark. Hava came out of the lavatory and saw the row of empty tables next to the waterline and facing her the Carmel, which her father had seen in his youth, a little blurred, overcast by the shadows of the late afternoon which was already clarifying the water but spoiling the perspective. The mountain looked wounded, slashed, but the line of the slash was elegantly aligned with the awning above the empty tables and

Hava said, I'll sit here and rest, you go with them, come back for me later, I want to be alone for a while. Her face was cold and the purity in her eyes which Hanoch had loved so much and which Käthe feared, was now concentrated on the view of the Carmel. Her friend did not argue, she knew that there was no point in arguing with Hava, she said, alright, we'll come back later, and went off.

Hava approached the water and saw tiny fish swimming in agitation. She sat down and ordered a glass of white wine. Abu Cristo, who was sitting in the doorway next to a woman with a gleaming gold tooth in her mouth, looked at her and said, that girl over there, give her the good wine. Abu Cristo was waiting for the fishing boats which were now beginning to come in with their haul. A soldier stopped his jeep outside the restaurant and yelled, get *humus* ready for ten people tonight. Abu Cristo looked at the soldier contemptuously through half-closed eyes and Hava sensed the glance he exchanged with the woman next to him. She sipped the cold wine. Small boys, their bodies dark in the fading light, were jumping into the little jetty separated by a reef from the bay, from a rock jutting up at her right. It looked dangerous but Hava watched the daring leaps, which were to some extent being staged for her benefit, without anxiety. A kind of serenity had descended on her. For the first time since she had been wounded she did not feel superfluous inside her body, an inner warmth flooded her, a pleasant smell compounded of mint, fish, vinegar and lemons pervaded the salty air. The waves slapping the edge of the terrace sprayed her with water but she paid no attention.

The bay darkened. Brightly painted boats approached the jetty partly hidden from her eyes by the restaurant wall. From where she was sitting she could see the bay spread out before her and the masts of the sailing boats in the jetty. She absorbed herself in the view and for the first time in years a tremor passed through her body, as if the little fish swimming crazily at the foot of the low wall where she was sitting with her legs crossed were escaping from her womb into the sea. A handsome man wearing a Mao shirt and an expensive jacket appeared from the direction of the little jetty which was half shut-off from her view. Holding a cane in his hand, more for effect than out of necessity as Hava, who had limped for a whole year, immediately realised, he walked very slowly, without seeing her, towards the water line. His eyes were fixed on the sea and the distant mountain and the way he looked at them gave rise in her to longings to which she was only later able to put a name. He walked like a blind man, as if every step he took was part of a well-rehearsed and time-honoured ritual, a hundred years of walking along exactly the same line. At the precise moment when his figure would be outlined to the greatest possible effect against the last dazzling light of the setting sun, the man reached the edge of the sea. Hava said to herself, this man has staged his entrance to time with the sinking of the sun and the red glow in the sky, and she was jealous of him even then.

When he turned and crossed the terrace his steps fell into place like punctuation marks between the cries of the boys leaping into the sea. Without even looking he sat down on the chair that he knew would be standing there, put his cane on the floor, and smiled. She saw his greying temples and she could not take her eyes off his still figure, blind to beauty as she was it was not the man's good looks which attracted her but the game he was playing with the fire in the sky. Everything around him formed a composition of which he was the centre: the boy leaping off the rock, setting off his dignified posture in the chair, the lights going on in the restaurant before night fell, the music breaking out, soft but clear, from where Abu Cristo was sitting with the gold-toothed woman. The chair the man sat in was his chair, she knew this as surely as she knew that the chair she was sitting in was not her chair. She forgot her friends. The water lapping against the concrete gleamed with a dark, dull light, the sky blazed up in a glorious conflagration, touching the Carmel, the towers and the wall, the fishing boats sailing into the jetty with fire, and as he put his cane down and settled into his chair the red sun sank behind the rock and the little boys' bodies were suddenly transformed into colourless x-ray plates.

Hava felt a pain in her wounded leg. The man was directing the world. He looked to her like an ageing angel at the gates of paradise. She felt transfixed by the serious look in his pale grey eyes staring unseeingly at the water. She finished drinking her chilled white wine. The sea grew fierce, caught fire for the last time and immediately turned black. Only the little fish were left, teeming in the light which had gone on in the restaurant, the dull glow of the bodies of the invisible leapers and the splashing of the water in the little pool between the rocks, a dangerous place to dive. She gave herself up in utter relaxation to the contemplation of their leaps, inexplicably happy and at the same time tense in expectation of the man whom the violet of the falling night and the lights of Haifa suddenly going on in the distance suffused with a pale greenish light. The fist of the mountain which only a moment ago had burned so brightly sank into the gathering darkness. The man stretched out his legs and his feet touched two little pebbles which seemed to have been placed there to mark a boundary between them. Under Hava's penetrating gaze he raised one finger with a barely perceptible movement. She was delighted by the lordly air with which he lifted the finger for no more than a second, by the way in which he kept his hand resting on the table instead of waving it about in the air, and needless to say she was not in the least surprised when the waiter arrived the moment the finger was lowered. The waiter burst in upon the scene, swift and accurate as a well-aimed arrow. The tray he placed discreetly on the table held a *finjan* of coffee, a glass of cold water, a little cup, two biscuits and a slice of lemon. Hava said to herself, he didn't spill a single drop, and she was filled with admiration. The water stood in the glass as still as if it were sculpted there. Hava was charmed by the whole bravura performance, by the way in which everything seemed to conspire to grant a final intensity to the moment which ended with the sinking of the sun and the gathering power of the night.

The man raised his hand, turned his face and smiled at Abu Cristo who smiled back with a hardly perceptible twitching of his lips, while the woman beside him giggled in greeting. The water darkened at the edge of the restaurant and dashed against the concrete with a fierceness which was already dying. Hava envied the man who lifted the little cup of coffee which the waiter had poured for him to his mouth, sniffed the coffee, squeezed a drop of lemon juice onto the rim of the cup and emptied it with a gulp. A boy holding a fisherman's net appeared from the right and said 'Ahallan' to the man, who waved a finger in reply, Abu Cristo turned the radio on to wailing, seductive Arab music, someone switched on more lights, the music frightened the little fish away, a few people came into the restaurant and greeted Abu Cristo and Hava marvelled at the way in which the impressively good-looking man had tamed the sunset and confined it to a little cup of coffee.

He finished his second cup, stood up without haste, and Hava, who kept her eyes averted, knew that he was walking towards her. She was filled with a sweet dread. She knew that he was responding to some signal of hers, some gesture or glance, but she didn't know if she really wanted him to come. She was quite content with the role of spectator at the repeat performance of the ritual being enacted this time against the backdrop of the sea instead of the rocks of the Judean mountains. The man was already standing in front of her, she still had not looked at him, the waiter suddenly appeared with a tray of coffee and when she lifted the cup which he poured for her with a trembling hand and put it to her mouth the man said, in a voice which was neither sad nor mocking, Look what a beautiful country you've got here.

Hava sipped her coffee and felt the knife twisting inside her. She raised her face to him and said with a smile, if violence is a form of seduction, you're wasting your time. He laughed and said, may I sit down? and she said, why ask me? In any case the place looks as if it belongs to you. He looked at her and said in a voice which sounded like a caress, if I sit down next to you now it's because you're here now and you weren't here before.

Azouri told me that when he saw Hava he felt as if she had taken Acre away from him. He said to me, our first meeting was in anger. She sat there, beautiful, alone, remote as if she belonged to another world, strong and submissive at once. I looked at her, she didn't see me looking at her, and she was alien to me, as if she had come to rob me of what belonged to me, and you know that that's not the way I usually think, that's not the way I see things...

They sat in silence, feeling each other's presence. Abu Cristo himself brought them a tray with calamari, shrimps, tiny grilled fish, *humus* and *tehina*, salads in little saucers, lemons, and a bottle of chilled white wine. There was a breeze blowing and a faint, agreeable chill in the damp air. Wordlessly Hava allowed Azouri to feed her, she heard her friends returning and she heard Abu Cristo telling them drily that she had already left, he had seen her getting into a cab and driving off alone, she wasn't feeling well, he said. Azouri sat enjoying the fear which was contracting her stomach muscles. Later Hava said to Franz, Azouri was never so confident of his good looks as he was then, and he didn't even know that I was blind to his beauty.

The wind began blowing towards Haifa, towards the ridge of the Carmel looming dimly in the darkness, which was full of flocks of birds flying in stylish formation in the lights of two ships sailing into the port. Hava said, what's the matter, has the cat got your tongue? She saw how he had been taken out of his ritual and perhaps she was sorry, she would have liked to plunge right into his production and never to return to herself again. The confidence he exuded was absolute, and she still didn't know that he was the man on whose knees she had sat when she was a little girl listening to him reading Wilhelm Bosch in his precise but peculiar foreign accent.

Dina is always telling me that Azouri loved Hava against Käthe. Dina never knew Hava but for some reason she bore a grudge against her. I never got to the bottom of it, I never discovered the roots of that resentment. She said, Azouri wanted revenge. I laughed because I know that Azouri never dreamt that Hava in Abu Cristo was the little girl he had once known in Berlin. Azouri wasn't a ladies' man, and I can say that to his credit, with looks like his he could have lived in a harem and licked ice-cream from the fingers of infatuated women. He was and remained all his life a romantic boy translating his romanticism into a corny story about a little girl in Jerusalem or playing with the precise formulae of an imprecise science and the methodical investigation of elusive subjects like history and philology. If there's one thing Azouri wasn't it's frivolous, his suffering was about suffering itself, and he never looked for an easy way out. Hava was a sitting duck, said Abu Cristo angrily when they arrested Azouri after her death and he came back broken to the restaurant and broke the chair the waiter slipped beneath him. But Hava wasn't a sitting duck and Abu Cristo admitted to me that the meeting between them was the most beautiful and spontaneous thing he could remember seeing. It was Azouri's ritual that captured Hava, still obsessed with the face of the man who had shot her. Even Franz never guessed that the memory of the brown-suited man in the hat who had shot her had remained in her, filling her with a terrified awe from which she never recovered until Azouri miraculously, by the very act of his ritual entrance into the restaurant, released her from the spell.

Hava suddenly felt hungry and she ate heartily. Azouri dipped a piece of *pitta* in the *tehina* and drank the wine. There was a light hanging just above their heads, they could see each other with the utmost clarity. Sadness touched sadness, remote systems operating in other galaxies combined with the simple laws of beauty, something caught fire and brightened the air. She saw an aristocratic Arab, the kind of Arab intellectual she had met in Jerusalem before the war. Azouri saw a young woman and he wasn't used to courting women, he was used to them courting him, when he would usually withdraw, or occasionally respond, he never looked for anything beyond what he found in these casual affairs and Hava suddenly seemed so unreal to him that he was embarrassed, and anyone who has ever seen Azouri embarrassed knows what an idiot he looks.

He was so awkward in his attempts to woo her that it made Hava happy. It pleased her to see how tongue-tied he was as he groped for the right words to say and couldn't find them. Suddenly he was no longer clever or witty, but moved by the sadness shining from her face. When he suddenly said that she should look after herself and eat more – she burst out laughing. Even my father doesn't talk to me like that, she said. To the women he met in the Party he was hard and casual, they went in and out of his bedroom without complaints. Azouri was the blue-eyed boy of the town, his reputation had spread to Haifa and Nazareth as well. His importance was recognised in the alleys of dozens of villages, although his actual power was less than that of the meanest and lowest of the power-drunk military governors his father served. He had come to know Käthe and Franz's brothers from their least charming side. Women from the Jewish-Arab Friendship League came to protest, violent demonstrations took place. Azouri did not go to demonstrations, he wrote pamphlets and edited a newspaper, he studied and taught, he was loyal to the Party without trying to become prominent in it, he agreed to serve on the local council because it was a necessary condition for the regulation of an intolerable situation. The people were desperate and full of doubts. No Arab knight came to rescue them when the three-inch mortar rained its shells down on Acre. A web of submission and rebellion began to be woven, a web and woof of contradictions, and he, Azouri, expressed it in a way that was appropriate to the time. Right or wrong, I'm not judging. In any case, he turned Hava on, of that I have no doubt; my mother, whom I loved, loved that man. I was jealous of him for that. I hated him for the two women who desired him, Käthe and Hava. But Azouri was honest with himself, he was fair even when he was hurt, he had learned the art of survival from the Jews and he saw it being squandered on the insanity of fanatical nationalism, both Jewish and Arab, here in the Jewish state. Years later he once said to me, you may belong to a persecuted race but you also belong to a race which was once persecuted and which is now revenging itself on those weaker than they are for what others did to them in the past. I understand them, he said, but don't think it's easy. There were only two women I ever wanted, and one of them I loved, Käthe and Hava. All the rest were women for a moment of pleasure or oblivion. Hava fell in love with me and don't you ever judge her for it. She struggled but she was too weak. The combination defeated us both. There was no victor in the duel we fought so clumsily.

Hava saw him groping in vain for tried and tested ploys and failing to find them. She was enchanted. At the end of two hours of halting conversation she said, my name is Hava and I'm living on borrowed time. He did something that was completely out of character, he took her hand and read her palm and said, with a profound gravity which they would later laugh at, you will live for a very long time. As if he knew. She said, what are you, a fortune-teller? And he said, I know, and then she smiled and said sadly, I don't know anything.

In the end she moved her hand on the table from where he had placed it and it touched his hand. They held hands and Azouri told her about how he had come back to Acre and found his flat filthy. How they had uprooted the lemon trees. He even told her about his father. He was a middle-aged man, he felt ashamed of himself for falling in love so childishly. I feel sorry for them, I pity them for the painful moments that they endured on their way to one another. He told her how his father sat paralysed in his room, how his stepmother despised him for failing to avenge himself. He seemed to her ridiculous but lovable. She knew that it was love even before the words were said. Her hands froze in his. His own hands were warm. He wanted to move for her, breathe for her, inhale for her the pungent smell of the sea. He told her about the rejuvenation of his mother at the age of fifty. How she fell in love with an officer in Kaukji's army and went off with him to Tunisia, without leaving a single belonging behind her for her husband and five children. How the stepmother demanded revenge. How his father refused to avenge himself. How the woman died before their eyes in the big room facing the sea. Even then she wanted to kiss his eyelids and she asked, and you? How old are you? He said about forty-five, more or less. He added more or less because he couldn't quite remember. She laughed and said, I'm not a child you know, I'm not a child any more either.

My stepmother, he suddenly said, and only I who know him so well know how strange it was for Azouri to talk about himself in this way to a strange woman, my stepmother came from the country, she wore a *galabiyeh*, her first husband was killed in the war, a hero, she said, she brought her daughters to see us, one of them was intended for me, even Abu Cristo that slyboots you see sitting there tried to push her into my arms, and then her mother, a proud woman, married my father, perhaps for the family prestige, perhaps she was fond of him, perhaps she was lonely, and there was the family money too. She was a woman with fire in her eyes, full of rage, she screamed at my father, what did your son learn in Germany? Can you kill Jews with those degrees? How many Jews can you kill with all the words he writes? And the whole town was laughing at my father then, his wife had eloped, he sat at home and went to work for the military government. Azouri poured Hava another glass of wine and stared at the sea. Later on he said, surveyors came and measured the houses we had left. We asked them, who decides? And they said, it's written in the Bible. And I asked them, what's written in the Bible, how many of our houses you need for the custodian of enemy property? And they laughed. I'm not angry, I understand, I said, but doesn't the Bible say 'Justice, justice shalt thou pursue'? They said, what do the Arabs know about the Bible? Hava listened to Azouri's anger, she felt that he was acting an angry man for her benefit, later on I myself would come to know that feeling of hanging pictures of hell on the walls of paradise. Azouri said, at the window stood my father, and Hava smiled at the order of the words and he saw her smiling and he blushed, and sweet man don't stop blushing, Hava thought to herself, facing the waves which had begun to woo the eroded concrete with a stormier passion. Azouri said, jeeps full of fair-haired soldiers began to drive through the alleys, driving away the Arabs who had begun to come back, giving them a punch in the belly or a kick in the pants to help them on their way, to help them understand that Arabs can only understand one language and that's the language of force, because that's what's written in all the books, the books they read in Poland, Arabs only understand the language of force. And my father's second wife kept on cursing him, go and do something, she screamed, and he did nothing. It's an entrance ticket to paradise, she said to him but he wouldn't go. He had a sword which he had received from my uncle abu-al-Misk Kafur but he didn't stick it in anyone's heart, not into his first wife's heart in Tunisia or into his own either. And his second wife was going insane with loathing and contempt. The shame was eating her alive. Her first husband died like a hero in the great battle for Palestine and her second husband sits and stares at the sea. She didn't hang herself like people said, she slit her throat in her room and came and stood in the door and the blood poured out of her and my father stood still and his eyes were dry and empty as he asked, how can the blood reach her legs when it's gushing out of her throat, and afterwards he said, I killed her, one of them I drove to Tunisia and the other one I killed, why aren't I like Haj Amin el-Husseini, like the knight in armour I was meant to be? But my father didn't have it in him any more. The woman died so that they would be able to lay another brick in paradise. She was a Moslem and believed that her death would enable Allah to lay a brick in the wall of paradise which develops cracks every now and then. She was a proud woman.

Hava looked at him. She sensed the savagery with which he was choosing his words, to insult her, to tell her, you came and took Acre away from me. She felt a shadow of fear, she had almost found what she didn't know she had been looking for all her life, she didn't want to lose it, and she said: I was escorting a convoy to Jerusalem and they shot me. He looked at her and she said, I'm a lost case, they'll never be able to put me together properly again. And then he asked her what her name was and she told him. My name is Azouri, he said and he looked at her. He took his hand out of hers and stood up. He paced up and down and Abu Cristo stared at him in astonishment. A waiter ran after him with a glass of arak. He swallowed the arak and threw the empty glass furiously to the ground. He came back to her. She sat there calmly. In any case everything was lost. The sea was full of sharks and devils. She knew there was no way

111

back and she didn't care. He said, are you Franz's daughter? and she said, I'm Franz's daughter. And Käthe's, he said and when he said 'Käthe' his voice was full of longing. She stood up and glared at him, and then Azouri's enormous tears spilled out of his eyes. She was amazed, she had never seen such enormous tears before. She looked at Azouri incredulously, his long lashes were studded with teardrops and he wept as he should have wept years before when Käthe allowed him to come close to her and then pushed him away again, and now that he had found love at last it had to be Franz's love again, it had to be his daughter he would rob him of, another Käthe all over again. He found himself hoping that she was married, that she had children. No, she had no children, I'm not married, she said, and I haven't got a boyfriend. And at three o'clock in the morning he took her to the military governor's office to get a travel permit and the young officer who owed his father a debt of honour agreed to give him one and he drove Hava to Tel Aviv in his little Ford. She asked him, if it means so much to you why didn't you get in touch all these years, why didn't you contact Franz and Käthe again? And then he said to Hava what he said later to Franz, I tried to phone but the line was engaged.

12

After Dina and I had separated, after I had tried to fuck her uniform, after my friends had returned from the war, there were some painful moments in store. Giora, one of my closest friends from school, was killed in the battle for Suez. I went to his house, I wanted to console Giora's father, Nachie. I'd known Giora ever since we were in the fourth form together. His mother was in a state of shock, all my old school friends were sitting there. A young soldier wearing a tank crew uniform sat staring into space and speaking in a monotonous tone of voice, as if he was shell-shocked. They all sat there stunned. Nachie said, they've killed my son and suddenly he saw me standing at the door. He had to blame somebody, Golda and Dayan were far away, I was the enemy. And he stood up and threw me out of his house. I had come to console the father of a friend, perhaps the only real friend I ever had, the only one who never attacked me for my relations with Dina, for destroying her parents who hadn't come to their Jewish state for their daughter to marry an Arab, and all of a sudden Giora's father, Nachie, who used to demonstrate against the military government, who was always on the right side, whose heart was in the right place, stood up and threw me out of his house in a rage. I went home, Franz was sitting and listening to the news. He said they're blaming the whole thing on the Intelligence, the Intelligence made a mistake and two thousand six hundred boys paid the price. I looked at my grandfather, the furthest thing imaginable from a typical Israeli

113

chauvinist, and I waited, but he didn't say anything about the twenty thousand Arabs who were killed too, Egyptians, Syrians, maybe relations of Azouri's. He said, two thousand six hundred boys were killed. He saw me looking at him, the words of the radio announcer had taken over the words in his head, the air was heavy with the sense of failure and grief. I went to Haifa and kept away from Franz for several months. That was my Arab period. I went to live with Kassem who wrote protest plays. We were a small group, poets, teachers, students, a painter whose nationalist paintings I thought were lousy, but I didn't say a word. To myself I said, Yosef, no half-measures! I thought of Giora's father, of the moment his eyes met mine like the eyes of a stranger and a fire of hatred and despair was lit between us. I met Laila again. I had to take a lot of crap from them, I was too cool, arrogant, they accused me of patronising them, but after the arguments Kassem would roll me a joint in the two-roomed flat where I lived with him in Abbas Street, and we would sit and talk about Pablo Neruda and Brecht and Picasso, he taught me about poets I had never heard of. I forced myself to read Arabic, I even wrote a couple of poems. They turned me into a poet and I made some illustrations for poems, abstract but with a lot of anger in them. They liked my anger. Laila fell into the trap I set for her, I had my eye on her from the beginning, on her shy well-groomed beauty, so different from Dina's. She was trying to find a place for herself in the Party framework, she talked about Marxism without understanding the first thing about it, she needed something to cling to and I understood her because there in Haifa I was a refugee too, and that was exactly what I wanted. We were like brothers. The comrades went out with Jewish girls and smashed the holy wombs of the bereaved fathers lamenting their loss on every street corner and planning preventative action against the Arabs coming to rape their holy Jewish daughters. I understood them, I understood the cunning of their insult. Every one of them came from a plundered family, with time and imagination the extent of the plunder was exaggerated, the number of the stolen hectares grew. Every one of them bore a scar. Anyone who was ever arrested on a bus by a Jewish policeman and told, come here, Arab, knows that scar. I understood, and what I didn't know from my own experience I knew from the look in Nachie's eyes. I had a passport in the name of Rosenzweig, but I had another one too, in the name of Yosef Sherara. I went to Franz and told him that he was a maniac, I told him how he had hurt me when he sat there listening to the radio and talking about 'our' boys. He remembered and tried to explain but all I really wanted was an excuse to get some money out of him, I had savings schemes from both Franz and Azouri, and money in Switzerland, but I wanted him to pay for my trip. Franz took out his cheque book and wrote a cheque. I went to a travel agency and bought a ticket to Athens. Laila said, you'll meet Murad there, he writes poetry. I went to Athens. I sat in my hotel for five days. I went to see the Acropolis every day, I walked around a bit, I wasn't crazy about Athens, I sat in a bar and drank ouzo, I met a woman who wanted to be my mother for the price of a few dollars, I took her into a dark corner and I beat her, I stole her purse and scattered the contents in the street. In the hotel they called me 'Mr. Sherara' respectfully, as if they could see the dagger I was holding next to my heart. At the end of five days I took two suitcases and filled them with worthless trash, I wanted to see the customs officials and security police getting their hands dirty. I poured sticky orange juice over my old underpants, over cheap books in Greek, I threw in some rubbish from the bin, and I took an Olympic flight back to Israel. When I got out of the plane there was a border patrol car waiting for me. In front of everyone, the only passenger out of that huge jumbo jet, I was led away to the car and the cop sitting in it asked me where I'd been. I told him and

115

he pushed his face into mine and dug his elbow into my ribs and said, did you meet Murad? Abu Zaidan? I said, I didn't meet anybody. They took me into the middle of the hall. The returning passengers stared at me as if I were the terrible danger they'd been waiting for, some of them quickly lowered their eyes. I was taken into a little room and interrogated for three hours, they opened my luggage and stuck their hands into the mess and swore, they brought me a glass of water and spilled it on me accidentally on purpose, they offered me cigarettes and lit them for me so that the match burned my lips, and I didn't say a word. I felt the blood beating and splashing against the walls of my brain, before my eyes I saw the olive trees that Laila was always talking about. At the end of three hours they had finished with me. They said to me, don't complain or we'll shut your trap so tight you'll never complain again. I went outside. I called a cab and the driver said to me, aren't you the Arab they took in for questioning? I said yes, and I had to wait for a long time before I found a cab that would take me. I arrived in Haifa, threw my suitcases away and went to Laila. I phoned Dina and said, I've got an Arab girl. Laila and I began our affair. After a few days she was already bad-mouthing her friends. She said they only fucked Jewish girls but in the end they married the girls their fathers told them to. Some revolutionaries, she said, but they're the only ones we've got. She lived with me openly, she wasn't ashamed, she wasn't afraid of her brothers coming with knives any more, but she was afraid, she said, of loving me, and it was then that I started playing the Arab macho bit for her benefit, I insulted her, I sat there waiting for her to bring me coffee. I sat there drinking coffee, and suddenly she screamed, why do you have to act the Arab with me? I said, what's wrong with being an Arab, and she said, nothing at all, but why lay on the middle-east macho bit so thick? I had a Jewish boyfriend once, he was so sweet, he came from South America, he had a beard, he taught me to respect myself, and then I hit her and she cried, you're a lousy Arab, Yosef, you should have brought me Hava's son, not Kafur's nephew. I was furious and we fought the whole night long. She was hungry for love, but she began to detest the Yosef who had come to Haifa to be part of her scene. She began to play herself and the barrier she erected between us was more real and more authentic than anything I could have imagined.

And then they chose us to go on one of their joyrides to the Soviet Union and the Eastern Bloc countries. I told Franz over the phone that I would look for the graves of his parents in Posen and he laughed.

Kassem wrote a protest play and Laila played the part of the oppressed Arab woman too shockingly for words. In real life, the oppression is far more credible. But they had built a kind of totem, and they were doing their best to live up to the role which Giora's father's eyes had cast me in when I came to weep with him for the death of his son. We set out united in our submission to the big words about the brotherhood of man and the world of the revolution. None of us was a great believer, but we played it for all it was worth. Questions were asked about me, by the Agencies, and by Franz as well, but in the end they said, if he chooses to be an Arab he may as well be their Arab.

In Moscow they were obliged to be friendly. Thirty thousand enthusiastic boy scouts arrived at the stadium in trucks to see us. They brought them from factories and plants, every group leader carried the flag of his plant, and they cheered and clapped in time to professional applause directors. Kassem fell into their trap, he loved that applause, all that instant love produced on demand. Laila could see how phoney it all was but she wanted to be loved too, she wanted the applause and she played the holy Arab woman martyred by the Jews, the Israelis, the Zionist imperialists, to the hilt. And she did it so well that they all clapped wildly, like a machine gone mad. Kassem beamed with happiness. They translated his play into

117

seventeen languages, into Georgian, Caucasian, Ukranian, Polish, Kurdish, German, Russian and God knows what else. Tank builders clapped mesmerised hands and shouted slogans about the tractors they were building for the world of tomorrow. It all seemed infantile to me. I felt fed up. When it was my turn to read a poem I saw the interpreter looking at me with cold contempt in his eyes. I caught his look and in the middle of that stadium, opposite thirty thousand tired but enthusiastic-by-command faces, I began to read and the interpreter began to translate, and I said in Yiddish – a mixture of the little imitation joke-Yiddish I picked up in Israel and the German which of course I knew well – I said: I have a father who had a mother who ran away with a terrorist who cut off Jews' heads and stuck them up on broomsticks, and a stepmother who thought you could buy a ticket to paradise with a knife. The man tried to translate, got mixed up, muttered a few words to me in Yiddish, went pale, turned to that vast audience and began declaiming whatever came into his head. He said, who can avenge the death of a little child, blood gushes from the olive trees, crosses burn in the wasteland, cry the beloved country, weep for the fallen, oh eyes which have seen your disgrace, only the flag rotting in the prison cells will chop off the head of the stinking oak tree and the audience applauded wildly. I said to him in my broken Yiddish, so we're in the same boat, eh? And the next day he came to my hotel and sat in my room and asked me how I had landed up with these dirty Arabs, and he said to me, please, give me a book in Hebrew, I want to dream more in Hebrew, one forgets, once I knew a lot of Hebrew, but not today, and he wept on the banks of the rivers of Babylon and Zion and I took pity on him. I said to him, listen, don't have any illusions about me, I'm an Arab, I just happen to know a few things that other people don't know. He didn't know what to say, he was confused, a Soviet Jew playing forbidden games, he begged me not to say anything and I

118

promised. Kassem became aware of the fact that our hosts were laughing behind his back, but he pretended not to hear them. They brought girls to embrace him. They said to them in Russian, go to that Arab and put your arms around him. I heard a woman standing next to the interpreter cursing in Yiddish and I spoke to her and she forgot where she was, she touched the hand that had touched the holy wall in Jerusalem and she said, they only bring them for the propaganda. Everything was a mess and when Laila came to me that night I said to her, they're making fools of us, they're using us, and she cried and said, I know, but we have to play along, we're the representatives of the new world, the freedom fighters ground under the boot of the Zionist oppressor and that's what they want and that's what we'll give them because they're righter than you think. I said to her, Laila that's hypocritical cant and you know it, and she said, their hypocrisy is better than your insults and discrimination and racialism! You at least have got somewhere to run to, you've got a different mother, I haven't got anywhere to go to. And I said to her, you've got twenty-two Arab states, why don't you move up a little, why do you have to have this lousy little strip of land precisely? You belong to the great Arab nation, you've crushed Jews for a thousand years, give a quarter of a percent of your territory to my mother...But I had the right answer to that argument too, and I didn't need Laila to tell it to me.

When I was standing on that platform I thought of Franz. Franz always said that Azouri wasn't a communist and that his Marxism was only a refuge for his nationalism. From a distance I felt sorry for Azouri, I spoke to thirty thousand people about his father's second wife, and the blood gushing out of her throat and the interpreter recited rubbish about dead olive trees and I laughed and thirty thousand people laughed too. The interpreter refused to believe in my Arab half, he came to me to look for Yosef Rosenzweig and I gave him what he wanted. Laila said, you're making a fool of him, he thinks you're a Jew, and I said to her, so what am I then? And the interpreter recited a poem about how we had taken the holocaust and turned it into a bargaining counter in order to expel the poor Arabs from their country. A million Jews were killed, he said, and the Zionists who collaborated with the Nazis exaggerate the numbers, exaggerate their imaginary pain in order to squeeze more money, more arms out of Germany, in order to rob the peasants, our poor brothers, of their land. And that night he came and sat with me and asked me about Jerusalem and drank in every word I said to him and jabbered to me in Yiddish and said, you call them freedom fighters? Arab hooligans on heat.

They took us on organised tours, they applauded us. Laila recited in Arabic to audiences who then spoke other languages. And then towards the end, in the middle of an argument Kassem suddenly yelled, what can you expect of a Jew already? The fact that your mother fucked Azouri doesn't make you one of us, you never had to go through what we did, you can afford to be stuck up because you've got Franz. I told him that he had more places to go to than I did and he said, you see? I told you that he was a Jew! When we came back I went on trying to get what comfort I could out of them. Nachie's hostile eyes still bored holes in my heart. But relations were unenthusiastic, we were always quarrelling, in the end it became impossible for me to go on living with Kassem. Laila and I looked at each other with unfriendly eyes, she was caught in the black magic of her own loneliness. She started working for the Haifa municipal theatre, she said she would show them how to treat an Arab woman with respect. Azouri came and took me away, he said, this is no place for you, you're playing games, you have to decide even though the decision was made for you before you were born. I told him they were hypocrites and no better than the worst of the Arab nationalists, and he said, in this

120

tragedy you're not really on any side, that's your good fortune and also your curse, you'll always be the most convenient shore to land on, the closest to spit at. I phoned Dina and told her about the Yiddish in Moscow and she wanted to laugh but she was afraid to and that made me even madder than before.

13

In my luggage I found a folded note. I opened it and read: If I forget thee O Jerusalem may my right hand forget its cunning. I showed it to Laila and she said, the cheeky bastard. I said you can't stop people from longing, Laila. I went to Kassem to take my things. He gave me a hostile look but in the end we embraced. Laila said, you're the man I loved, what chance did our love ever have? You belong to Dina, you'll never be free of her, and I told her that that wasn't the reason and she knew it. She blushed and said that it would be better for us to think that that was the reason, and I said, okay Laila, if that's the way you want it.

Today, looking back, I'm no longer sure what I was looking for in Haifa, not in the town itself that is, but in the attempt to belong. I was Hava's son, after all, and apart from the dance of death in Koloniya Hava had no roots. Käthe belonged to the past, like the cobwebs on her furniture, and Franz belonged to Azouri more than he did to Käthe. When Azouri brought her home from Acre that night, he parked his car next to the house, leant his head on the steering wheel, and waited. Hava said, nothing can come of this but the yellow star all over again, and he didn't know what she really wanted but it was too late to turn back. He lied and said, I can't possibly go back now, they'll stop me on the way, they'll take me in for questioning and hold me for forty-eight hours, I'd better stay here. She said, come upstairs, the time has come for you and Franz to talk about what you left behind.

122

At five o'clock in the morning on the stairs of the sleeping house she led in the only chance she would ever have to return to who she was before they told her to acquire a new identity. She knew that Käthe would be there, and she wanted to see her surrender. Ever since her childhood she had been waiting for the moment of her revenge on Käthe, and nobody knew, not Hanoch, not Franz, nobody knew the gaping hole which her mother's pure beauty had left inside her. Azouri looked at the quiet street, the cypress tree and the casuarina, Franz's Kaiser Frazer parked below, and he thought of the time he wasted on negotiations between his neighbours and the military government, the lawsuits and evictions and arrests, he saw the position of strength this house represented and he remembered where he had brought Franz from for his daughter to be shot at on the top of a truck on the way to Jerusalem. All he really wanted was to give Franz back what he deserved. To let Käthe give him at last the daughter he had been waiting so long to beget from her. He thought of the military governor, with whom he read German poetry, how sure he was of his own rightness, how he loved the submission he thought he saw in Azouri's eyes. The war's just begun, he said to him. And in a dark room in Acre with a flyblown picture of Lenin on the wall people said, both Arabs and Jews, after the revolution there won't be nations any more, there won't be wars, and how he wanted to believe them, but he didn't believe them. He believed in this moment on the stairs in the city of the military governors with Hava, the apple of their eyes, the heroine of their war, waiting to go up and meet the enemy, the man who but for the fact that Azouri had smelled the fire would have been turned to smoke to decorate the sky of a tired God. Why do I have to understand him and who asked me to be his doorman to paradise, he asked himself?

He looked at Hava and was flooded with sadness, he didn't want revenge, but he didn't not want it either. He was afraid to

123

go inside.

Through the round window between the second and third floors he saw the trees haloed in the glow of the rising sun. It was cold in the stair-well and the smell of old lysol mingled with the smell of his fear. Hava opened the door, the flat was dark, he saw Hava tiptoeing in, leading him into the kitchen, putting the kettle on to boil, trying not to make a noise, looking for something to do. He stood still. He knew that Hava wanted to get inside his body and stay there. On the other side of the door he heard someone breathing rhythmically in their sleep, he sat in the kitchen with his hands around a steaming cup of coffee and watched the sun rising to touch the top of the cypress tree, and suddenly he wanted to calculate the exact moment of the sunset, to surprise Franz, but Franz seemed very remote to him, as if he wasn't sleeping a few feet away, as if he were a great distance from him. Käthe, who even then looked more like a dead soul than a living body, was sleeping soundly. The evening before Franz had given her a sleeping pill after an attack of hysteria. When Franz stood in the door and looked at Azouri, Hava withdrew into the corner and stood with her back to the pantry door and let the sunrise dissolve her into the pale yellowish grey of the paint on the door.

Azouri looked at Franz and thought, where is the pale young war hero with the noble wondering face in this respectable refugee from the vanity fair of history? Franz wanted coffee more than anything else. His tongue couldn't form the words he wanted to say. Hava smiled and embraced her father. He said, it's a long time since you were here Azouri, and Azouri laughed and then stopped and tried to fit the banal words into some conceivable context. They looked at each other, old war horses, thought Hava, out of the corner of her eye she could see her mother's locked bedroom door. She knew, without having to think about it, that Azouri was trying to penetrate to the other side of the door with his eyes.

They sat and drank coffee. Hava found some rusks and smeared them with margarine and jam. Good jam, said Azouri. Hava smiled. The light grew brighter and shadows crept up the walls and disappeared. Azouri stood up and suddenly he grabbed hold of Franz and lifted him right off his feet and kissed him on the face and Franz went pale. A single tear formed under his eye and he looked at his slippers and said, Azouri is here, and Hava said, he is going to be my man. Franz looked at his daughter, he felt embarrassed and he didn't know what to say. He wanted to run to Käthe's room to make sure that she still existed. Azouri said, I have to go, it will be morning soon, my permit is only good till ten, kiss her for me. Hava said, an hour has already gone by and I didn't even notice, and Azouri said, I should have stayed in the car.

The next day Hava sat at home and waited. Yona answered the phone. She said, Madame Käthe, a man from Acre wants to talk to Hava. Käthe said I don't know anyone from Acre, I'm going down to the sea to swim. She went down to the beach and she looked for Azouri in the sea and she began to swim. Franz ran after her and she shouted, I'm going to swim to Berlin, you can stand on your head but Azouri will never beget Hava from Hava.

What happened to Hava and Azouri was inevitable and the way they displayed themselves in public didn't help. They sat in cafes and the waiters, whose sense of smell had been sharpened in the camps, gave them hostile looks. Azouri wasn't angry but Hava began to feel like a wounded animal. She said, I don't know what to do. They separated and came back to each other. Somehow they managed to let a whole year slip by, how I don't know and after all this time Azouri can't remember either. All I know is that it was a year full of bitterness. They sat in cafes and people stared at them and they went down to the sea and Hava said, I don't know what to do, I can't go on with you and I can't go on without you. They went dancing in a nightclub where nobody asked any questions. At Abu Cristo's they said that Azouri never cried and the famous story about his tears was apocryphal. Azouri was kept busy trying to help people in trouble with the authorities, he was placed under house arrest again, because the military governor didn't like something he said about him in the Party Club, and then he was released again, both the detention and the release without any legal grounds. Azouri didn't even try to understand any more, Hava came and stayed with him for a week. Azouri's father shut himself up in his room. He had been ill for a long time and now he was dying. Azouri's brothers began to gather, not all of them received permits to enter the country, the brother from Jordan was refused entry, the brother from Beirut arrived on forged papers. Hava sat with them opposite Azouri's dying father. Azouri said, he's not going to where my uncle Kafur went when he died, he's going to his two wives. How romantic, thought Hava, and she found his body waiting for her. His brothers spoke about the struggle and he clung to them and avoided them at the same time. Hava said, I have to have your child Azouri, and he said, and where will we bring him up, how? They sat in the intoxicating fragrance of the orange trees and caressed each other, they surrendered to their love because there was nothing else to surrender to. Azouri came to visit Franz and they resumed the deep and ancient friendship which Hava could not understand because it had begun a hundred years before she was born. Käthe stood in the doorway and looked at Franz and then she stole a quiet glance at Azouri and she was reassured. Something which had once burned in her was dead. Yona said, what is that Arab doing here? Hava and Azouri sucked each other's blood, Franz said to me afterwards, but he spoke without bitterness. He understood. Käthe put on a white dress which she had brought with her from Germany and drove to Acre. She had some trouble getting in. A group of Arabs was standing next to a

126

truck and policemen were searching their pockets. Käthe looked at the wall and the towers and the minarets and she said, what a beautiful town. She entered the town and found the house. Hava opened the door. Azouri's brothers were there. The house was a fine two-storied building surrounded by neatly trimmed trees, full of men and women she did not know. It was very clean. Hava sat on the sofa in Azouri's room and bent over a book. There was a typewriter in the room and shelves full of books. In the window was the sea. In the sea was the death she had always wanted to marry. She said to Hava, don't marry him, and Hava said to her, mother, why have you come here? Käthe said, you never loved me, and Hava said, that's not true, it was difficult for me, I was looking for love and you lived only for your memories. Käthe sat down next to Hava and stroked her hair. Azouri came in and sat on a low stool in the dim light of the room. Hava said I'm a Jewess hanging on a hook in an Arab bazaar. Who'll buy me? Käthe said, don't marry him, don't do it just to spite me, and Hava said, it's got nothing to do with you mother, nothing at all. Käthe said, I could have died a beautiful death and I came here instead. I can find no peace. The sea calls me. I shall swim in it and reach the place where I was born. I'm an old rag, I didn't come here to rob you of your happiness but to rescue you from ruin. You don't know. I have lived here in the heat and the noise between sweating Jews and Arabs with daggers drawn, and I know. This is a hard place, a hard language, everything is strange, what will become of you with one strangeness stuck to another? And Käthe said, Azouri has only loved one person in his life and that person is Franz. That's why he never got in touch with us, he was afraid. Men are peacocks without feathers. She stood up and walked from room to room and back again. Azouri said to Hava, your mother is sick and she should be hospitalised, and Hava said, I hate her. Azouri embraced Hava but his eyes looked after Käthe. Hava said, why don't you go to bed with

127

her, that's what you want, and Azouri took Hava down to the beach and he pointed to the sea and he said, this is where we shall sail from to bring our son, and Hava said, our daughter, and so I finally brought them to the moment I had been waiting for for millions of years in order to be born. They went back to the house and found Käthe sitting in the room with the shutters closed and the light on, trying to protect herself from herself. She no longer knew exactly who she was.

14

When Hava came to her parents' house and said to Käthe, I'm pregnant, Käthe put on a cotton housecoat over her silk dressing gown and went outside. It was a cold early morning in February. She went down to the beach, took off her housecoat and stepped into the water. She sat in the shallow water, the rocks stuck out in the dull light of the winter morning and she looked into the gathering black clouds. There was no rain but there was an icy wind blowing. A man huddled in a coat saw her sitting with the waves splashing over her. The man called the police. The policemen came down to the beach whipped by the wind, the icy water dashed against them, and they tried to drag the frozen woman out of the water. Her lips were blue, her eyes were soft and shining with frozen tears. They looked at her and asked her who she was and she said, take me to the Red Cross. They pulled her up the sand and she whispered, she shouldn't have done this to me. The policemen, stamping their feet and rubbing their hands in the cold, asked, who? But she didn't answer. In the distance they saw a heavy cloud burst and pour its water into the sea. The cloud was coming closer. The policemen hurried her away. They took her to hospital and put her to bed. The nurse didn't know what to do, she saw a frozen woman with a beatific look on her face, she called another nurse who ran to fetch a doctor. The policeman went away. Hava sat at home. She knew that her mother had disappeared but she didn't move. Yona arrived and woke Franz up. He asked, where's Käthe, and Hava did not

129

reply. He began to shout but Hava retreated into her shell and refused to say anything except she's gone, mother's gone. Franz went out to look for her, the neighbour who was still sitting with his telescope and looking for the enemy shouted, the police took her away. Franz went to the police station, the sergeant on duty didn't know what he was talking about. They tried to calm him down, they told him that women who ran away always came home again. A policeman came in soaked to the skin and said, we found a crazy woman on the beach, and began writing a report. Franz hurried to the hospital. He found a strange woman there. She looked at him without recognising him. Her glazed eyes could not grasp what this man wanted of her. All her life she had been running away, now she had arrived.

At the end of a week they transferred her to another hospital, where she burnt her hand with cigarettes, slashed her arms, and said, this way I feel something. They tied her down, they gave her pills, but the moment they let her go she would find a cigarette or a match and burn herself. Her left hand was full of burns. She didn't cry because the burns didn't hurt her. She said, it's a sweet pain, and she smiled shyly.

Every morning Franz brought a bunch of white carnations and put them beside her. He sat and read the newspapers to her and when she grew bored he read her a book. Then he went to his own hospital and operated on people's lungs. He was very tired. He felt that Azouri had betrayed him and this made him feel even closer to him than before, he liked to sit and talk to him in the evenings. The bond between them was renewed, and Käthe, who had once been the only bridge for their love, paid the price. Hava did not go to visit her mother. Azouri began to wonder aloud what they would do with their son when he was born, and his only remaining brother in Acre took him to the Party Club and gave him a lecture. He said, I stood here on the beach and the Jews yelled at me through loudspeakers, they chased me away, our family lands have been stolen, our houses, our trees. What's left? One house, and the sky. You're a beaten man, Azouri, don't bring us a Jewish child. What will we do with him? There's a new story starting here, there won't be any more uprisings, they're too strong, they've got the world on their side, and we sit here dreaming about the world of the future. What future? They've bought the future too! Azouri knew that he had to arrange things so that Yosef wouldn't suffer, but he didn't know how. Hava came and went, she tormented him with her caprices. Full of loving tenderness she said to him, whatever happens Azouri you're the only man I'll ever love but you must give me freedom, move up a little, you're putting pressure on me with all these problems. And then they sailed to Cyprus in a little boat stinking of the vomit nobody bothered to wash off the decks and they got married by a Justice of the Peace and they came home and went to register themselves as a married couple at the Ministry of the Interior. At first the clerk refused to register them, there was a big fuss, a woman screamed, you've made your bed now you can lie on it! A young lawyer passing in the corridor intervened on their behalf. Azouri stood there without opening his mouth. Hava began to look about her with haughty hostility, stifling the scream that was rising inside her. Women who might have been more understanding were put off by her disdainful looks and they too said harsh things, which they may not have meant to say. Something deep and ancient, atavistic and full of hatred broke out without anyone meaning to unleash it. Hava was appalled and Azouri was unable to go to her rescue, they were her Jews, not his. She realised how helpless he was. She did not say to the people there, don't you know who I am? I'm a heroine, your children learn about me in school. She said, you're worse than the people my parents ran away from in Germany. There was an uproar. They ran to fetch a rabbi and he glared at her wrathfully and began denouncing her in a

131

loud, ringing voice, and then they escaped. Hava said, let's go away, and Azouri said, where to? There's nowhere to go, and Franz, whom Käthe no longer recognised, said, you'd better go. He was already very tired.

I was born in a hospital in Paris. On the day I was born I received French citizenship. Azouri taught at the Sorbonne. Hava said later that it was a great honour for a man who had been refused a job at a Tel Aviv secondary school to teach at the Sorbonne. At night he sat and wrote his books. Hava adjusted quickly to the European city. Something of her childhood had survived here and she found it waiting for her. Everything was clearer, and life was simpler. The complex tangle of loves and hates was far away. She had nothing to do but bring me up. Hava was a good mother. She lavished love and tenderness on me. Azouri said that I looked like Franz and she said that I looked like Azouri. Azouri didn't like Paris. Every door was open to him there, but he was forced into the position of representing something there and he didn't want to represent anyone but himself. The teaching was fine, he told me later, but afterwards I had to explain. And he couldn't explain, he wrote a vast study, two hundred years of Jewish-Arab relations in Palestine, and he came to painful conclusions. An Arab shouldn't come to such conclusions, he said to me. He came to the conclusion which we are only beginning to understand today, that there is no hope at all, that the tragedy begins long before the historians can locate it. That everything seems to have been preordained. That the fanaticism was inevitable. That the country was foreign to both nations, which invented national movements which did not stem directly from their histories, but only from their sufferings. I spent five years in Paris, the last two of which I can remember. I already knew then what was going to happen tomorrow, and I made the children in the Luxembourg Gardens where Hava took me to play laugh. Azouri grew sad and

132

nervous, he was homesick. Franz was sent by the Ministry of Health to represent Israel at international congresses, and he took Käthe with him. He thought that he would find a cure for her, but nobody knew how to cure her. He arrived in Paris to visit his daughter. Azouri took him for a walk, they went to visit Käthe whom Franz had hospitalised for the time being in Paris. Käthe smiled and said, our Arab has arrived, and then she laughed. Azouri left the room. In the evening we went out to eat in a restaurant and I sat on my grandfather's lap and he whispered words to me in German. Azouri said that he had to go back to Palestine. Hava said they were staying in Paris. Franz didn't want to interfere. Käthe said in the hospital, who are you? and Franz said, be a good girl, Käthe, and drink your juice. He was a most devoted husband. He brought her a bunch of flowers every morning, at home and abroad, he never missed a single day. Franz was invited to give a lecture in Berlin and he flew there without Käthe. Three days later he came back. He said that he hadn't felt anything, as if he were visiting a foreign country. Azouri tried to understand, he asked questions but Franz was full of a kind of fear which Azouri had never seen in him before. That night he disappeared. They heard nothing from him and Hava went to inquire. At the Israeli consulate they told her that Franz had gone to lecture in Copenhagen. Hava knew that no lecture had been scheduled in Copenhagen. She phoned all kinds of people and she began to feel hostile towards Azouri. Because of you, she said, my mother is sick and my father has disappeared. He embraced her wordlessly. Franz had taken the night train to Copenhagen. It was cold and the heating on the train wasn't working. He wasn't sorry, it was what he wanted. He wanted to feel what it was like to travel in a closed train through Germany. The policemen shouting in the gloomy stations of the night, the cattle grazing in the dark silent fields, the cathedral spire of Cologne, he saw them all slip by as he sat freezing alone in his first class compartment, and felt like a sheep being led to the slaughter. He came back to Paris and said to Azouri, when I was giving my lecture in Berlin the hall was full of the friends of my youth and I stood there and felt that everything was happening in a dream, I was moved and happy to be talking German again but I thought about Käthe as if she were already dead, as if it wasn't her who had burnt her hands like that but they who were burning her alive. Franz was eager to get back to the illusory past he was increasingly finding in the potsherds of the ancient kings of Israel, and Azouri said to Hava, if we don't go back the whole country will soon belong to Franz. He is robbing me of my country, but my longings are worth as much as his old potsherds. Hava went to the hospital and looked at her mother. She took me with her. I stood there and looked at my grandmother's beautiful face. She asked, who is this child, and waved her hand at me. Hava told her who I was. Käthe spoke to me in broken Hebrew and I answered her in French.

Franz and Käthe went back to Israel, leaving a trail of longings behind them. Like Käthe so many years before Azouri too began to pack his bags. He tried to understand how Hava could be so indifferent. She said, this child will grow up here and be free, and Azouri said, we've weighted the scales against him and we must teach him to be strong. There the borders will cut him in two but here he will have no borders at all and he'll grow up as lost and homeless as your mother. Hava cried and tried to resist him. Azouri's longings were like a noose around her neck. She had never longed for anything. She never thought of Tel Aviv any more than she thought of Hanoch after he was killed in the war. What's done is done, she said to Azouri, but he said no, that's not true.

And so, when I was five years old we went home to Israel. From senior lecturer at the Sorbonne Azouri descended to the level of member of the Acre local council and Party hack. Once again he sat in the dim room under the picture of Lenin and finished the proofs of his monumental book. I grew up alternately in my grandfather's empty house and Azouri's house. Hava and Azouri did not know where to live. There was an empty apartment available in Haifa. It was easier for a mixed couple in Haifa, but Hava wanted to bring Tel Aviv to its knees, and Tel Aviv hid behind a smoke screen of indifference and fought them. Wherever they went Azouri's name sent them right back to the bored estate agent. In the end they found a flat where the landlord said I don't care if he's an Arab and you're a Jew or vice versa, as long as you pay me enough and on time, I want a lot of money and I want it in dollars, and they paid.

Hava, my mother on Azouri's side, was the heroine of isolated moments: the moment when she was shot, the moment when she saw Azouri coming into Abu Cristo's, the moment when she came to her mother and said, I'm pregnant. Her homecoming was accompanied by more than regret, she followed Azouri down the ramp of the aeroplane full of bitter resentment. Dina says that Hava was always looking for an outlet for the anger she felt against herself because of what she did to her mother, but Dina is always looking for reasons for things. Her affair with me is the only thing in her life that she never had a reason for. Once, when Dina came home for the weekend from her basic training, she phoned me from the central bus station in Tel Aviv. I was sitting in Franz's house reading the Koran, Franz said I was reading it to spite Dina, but I really did want to understand, to know things that had been kept from me, my atheistic father and my mother had not provided me with enough ammunition in my struggle for survival. Franz left me alone, ever since the refusal of the army to draft me and his own outburst in the Chief of Staff's office, he had become more and more preoccupied with the attempt to put out the fire of loathing he felt for the people around him. Actually, Franz was the violent side of Azouri, and to call Franz violent is like comparing Albert Schweitzer to a Spanish bull-fighter. Dina was still living with her parents then. They were the most pitiful people I've ever met, they liked me but they wished that I was dead, they felt my foreignness more than anyone else, the very fact that my father was an Arab was enough to crush them to a pulp. They looked at Dina as if she were supposed to fulfill the dreams they hadn't even managed to dream. In their dreams there was always someone like Rammy asking them for their daughter's hand. They always treated me politely, and Dina's mother was even quite fond of me in her own way, as if in spite of everything my smile and my anger coiled like a spring, my ability to live for a moment in tomorrow, to bring the rain to Kassit, had a certain entertainment value for her, and she would ask Dina questions about me. When Dina and I broke up she didn't know if she was only happy or a little sad too. Unlike her mother Dina's father had no doubts at all about his dislike of me, and when he saw me arriving at the house an hour after his soldier daughter had come home on her first leave he couldn't control his anger. He got up and walked out of the room in order not to have to sit for a minute with her Arab, as he called me behind my back. I said to Dina that I was sure she was going to make a great soldier. She sensed the scorn in my voice and she felt guilty, she really didn't try but in spite of herself she was a good soldier, perhaps not the most disciplined, but with her drive to excel in everything she did it bothered her to be the only soldier on the base with an Arab boyfriend. She may not always have put all her hair up under her cap, she may have chewed gum when she shouldn't have, but she was ready for inspection in five minutes flat in the morning, she was physically strong, she was the favourite of the corporals and the officers, she was the first to volunteer, even when she didn't want to, she was a good shot, she did well on all the tests, she tried not to be the best recruit on the base but she knew that I was right. In two weeks' time she would graduate from basic training as the outstanding soldier of the course, and she knew that it would make me mad. I said, you won't only be the outstanding graduate of your course, you'll be a corporal too. She said that she wouldn't, but she knew that they would recommend her. She knew that she would try to resist them but that in the end she would do the course, pass it, and be a good corporal.

When I began to fuck her uniform she burst out laughing. But the laughter ended abruptly. I could see how, and from what depths, depths I knew in my own soul, as if against her will, she was forced to fight for something Jews had prayed for in their cellars, suddenly she had to defend that bloody uniform, make it into more than it really was, even though she hated herself for doing it. What's a uniform, she said afterwards, but at that moment the uniform was a symbol for the two thousand years they had washed our brains with in school, dinning them into us with pained expressions, gritting their teeth, with pride, with arrogance, the two thousand years which were always used against me, against Azouri's son, not Hava's son on Franz my grandfather's side. She didn't say that I was desecrating it but after the short-lived laughter she began to fight me, to save her uniform from disgrace, perhaps to protect her father. She said, even when there's no need to you have to hurt me. I said all I was doing was fucking a uniform, and what the hell was a uniform anyway, every army in the world had uniforms and heroes, the Germans had them too. She said, but it's not just any uniform to you Yosef, and I knew that that was what she would say. From the day she joined the army all I could think about was the day she would come home on leave and I would find, here in the room I had known for four years, a Jewish soldier, who would one day search my pockets in buses, enter the homes of Azouri's cousins in Sakhnin to hold the baby while the men searched the house, the comrade-in-arms of the people who would put his cousin

137

in administrative detention or torture him with all the ingenuity at their command in order to justify those 'two thousand years'.

I said to her, for all your so-called liberation and left-wing views, all you really want is to have a strong army, and she said, yes, that's right, and I said, my nation is at war with my state, and vice versa, and what am I? And she said, you're my lover, but I'm part of something and I can't help it, I belong to its genetic code, and I asked her, what? What do you belong to besides me? And she wanted to answer but she knew that whatever she said would be wrong and so she didn't say anything.

She was confused and tired, the basic training was rough, she hadn't slept for a week, she didn't look well, her nose was red and peeling from a forced march in the sun, she'd lost weight and I even wanted to respect that uniform because it was my mother Hava's uniform too, and when I hurt her I was hurting myself where it hurt most. I always envied Azouri for being a full Arab, free of the accursed blood of the Jews who in the name of their absolute justice forced me to be my own enemy.

Dina was ashamed of herself for losing her temper and she got into bed, curled up in the blanket and looked at me anxiously, biting her fingernails ferociously.

Afterwards she said with the hostility that always came out when she was happy, you probably enjoyed fucking my uniform more than fucking me. She lay next to me and I held her relaxed body close to me, we had just finished re-discovering our real secret, the passion which neither of us would ever be able to overcome. The near demonic desire to merge into one – the soft blow falling, the trembling participation of every inch of our bodies. She looked at me, she was exhausted from the army, from love, from fucking, from everything together, her face was distorted, she looked like a trapped bird, the light fell onto my half-closed eyes and I couldn't resist saying, yes, your uniform was sexier! And she said, that's what every Arab boy dreams of, fucking a Jewish soldier, fucking her uniform...I closed my eyes furiously, for a moment I wanted to hit her, but then I thought of what had just happened between us and I knew that she was right. When I had been with her now, perhaps because of our quarrel, perhaps because of things that went far deeper, things that only Bunim knew how to set before me in all their cruel simplicity, I really had enjoyed myself more than usual, it was a moment of pure happiness to fuck not only Dina, whom I loved so much, but a Jewish soldier, a fantasy toughness, a woman with an Uzi glued to her body, who could walk into my house whenever she felt like it and arrest me, who could humiliate my father. For the moment she put on that fucking uniform she was ten times more powerful than Azouri, who had stepped into Franz's shoes and become a refugee in his own country, which in a curious way made me stronger than she was precisely because I had no uniform, but of course immeasurably weaker too. And if Azouri's cousins on the other side of the border had uniforms and guns, that made me stronger, but it also defeated me utterly, and whichever way you looked at it I was trapped, I had to fuck my mother's uniform to kill my father.

Later on we tried to forget. We drank cold beer from the fridge. Dina's mother bought the Tuborg specially for me. Her father came in with the needle and said, listen Yosef, why don't you give us a chance to see our soldier daughter too? We haven't seen her since she was drafted, you can come back later. I looked at him, I felt sorry for him but I said, I'll go when she tells me to. She sat there naked under the army issue parka, it wasn't particularly cold but she was shivering, and she didn't say a word. Her father looked at her, full of longing for his only daughter, and she tried not to see him, but not to see me either. He was a sensitive man, he was hurt and he went outside in order not to let me see how much I had hurt him. I began talking to her about Azouri and Hava in Tel Aviv, when I was five years old, I said to her, imagine how many times they had to leave the room like that, to stand facing a decent person like your father and feel that they weren't wanted. She cried soundlessly. I knew that she only wanted to be with her parents a little, not against me, not without me, but with them, to let them spoil her a little. She was a woman in bed, but we were still children then, she was an eighteen-year-old girl who had just come home from a backbreaking month in basic training and she wanted her father to be proud of her, to tell her how good she looked in her uniform, so that she could say, oh, you're only saying that, you know it's not true, I hate my uniform, but to me she couldn't say that she hated her uniform. She could only say it to someone like her father, and this infuriated me. Perhaps that was why I was sitting and reading the Koran when she phoned. I had never read it before, it had been lying in my room for years, but I knew what would happen, I guessed. Sometimes knowing what's going to happen can drive you crazy. This whole situation had already been lived through before, I knew it inside out, and she knew that I knew it, and it maddened her to think that she was playing the game according to the rules that I had invented for her when she phoned me from the central bus station.

I sat talking to her for a long time while her parents waited, she was so tired that she fell asleep while I was talking. Her father came in and touched her forehead and said, she's worn out. You don't know what basic training's like, they give them hell. I told him that I did know. He looked at me and said, you can go now, you haven't left us much anyway. And Dina's mother who was fond of me in her way but no less hostile, trying to control her growing anger said, you've already got what you wanted, haven't you?

140

15

When Azouri began to stand opposite Kassit, sombre and controlled, a sad, silent reproach, I needed him there as a challenge. I drove to the desert, I sat with Rammy and Dina, I was jealous of everyone. Azouri was necessary to me there because I loved him, I wanted him to relieve me of the terrible need to always know my limits, to know how far I could go and where the border was. The more I tormented Rammy and Dina the closer I brought them together. Dina phoned Franz one day and he told me that she wanted to talk to me, outside in the yard. I went down, the garden which Käthe had watched being planted was wet with the rain which had fallen during the night. Dina was sitting huddled on a bench. Perhaps she asked me to meet her here because she didn't want to see herself from her balcony looking for a lover's bench to meet me on. She hardly moved as she spoke, she kept her eyes fixed on the gap between two buildings through which you could still see the sea. The sea was stormy and there was a ship sailing towards the port in Ashdod. Dina said, I want to marry Rammy. I didn't react. I had nothing to say. She said, he's the sweetest thing that's ever happened to me, he came to me with your recommendation, you went to the desert to play games with a Danish tourist so that I could meet him, you're responsible for this marriage, if you could have taken me as I was I wouldn't have been so lonely.

I told her that I looked for Azouri on the other side of Dizengoff street and I couldn't find him there. She said, you know he won't come any more. How long can he go on waiting for you? I said that I spent my life waiting for her, and that if you wanted to wait for someone you waited. She said, don't be melodramatic, Yosef. You spent your life waiting for me! You weren't waiting for me, you wanted to break me! Why did we separate? You said you'd never marry me because I'm Hava. You said you saw the deaths of Käthe and Hava in my eyes. I'm not them, I'm Dina, and I want a man of my own, and a home of my own and everything that goes with it. I looked at her, she was embarrassed and withdrawn. In the distance, on the corner of the street, I could see Rammy's mop of hair. The poor boy was trying to hide behind a pile of planks some builders had left there. I didn't know if she had come to ask for my permission to marry, or perhaps for my refusal to give her permission. I said to Dina, I can't tell you what to do, I can't stop you, and she whispered, you can, and stood up. We looked at each other and I said to her, you'll always know where to find me if you want me, and tell Rammy he doesn't have to stop coming to Kassit, I like him, no good will come of this, perhaps in the end I'll paint the desert red at last, and then I'll get out of here.

I didn't go to their wedding, and later on when they got divorced I didn't go to console Rammy. Franz was sad, Gertrude had already snared him in her net, the house was empty. Azouri hardly came any more, and I thought then about Hava, my mother on Azouri's side, and their love, about how they had brought me up in Tel Aviv, how they had taken me to Acre, to Haifa, to the Party. Hava's body withered, she sat at night with a bottle of wine, ready for the glorious death for which she was fit and which she had wasted on the small change of bitterness and defeat that had made her old before her time. She said to Azouri, look at me, I'm falling apart, Yosef's growing up in a foreign country, surrounded by hostility, and Azouri said, it only seems that way to you, I'm working, I've started teaching at Haifa University, things are getting better, the struggle continues, even if I'm not part of it any more, the Jews and the Arabs are one story and we two are together. She said it wasn't true, and if it was the same story it was a lousy one, and Franz said, let's forget the past, why do things have to be like this, and Hava said, I can't go on suffering in this world both as a Jewess who was meant to end up as an ashtray on Ilse Koch's table and as the target for the hatred of all the refugees who have taken over the state for whose establishment I fought and who don't want me the way I am and who reject my son. They look at me and think that I've sold my soul to the enemy, sold a Jewish body in an Arab bazaar, and I feel degraded. Yosef is living a double life which is destroying him, even if he doesn't realise it yet, he says, I'm an Israeli, I'm a Jew, my name is Yosef Rosenzweig, not Azouri, not Sherara, Rosenzweig, but who am I? and Azouri said, what did Franz come to Palestine for? For his grandson to grow up in Paris?

I thought about them when Dina got up and left me alone in the garden. I knew that Franz was peeping out of the window at me with a book in his hand, he was already wearing spectacles, soon he would be embraced by Gertrude whose three fat daughters wanted to be the aunties of Franz Rosenzweig's Arab grandson. I thought about how they had said in Acre that Azouri was sick with a Jewish disease. I only found out much later that Azouri went to Germany to make the Germans give Hava reparation money, although Hava herself said, my parents took their property with them, and the Germans can't give me back what I lost. But he went anyway, he insisted on going, he met the friends of his youth, they tried to iron out the difficulties for him, but perhaps it was precisely the difficulties that Azouri wanted, they said to him, what's this Jewess to you, and he was insulted and said, she is my wife. He came back with the reparation money the lawyer had obtained for him, and Hava refused to touch the money and it was put into a trust for me in Switzerland. A tidy sum accumulated there for Hava's son, Hava knew, I knew. Later I said to Azouri with a sneer, you married Hava for the German reparation money. Dina had suffered every possible abuse from me and she had waited, how many years could she wait? She threw me out of the little flat in Nordau Street for which I had paid the key money and the rent, and in which Rammy and she were living now. When she came and demanded that I take the money from her and said that she and Rammy would buy the flat from me, I said, out of the question. And then, when I was about to take off with the pilot of a crop-spraying plane and paint the desert red at last, Rammy came to Franz's house and spent the whole night talking to me. He tried to explain to me that he loved her and they were living together, he knew that she would always love me too, but he couldn't possibly go on living in a flat that belonged to me. I would have to give in. I said to him, look here, Rammy, your mother's dead, your father abandoned you, you haven't got any money, Dina wasted the best years of her life on me, now she's got you, you two are good for each other, I've even stopped following you around, what have I got left of you and Dina? All I have left is the flat, let me feel that I belong. Think of it this way, imagine you married a widow, her husband's dead, the flat was his. What would you have done? I'm the dead husband.

Rammy put pressure on Dina but she didn't want to leave the flat. I knew in my heart that she was glad that I wanted to hang on to the flat. She married Rammy but she wanted me to stay in the picture. She would phone me up and say, the rent's gone up and we need something done to the plumbing, the neighbours say the landlord has to do it, and then I would appear, the saviour with the moneybags. She liked taking that money, although Rammy could have paid it, he was earning quite well, but she was living it up, buying dresses, an expensive stereo, records so she could sit and listen to music. Her books of poetry came out, people wrote about her, she was interviewed on television, she received official recognition as a powerful poet. If I'd had a son in high school he would be learning the poems she wrote about me in our private codes now. She enjoyed the idea that I was keeping them and Rammy realised this, he wasn't a fool, he was really the last of the romantics after Azouri, he understood that she needed my hate to pad out their love, just like Azouri can say what he likes today, he didn't go to Germany to get reparations for Hava because he thought it was her due, but because he wanted to show her that he could bring the Germans to their knees and force them to give him money for a Jewish girl. I saw through Azouri when I was sixteen-years-old, and later when I was having my affair with Laila he would come to her house on the Carmel, above the Polish woman who played cantorial music all night long and who loved Laila and looked at me like a kindly Madam looking at a client she's too old to service herself, and he would say to her, Laila, you're wasting your time, Yosef won't stay with you, he belongs to another woman, and Laila would go into the other room to cry, because she really loved me and she didn't want to face the truth that Azouri was trying to force her to face, and nothing I said could make her stop crying. I realised then that Azouri was a much more complicated character than he seemed, writing so lucidly, with such careful objectivity, paying lip-service to the idea of co-existence, but at the same time hanging on to his membership of the Party which he believed in about as much as I did. Azouri played it safe, but he really was free of the curse of his generation, the dreams of the restoration of the Umayyads, the vainglory of the past, even if he did have a rather romantic attitude towards the Organisations. They killed children on a kibbutz and Azouri didn't sound too convincing when he condemned them, perhaps in the depths of his heart he admired them for the single-mindedness which he lacked. Sometimes when I look deep into my own heart, trying to understand the tragic conflict on which so many patriots on both sides have taken out a patent as if it were their own private invention, I think that the gap between the moderates, and Azouri really is a moderate, is wider than that between the extremists, because at the heart of everything is Hava and the plundered land and ancient wounds and something even deeper. Franz's Europe burnt and Hava jumped out of the fire and landed on Azouri and gave his brothers, my uncles, a brave new identity which crystallised during the struggle, and the field was left to the extremists, and the war, I know it in my guts, will be very long, it will last for generations. It won't be solved by any half-measures, in this game there will have to be a winner, and the victory will also be a defeat, for the victor, whoever he is, will bear all the scars within him and he won't have any peace, neither for himself nor for his enemies.

Azouri and Hava trod a fine line between the opposing sides but the only result was Yosef, in other words, me. They were sewn into the fabric of events, and whatever they did was doomed to fail. They had an alternative, they could have stayed in Paris, but then Azouri would have remained a foreigner all his life and he wanted to live in his own climate, his own country. Hava didn't belong anywhere, she could have brought up a French son and today I agree with her and not with Azouri, and perhaps that is the root of my anger against him, that he deprived me of a dignified way out, a possible refuge. When it became clear to me that I didn't have to stay here, that I could escape, go abroad and live on the money that had been invested for me there, it was already too late, I was already part of this lousy country and its curse. Today, as I write these words I'm not living in any real place. I'm existing, a stranger to myself and my surroundings, I see Israelis standing at the newspaper stand, buying the Hebrew papers, I look at them, I listen to them talking Hebrew, they don't know me, there is no danger that any of them might recognise me, but still I go round to the other side of the kiosk and wait for them to leave, and then I buy Arabic papers, Egyptian, Syrian, Lebanese, and then I go home to my little flat to carry on my war alone. I have no steady girlfriend, sometimes I go out to meet French acquaintances, they think I'm Lebanese, a native of Beirut, engaged in the import-export trade, an art lover, sometimes I go to the theatre, or the opera. The poet I read all the time is Heine, the German Jew who loved and hated his Jewishness and his Germanness and lived in Paris and revenged himself on himself, writing lines of love and accusation against himself. I must be the only person alive still looking for the lesson which Heine left in Paris. Paris is a capricious city, many strangers have perished here and been forgotten. Paris has forgotten the exile who sat here writing his ironic barbs, his sad Jewish poems, his German love poems, I know that I won't find him here, but I look for him, I like to think of myself as an Israeli Heine sitting and waiting for the miracle which will save me so that I can go back, but where to? If I go back I'll have to pay duty on my treacheries, not great treacheries but treacheries just the same, I'll have to pay a price which seems unacceptable to me even now, as I sit and write these lines, and I know very well that they're looking for me, when I phone my friends I hear the message they're trying to convey to me, I hear but I pretend not to, even now, when I'm so close to the meeting that will explode everything – I'm quite calm. If the meeting I'm waiting for takes place and I surrender to the curse, Bunim will be waiting for me, he'll say, I knew you'd be back one day and now we'll let this phoney Jew, this non-Arab Arab pay. Bunim once said to me, if I were an Arab, not an Arab like you but a proud Arab, I'd join the Fatah, and I smiled my special, obsequious 'Arab' smile for him and went on describing what was happening in Arafat's camps, what I saw there, what was going to happen, and he looked at me contemptuously and said, there isn't an Arab you can't buy, all you have to do is name your price, and then he stared into space and I knew that he was thinking, and how many Jews can't you buy? When were pride and patriotism exactly Jewish virtues? And then he must have felt very lonely in his desperate struggle to justify the injustices he caused, but his conscience didn't bother him, he had rubbed out the humanity he was brought up on long ago so that he would always be right, even when he wasn't right, because there were plenty of people on the other side who were just as right as he was, each of them a Bunim in his own right. The world is full of Bunims and I'm dying here alone, homesick, thinking if only Azouri had let me grow up here I'd be a French painter today and I wouldn't have this terrible hole yawning inside me, dripping tears onto the pages that you might be reading, but that I'm tearing out of my heart.

16

My moment of glory was the flight over the desert. We took off from a small airfield next to Beer-Sheva. Ami, the pilot, asked me where I got all the paint from and I told him that I had a grant and a paint company had donated the paint. We flew to a point we had marked out in advance and I began to spray the paint I had been mixing for the past month in an abandoned military hut with holes in the walls. We flew about five hours every day for a week. My nose was full of paint. The air was red with paint. Ami laughed and put a mask on, but not me. Gradually the huge square I had marked out began to change its appearance. The red began to sink in and bloom, sprouting like a plant from the sand, the rocks and the low-growing vegetation. It took me a long time to find the right place. I spent a month taking measurements and building a nylon fence around an area of one and a half square kilometres. Filling a space like that with paint was a hard job and an expensive one, and there were places where the paint was a little thin, but anyone who has ever seen a huge square painted red in the middle of the desert, cutting through the blazing yellow which faded into a soft grey, and then turned harsh and threatening as it rose in a line of jagged hills, can imagine the happiness which filled me to overflowing and poured out of me so thick that I could bite it, I didn't need anyone, only that huge red square, the plane and the view.

Ami didn't understand exactly what I was doing but he needed the money and I think that he liked me. He was in the same unit in the army as Rammy and flying was his hobby, he had dropped out of a pilot training course before he joined Rammy's commando unit. They said he didn't have enough fear, and that could be dangerous. He was the bravest person I've ever met, a loner, he lived in a little hut in the desert next to a roadhouse owned by a friend of his, and at night he would sometimes pick up a pretty tourist and sell her his peace of mind. He tried to get me to take an interest in his women but during the month I was working on my red square I didn't want anything else. I would get into bed at night in the tent I pitched next to the isolated roadhouse and fall into a deep sleep. I never even dreamt. Ami would come in and wake me in the morning with a cup of coffee and a smile, and we would go into the dark roadhouse with the lust of the night before still imprisoned in its walls. I could smell the tourists and the hippies Ami had met the night before, on their way to Sinai, or back from Sinai, German and English, Norwegian and Danish and Swedish kids, and Ami would stare at a point in the distance and I could see his night spread out before me, picking up some girl with a bored expression on his face, plying her with beer, and finishing the night with her in his hut, which inside looked like a palace. He had built himself a stove and he would roast meat in it and make coffee and play his banjo. We would go to the airfield, take off in the plane, and I would spray the paint. Until it was finished. The square was complete. Ami said goodbye and he told me that Rammy and Dina had phoned to ask how I was getting on and that they were planning to take a trip. I told him to tell them that if they needed any money they should let me know. Ami smiled, perhaps he was the only one who realised that I was footing the bill for their romance, because Dina helped Rammy spend all his money in order to arrive at a situation where I would step in and pay. It was some game we were playing, Dina and I. Ami laughed and asked me if I would introduce him to Laila, and I told him to go to Haifa and give

150

her my regards and tell her that I had finally conquered the desert from the Jews and made it bleed, and he smiled mockingly, but rather affectionately too. Yosef's a man to be reckoned with, he told the Norwegian and Danish and Swedish girls, he spends all day in a plane painting the desert red. I gave him a week's leave and spent it sweating in the scorching sun, pulling up the nylon sheets and moving them far away from the square, and when Ami came back we flew over the square and spent a whole day taking pictures of it from the air, six hundred pictures I took and even Ami said that it looked good, especially in the late afternoon when the shadows crept over the desert and the evening approached with the pink and violet colours of the sunset and the square grew opaque, full of power, huge against the white of the desert which was still soaking up the last rays of the sun. And then I set up the mikes and I was ready to hold my happening. I invited reporters, art critics, there were articles in the papers about how I was painting the desert red, people were interested, Rammy roped in a few big names without telling me, we chartered planes, and the happening was scheduled to take place on Saturday, a Saturday at the end of spring. And then a jeep from the Nature Protection Authority arrived with another jeep from the Border Police and they told me that I had to clear out because it was a military area and the army was about to hold an exercise there. Azouri heard about it and he came down, he phoned Kassem and Laila but they said they weren't interested and my games with Israeli art were my affair and had nothing to do with the national struggle, Rammy tried to alert public opinion, Dina wrote a hard-hitting article, even television crews came and took pictures and interviewed me. I was threatened and confused and in love with my square, I wanted to live the moment I had been dreaming about for so many years, but nothing helped. Facing me stood a broad-shouldered, middle-aged man, I knew him as a famous ex-army officer, Rammy

151

had once served under his command, now he was working for the Nature Protection Authority, and he said to me, sorry, I can't help you, the area has been declared a military area and tanks are going to practise manoeuvres here, you can be grateful to me for not making you give the desert back its natural colour. His tone was aggressive and I could hear the pleasure in it too, the pleasure he got out of showing me who was the boss around here and who decided whose desert this was. I said to him, there have never been any army exercises here before and he said, it's none of your business where the army holds its exercises and where it doesn't, you're not supposed to know anything about it, and anyway the State of Israel didn't come into existence so that Arabs could paint the desert red. It was the red that got to him, he knew whose blood it was. He was aggressive but there was a note of dry humour in his voice too, the sense of his power over me gave him a kind of grim, dry happiness, he didn't want to hang me on a tree, he even said with a heavy irony which wasn't lost on me that maybe the Syrians would let a Jew paint their mountains red after they'd hanged him first, of course. Rammy arrived and began to argue with him. That evening they announced on television that an Arab Israeli painter was fighting for his right to create a work of environmental art in the desert. The battle was on between journalists from both camps, one for me and one against, but the ex-army officer won and he knew that he would win. He didn't even try to explain why they had to choose this particular square out of all the thousands of squares for their manoeuvres. He wanted to show me who was the boss and he did show me. Ami took pity on me, he went to the C.O. Southern Command, but he was told that the decision had already been taken and that it was irreversible, and afterwards it turned out that this 'irreversible' decision had been taken on the spot by Rammy's ex-officer. He didn't like my square, it offended him. The bedouin came from all around to console me, I saw the open wounds in their eyes, we were together in our pain but they didn't really feel comfortable with me. Dina tried to comfort me, all kinds of people I didn't know came to interview me but Bunim said to me over the phone, it's a lost cause, Yosef, come back to work. You can paint the desert after the next war, maybe we'll conquer another desert on the way and there'll be more sand for you to play with. Today when I look back on what happened and try to reprogramme my life as if only I knew where I went wrong, where I tripped up, as if I could live it over again, I know that the moment I stood facing that man in the desert and saw that nothing would help because he had decided with calm malice, with brute force, that no Arab was going to paint a Jewish desert, that moment was the most humiliating in my life. More humiliating than all the searches at airports and in buses, more humiliating than Azouri's stories about expropriations and dispossessions, about his uncles sitting and looking at the green fields of the kibbutzim on their plundered lands, more humiliating than the sad tales of Laila and Kassem, of all my Arab friends, than the whole great Arab lament arising from the land of the Jewish refugees. All that was somehow understandable, there was a war, battles, just, unjust, Jewish refugees against Arab refugees, all or nothing. I know, justice hurts. I've lived it on both its sides, but it can't excuse the moment when I stood facing the efficient, well-oiled engine of hostility underneath the innocent smile of that kindly nature-lover, father of two little girls, officer and blue-eyed boy of artists and journalists, true pioneer and barefoot farm boy, who loved his country and was renowned for his wisdom and even a certain moderation. He wasn't particularly cruel or wicked, but the idea that I would be the artist who would paint his desert just didn't fit in with his scheme of things – and for that all my work was wasted. A few days later a wind blew up and the colour began to melt into the ground. There wasn't a tank to be seen anywhere in the whole area, Ami told me but he said, look Yosef, he's a stubborn man and he doesn't want you to do it and if he doesn't want something there's nothing anyone can do about it.

Dina wrote another article, Rammy got signatures on a petition, but it was all pointless. I sat in my tent, I didn't want to go home, and when there was nobody there I cried. I felt the hatred whose roots had been growing in me since I was a child swell and harden until it was like an ugly bump on my back. I said to myself, this is it, I'm not working with them any longer. I went home and shut myself in Käthe's old room. Franz tried to talk to me. He was so angry that he trembled when he spoke of what that man had done to me. I went to Bunim and I said to him, Bunim, I'm not working for you and Bunim said to me, you can't just get up and walk out like that. There'll have to be an inquiry. A young man with nice eyes and a brisk business-like air arrived to talk to me. He looked at me with interest, he had heard about me, he had read about my fight in the desert in the newspapers, I felt that he understood me, that in contrast to Bunim he worked in the Mossad but he wasn't a crusader or a Jesuit. He took me into another room and Bunim ground his teeth while we talked. I remember that conversation, we talked for hours, he said, you know it's not so simple to leave, you came to us of your own free will, you know too much. I said to him, you can burn me and he pretended he didn't know what I was talking about and he said, what do you mean 'burn' you, and I said you can leak it to the Organisations that I worked for you and they'll take care of the rest, the first time I go abroad they'll get rid of me for you, and he said, Yosef, we don't do things like that. I said to him, you know and I know that you do things like that and you'll go on doing them. I don't even blame you, I said, that's your business, what I can't understand is meanness for its own sake. That ex-officer from the Nature Protection Authority shouldn't have stopped me from holding

154

my happening. The young man said that he sympathised with me but that it would be foolish of me to cut myself off, and then after a session which lasted the whole night and during the course of which I realised that in spite of all his friendliness I really was going to be burnt if I didn't go back to work, they decided to take me to one of their safe houses for another talk, the famous 'palace'. And there in a pleasant room, with reproductions of Cézanne and Manet on the walls, I sat facing a number of men, one of them wearing dark glasses. I said to him, you look like a spy in the movies, and he smiled politely and went on looking through me at the wall. One of them was an affable young man who spoke to me about environmental and conceptual and performance art, he really knew what he was talking about. In the end they came to the point. They couldn't let me run around loose, they needed strings. I was afraid of being burnt. The full force of my humiliation hadn't really sunk in yet as it did a little later when I'd had time to reflect on that ex-officer and his indifferent stare, a kind of overgrown Rammy who, like Bunim, had been over-exposed to war and something had been blunted in him, perhaps in all of them, perhaps it was a hereditary disease that came from the smell of fire, I don't know. I said okay, I'll go back to work but not now. I was free to go, but not to leave the country, if I wanted to go abroad I had to inform them, and in the meantime, they said, keep in touch. Bunim ground his teeth and said, you'll be sorry if you let him go. Remember, they said, don't go away, stick around, keep in touch, and if you ever want to paint the desert again let us know, we've got connections, we can help. You see, said Bunim with a sneer, we look after our Arabs. I tried to laugh but my mouth wouldn't move and it was then I think that I caught a glimpse of Nissan slipping past in the corridor, although I'm not positive that it was him, and I thought to myself one day I'll still meet Rammy here and Dina and Franz and Käthe and my teachers from school and my mother Hava.

Today I know that it really was Nissan. Today I know that it was Bunim who phoned the ex-officer from the Nature Protection Authority and said to him, what's this I hear that you're letting Arabs mess around with environmental art in a border area? And then the ex-officer asked Bunim what he was talking about and Bunim said, it's Yosef, he wants to paint the desert red, desecrate our soldiers' blood, talk inflammatory rubbish into a microphone, we don't have to give him our desert for that, if he's got something to say let him write it in the newspaper, a desert full of blood will attract too much attention. The ex-officer said, I never knew a thing about it, and he phoned Ami and Ami told him. Ami knew a week in advance that the game was up but he let me carry on as if nothing had happened and he never said a word.

17

Today the whole thing seems like a joke. The panic flight from the Organisations, the ludicrous chase through the streets of Copenhagen in a Volkswagen Transit with two young men, whom the Israeli papers would doubtless have described as 'minority group members' hot on my tracks. They didn't have a chance, they stopped to ask people the way, and I got away from them with insulting ease. What I think about today, in Paris, is love. Paris knows how to put love in its proper place, to trivialise it out of existence. I think of my mother Hava, who announced that love had died at ten past nine. That was when she was standing over her mother's body. Afterwards she clung to Azouri to save herself, and after that she began to die.

I sit in a little cafe near the Pompidou Centre. In the distance I can hear the organ grinder playing for the fire-swallower, and I remember love. I embrace love from afar and feel the jaws closing around me. Once when I was a student at Bezalel an American director arrived in Jerusalem and decided to put on the classic old melodrama the *Dybbuk* with us as an exercise in consciousness raising. And guess whom he chose to play the part of Hanan, the dead lover who takes possession of the soul of his beloved the day she is wedded to another? Me. Dina was then in the officers' course she was later to be chucked out of because of me, and she came to see the play. She was the only one who thought that I was the right person to play Hanan. When I played him I thought about my mother in an abstract sense, not about the real Hava. Not about how she

157

had adjusted to life in her new country, nor about her childhood, haunted by the dreams of another place, and her jealousy of her mother's beauty, but about the woman who had given birth to me from Azouri's seed. I thought of Hava among the British armoured cars in Jerusalem, the divided city, the struggle between the Jews and the British, the shots on every side, suddenly finding herself a heroine in spite of herself. When Hava and Azouri went to register themselves as a married couple in the population register, a woman there said to her, Look, lady, you're a problem! Time will solve the problem, but not in your favour. In Paris her mother's devils came to visit her. Azouri's homesickness filled her with an obscure fear that he was beginning to feel too much like an Arab. It makes me laugh to think that Azouri wanted to be a liberated man, a communist who despised nationalism. Hava asked him then, what exactly are you homesick for? There are olive trees in Provence too. She saw how the streets with their Gallic-sounding names revived in him the grandson of the wealthy Arab with land in Acre bay. Azouri hung a picture of Acre above his desk. Hava hung up a picture of Tel Aviv, but she wasn't homesick for it. The battle between them was a game they needed. Each of them needed to blame the other in order to prove that I was growing up outside the vicious circle of opposites which they had tried to break. Hava said to Azouri, you want to chew Jewish soil, and he said, there's no such thing. They argued about Zionism and the Arab national movement as if they need weapons to put out the fire burning inside them. In the city which plays with love like a bored gourmet playing with an expensive meal they loved each other so much that they thought their love was the reason for their fights. They compared her forefathers' longings for Zion with his longings for Palestine, but it was impossible to measure the longings and they concluded all these superfluous arguments by coming even closer than before. I was three or four years old

158

then and I remember. When I played Hanan in the *Dybbuk* I tried to feel like an old, pre-Zionist Jew, and then too Azouri's face would frighten me in my dreams. I have never known a love as great and as doomed as my parents' love, a love which devoured them and drove them crazy. Perhaps they met too late, perhaps it was because of the curse of Franz and Käthe, perhaps it was because of me, the child who should have been born not to Hava but to her mother, I don't know.

And so it was very strange to hear Hava saying over her mother's dead body, Love died at ten past nine. When Käthe lay on her death-bed she never removed the broken watch from her wrist, for her time had stopped at the terrible moment when she had arrived in Palestine. She always said, I don't want to be here, but she never said where she did want to be. She hated the country so violently that she would escape to her room and shut herself up in it for days, even before she became so ill that she had to be hospitalised. When she lay dying and they all stood around her bed she looked like a still-quivering butterfly stuck on a pin. Her eyes smiled, the end of her suffering was in sight and she wanted to keep it there as long as she could. For two days she lay there dying, holding the thread of life in her hands. It was a melancholy sight but not without beauty.

Hava stood there and begged her mother to forgive her, but Käthe pretended not to hear, not out of cruelty but out of absent-mindedness, perhaps at the back of her dying mind she even felt pity for her daughter, but she certainly didn't remember what Hava was begging her forgiveness for. Azouri made her angry, her face contracted when she saw him, but it seemed that she no longer remembered what she was angry about. She asked who I was and when they told her she said in German, whose son? Who's my son? And then the pure, lucid look suddenly left her eyes, she stretched out her arms, the life began to race as if it wanted to leave her, she tried to hang onto

159

it for a little longer, so that she could go on looking forward to her approaching death, her face was as beautiful as clear water troubled by a stone, and suddenly we saw her soul depart.

Hava said to Azouri, your first love refused to forgive me, and she wept over her mother's body. She hated Azouri then and she squeezed my hand so tight that it hurt me.

As soon as I had finished playing Hanan in the *Dybbuk* they threw Dina out of the officers' course. In an argument with her officers she had spoken up in favour of a Palestinian state alongside the state of Israel with security safeguards and mutual respect for each other's rights. Some of them even agreed with her, but there was someone there who didn't like the idea that she was living with an Arab. She didn't say that my name was Yosef Rosenzweig and I was playing Hanan in the *Dybbuk*. Today Dina never mentions the military episode in her biography, but then she wanted to be an officer and she was upset about being thrown out of the course because of me. Later she married Rammy, the blue-eyed boy of all the Jewish mothers who threw me out of their houses when I was a young boy coming to visit my friends and listen to music with them. I didn't even think of myself as an Arab but then their mothers knew and they said, you have to go home now, Yosef, and I would go home and cry to Franz, and he would look at me with eyes which Käthe's devils were beginning to haunt, and try to comfort me.

When I was in primary school I wrote an essay about making the desert bloom. Our teacher gave us the headings for the essay: the desert; the swamps; the opposition of the Bedouin and the Arabs; the pioneers; the colonies set up by Baron de Rothschild. I wrote about how we had come to an empty wasteland, how everything was full of swamps, how we got malaria, how we wanted to civilise the one and only country we had ever had, which no one else had ever claimed since we were exiled from it. I wrote about the wicked Arabs who came

160

at night to burn the haystacks, about the brave Zionist pioneers. I wrote a very dramatic essay, but my teacher wouldn't let me read it aloud to the class. When I read it to Azouri he burst out laughing. I was furious, I wanted to revenge myself on the wicked Arabs. Believe me, I know the whole story off by heart, I know it in the marrow of my bones, and believe me, I'm sick of it.

For two thousand years the country was empty. There were Arabs in it but there was no Palestine. The Jews could have come but they didn't. The tragedy began the moment the Jews suddenly remembered too late and the Arabs in Palestine suddenly realised they were a separate nation. One nationalism fed the other. Justice belongs to God alone. I try to fish for memories of Käthe . The day of her death, the day my mother said, love died at ten past nine. How Käthe stopped time, how she saw the world through a fog and wore a watch without hands on her wrist, how she looked at us with shy surprise, with suppressed rage, and began to disintegrate. How she let death enter her and her soul departed. My mother said, love died at ten past nine, she clung to Azouri, she squeezed my hand, she hugged me so tight she almost choked me. Franz stood there like a Prussian officer, grotesque and out of place, the death-bed scene was over, we went outside into the fierce light of Eretz Israel, of Palestine, we rubbed our eyes as if we had come out of an afternoon show, Franz marched erect, only Azouri looked like a broken-down old Jew.

We went to Franz's house. Gertrude had prepared a light meal. Franz, a little Job who had lost his parents, his sister, his son, and now his wife, stood there trying to digest the fact that the rooms of the house were already Käthe-*rein*. He said, Käthe made a will, she made me bring Ernst and she wrote it with him standing over her, and then Ernst died but the will is still legally binding and we have to read it now. I don't know why Franz couldn't have waited a few hours but he was a

161

stickler for formality and he liked to have things cut and dried. Azouri sat in an armchair and pretended to read the newspaper. He felt uneasy, he was worried about Hava, about her feelings of guilt towards her mother, he was always the mast of our floundering ship.

There were a few friends there, Moshe the secretary of the symphony orchestra, Walter Stepper from Jerusalem and his wife, another couple, Gertrude who had already sewn her wedding dress in her imagination. Once I broke the pretty teacup Käthe drank from and when she came home for the week-end, walking around the house in a silk dressing gown and counting the pieces falling off her she said to me, I'm a teacup, look little boy (she never called me by my name), I'm a broken teacup, and here are the pieces lying on the floor, *eins, zwei, drei, vier....*

Franz read the will. It ended with the words: I want to be burnt. My broken pieces are ground to dust. (Here she started writing Hebrew). Strong sun. Hard country. My ashes to throw in Acre. The child born in Acre. A little ceremony to have there, only family, if anyone wants to read a poem he can. Käthe Rosenzweig, yours in surrender.

There was a silence. Franz went on standing there like a scarecrow, staring at the painting by Klee, whose frame needed dusting. Hava said, Yosef was born in Paris, not in Acre, but nobody took any notice of her, we were all thinking about Käthe. Hava knew she shouldn't have said what she said and she felt in the wrong. The tears shining at the corners of her eyes didn't help. Azouri tried to argue, his anger seemed exaggerated as he demanded that the will, written by a sick woman, be annulled. But Franz insisted that Käthe's last request be carried out. Everyone in the room felt that the will concerned Franz and Azouri, even though he wasn't mentioned in it, more than anyone else. Franz said, we never understood her, Azouri, and if she asks us to do this for her

162

then we must do it. His voice was that firm, angry voice that I heard when I waited outside while he went in to talk to the Chief of Staff on my behalf. She'll get what she wants however hard it is, he added. Not hard, cruel, said Hava, and Franz said, not cruel, we, I, was cruel, not her. And Hava said, I was! And he said, no, not you, Hava, not you, we – Azouri and I, and he went out of the room. Deep in her heart Hava my mother thought that she was the real glue which had stuck Franz and Azouri to Käthe. When Käthe died she felt there was no point in living. Funny how women can twist things, marry an enemy because they misinterpret their own answer. I looked at him then and, of course, I thought of Dina.

After Franz walked out of the room Hava began to cry, she clung to Azouri as if she were trying to creep right into his body, she hated him as much as she loved him, she said to him, it's all because of you, all our catastrophes are because of you, including the fact that we came here in the first place, and suddenly Azouri didn't know what catastrophe she was talking about. Later Hava was moved by the look full of pity which Franz gave Azouri when he came back into the room, the way he patted his shoulder and clasped him to his breast. Azouri sat inside Franz, Hava inside Azouri, and Azouri felt that he was losing Hava precisely on the day that Käthe died. Hava hugged me tightly, perhaps because of the big hole that had opened up inside her. A hundred generations of ancient knights, both Latin and Arab, had made Azouri, with his eyes like northern lakes and his dark oriental skin, suspicious of outsize dreams like the revival of the glorious Umayyads and the Zionism which had no option but to be a junction of prayers and cruelty with a Ministry of Defence where they played chamber music. Suddenly he felt more lost than ever at the idea of Käthe's ashes being scattered over the town he had once told Hava was beautiful and belonged to her.

Everything was arranged. Franz was a man with a lot of

connections and a lot of money. Doors opened and eyes were closed. The burial society made more money from not burying Käthe than they would have made from burying her. The permit to take the body to Germany was obtained. An impeccably orthodox rabbi wrote out a certificate of burial in a little town near Hamburg. Käthe's body came back in an urn inside a box bearing the words 'toxic matter, to be delivered to Professor Franz Rosenzweig in person.' The dockers were afraid to touch it and Franz drove down to Haifa to fetch it. One fine, warm day we drove to Acre, to a place which Azouri was obliged to choose. From where we stood we could see Acre spread out along the water line, the towers and minarets shining in the last rays of the sun. The sea was smooth as silk. Franz took out the ashes and scattered them next to an old fig tree, opposite the beauty of the wall weeping into the bay, between the rhododendrons and the nettles, and then he covered it with dry fig leaves. I was a child and I was afraid. This was what my beautiful grandmother had come to! Franz read a passage from Psalms, in Hebrew, for some reason: 'Who forgiveth all thine iniquities, who healeth all thine diseases, who redeemeth thine life from destruction, who crowneth thee with loving-kindness and tender mercies.' Hava, detached from everyone, sang a Schubert lieder. Azouri recited Heine's '*Schöne Wiege Meiner Leiden*' which was a favourite of Käthe's.

Lovely cradle of my sorrow,
Lovely tomb where peace might dwell,
Smiling town, we part tomorrow.
I must leave; and so farewell.
Farewell, threshold, where still slowly
Her footstep stirs;
Farewell to that hushed and holy
Spot where first my eye met hers.

164

....And I take my staff and stumble
On a journey, far from brave;
Till my head droops, and I tumble
In some cool and kindly grave.

The sun was sinking, Azouri recited slowly, in his peculiar
German accent. I was full of dread, I approached the ashes.
Franz's eyes were dry, the ashes were beginning to scatter in
the wind, church bells were ringing, as was the bell of a fishing
boat sailing towards the jetty next to Abu Cristo's restaurant. I
said, you were the biggest and the most broken and the most
wonderful of all, you never said anything to me and so I've got
nothing to say to you, Blessed art thou O Lord our God, King
of the Universe, I'm Yosef, and I ran away. Franz sprinted after
me and hugged me, he said, she loved you Yosef, but I knew
that he was lying. I looked at him, all the sorrow that was to
continue collecting in him was already hardening in his eyes,
he took all our tears into himself, I have never seen anyone who
took such enormous grief onto himself and hid it underneath
his collar. And then I felt a great emptiness, the shadows crept
up the tree, the wind blew and the sea rippled. Hava, whose
love had died a month before, at ten past nine, entered
Azouri's arms and said, even if everything is already over
you're all I have, the only question is for how long, and I said to
her, Mother, and what about me, and suddenly she looked at
me with Käthe's eyes, she tried to focus on me, she blinked her
eyes, and I saw that she couldn't remember who I was, and
Azouri took me by the hand and said, look, have you ever seen a
sunset like that anywhere else? And he tried to smile, and
Franz scattered more leaves to protect his beloved.

18

After the funeral we went to Azouri's house. An old woman who may have been Azouri's aunt or his stepmother's sister served *kubbe* and rice and meat and *tehina* and salads. We sat there, Franz looked at the night sea, the lights of Haifa twinkled in the distance, Hava went into Azouri's room and came back wearing a white dress. Even I knew that after a funeral you were supposed to wear black. Today I can remember little details, glances exchanged. Azouri said, Hava is wearing white now too, and Franz said, Yosef could have been Käthe's son and he laughed a painful, ironic laugh, and Azouri took his hand and kissed it as if he were a short-sighted Polish count. Afterwards we drove to Tel Aviv, Hava didn't come with us, I remember that Moshe, Franz's friend, drove the car and Franz kept his arms around me all the way, and later I remember dimly going back to Acre, Azouri and Hava must have been living there then, Azouri suddenly began to go fishing in the bay, which I could never remember his doing before, and the woman, who might have been Azouri's aunt or his stepmother's sister, sat and tested my Arabic and laughed when I got a word wrong or mispronounced something. He talks like a *Yahud*, she shrieked, he talks like a *Yahud* – as if she found this excessively amusing.

Hava began pacing up and down her room. I remember going to a different school, not in Tel Aviv. That year is misty in my memory, I was taken out of one school and put into another. For a while I went to a Christian school in Haifa and I wore blue trousers, a white shirt and a jacket, and it was hot, and the children laughed at me. In the evenings I sat next to the fig tree and looked for Käthe , who had been so mysterious to me. I knew what was going to happen tomorrow and I said, it's going to rain and the children laughed at me, and then it really did rain and they brought a witch-doctor to the school to exorcise my *jinn* and Azouri came and shouted at the headmaster, who was a nice man as far as I can remember, and he took me out of the school. Azouri was angrier than I have ever seen him and Hava swallowed medicines, her internal injuries had begun to trouble her, she groaned at night and they took her to hospital in Tel Aviv and Franz stood over her all night long while they operated on her, they told me that she had a bad case of flu, but I knew that they were really removing her gallbladder. Hava was fading away and she said to me, I remember exactly, she said, I think too fast, the words escape me, I try to run after them but I can't catch them up, I have dead people in my stomach, I know they're not really there, but I dream about Hilda, my aunt who killed herself, and I never even knew her. Azouri was worried and he was strict with me. I kept getting under his feet and the old woman, Aunt Houri, laughed at my Arabic although Azouri said it was excellent, and then one day after Hava came back from the hospital she took the car and drove without lights all the way to Rosh Hanikra. She was arrested and they took away her licence. She cried and told me to look after both my fathers and Franz came with Gertrude and the eldest of her fat daughters, who was married to the insect investigator, and Gertrude tried to feed Hava on vegetable soup or meat soup with noodles which she thought was a cure for all ills. And then one night, with the aid of a bottle of wine and some pills Hava tried to connect the lemon trees which the Jews had not succeeded in cutting down with herself and she couldn't find the glue, and she said to me, I remember the words but not their meaning. And then she fell asleep with a cup of coffee in her hand, sitting on a chair with her mouth open like an old woman, and Franz arrived and tried to persuade her to go back with him to Tel Aviv. Azouri begged her to let him take us back to Tel Aviv, but for some reason she had decided that the only place for her was Acre, where people nodded to her in the street and she would go and sit in the middle of the enormous courtyard of the old Khan and look at the sun setting through the exquisite arches.

Hava cried in her sleep and her eyes were tired and full of something which looked like despair, she was enveloped in a kind of sorrowing hopelessness, and Azouri looked after her. Franz came almost every other day, and one day, I remember it dimly, I was sitting with her, Azouri had gone to Haifa, and she said to me, there's a man with a moustache who sharpens bayonets and wants to kill you. I said, nobody wants to kill me mother, and she got into the bath with all her clothes on and came out with toilet paper wrapped around her head and sticking to her fingers. Bits of wet paper fell onto the clean floor, Aunt Houri shut herself up in her room, Azouri came home and said to my mother, think of the child, and she said, he's Käthe's child, not mine, and after that she began calling me Mahler's illegitimate son, and she added, that's why I sing, and Azouri asked her, since when do you sing? And she began to sing and they told me to leave the room but I heard their raised voices through the door. Hava began to sing so loudly that all the neighbours heard.

This went on until evening. Azouri phoned Franz and Franz told him to bring her to Tel Aviv at once. Azouri dressed her, took off the toilet paper, put her in the car and late in the evening he began driving to Tel Aviv. She sang all the way, he trembled and smoked one cigarette after the other, and next to Kfar Vitkin she began to play with the steering wheel. Azouri fought her off, he tried to press down on the brake but her foot was there and she wouldn't let him, she tickled him, pinched him, shrieked a song by Mahler about the death of children into his ear and made it impossible for him to concentrate. Suddenly she was strong, as strong as small children can sometimes be, he tried to fight her off but the car veered, he couldn't stop it, he tried to bring it to the side of the road but she pushed him, she turned the wheel with her foot on the brake, he pressed down on top of her foot but he couldn't stop the car and then....

And then they found them in the overturned car, Hava's lifeless hands on the wheel and her head hanging crookedly. Azouri was sprawled in the space between Hava's hands and the wheel, he was scratched and his head was bruised. An old man from Kfar Vitkin called the police and they came and found a slightly wounded Arab in an overturned car with a dead Jewess. They took him to the police station and they took her to a hospital in Hadera. The police insulted him and one of them hit him, but he sat and stared into space, he couldn't see anything. Afterwards one of the policemen said to a Jewish journalist that Azouri was in shock, he didn't say a word. They roughed him up a bit, he said, but you have to understand what they thought, what kind of impression they got, a beautiful blond Jewess with an Arab at the wheel, him with nothing but a few scratches and her dead without a drop of blood on her. Azouri came to his senses quite quickly. He wanted to see her but they wouldn't let him, they asked him who was her family and he said, me! They laughed insultingly and said, who else? And he said, Professor Franz Rosenzweig, and in the middle of the night Franz arrived, cold and practical as never before, on the way there, as if he expected the worst, he brought the pathologist from the hospital, and as if he knew in advance that the more witnesses the better he also brought his friend Moshe from the orchestra. He looked contemptuously at the police-man who was trying to show him how good they were to his dead daughter and how they put that Arab in his place, he never opened his mouth and he allowed his friend the pathologist to examine Hava, a police specialist went with someone from the hospital to examine the car. All the evidence confirmed what Azouri had said, but Azouri suddenly looked at them and said that he had driven like a madman and he was to blame, the policemen wanted him to go on, but Franz wouldn't let him, the speedometer showed twenty kilometers an hour, the evidence was on Franz's side. In the meantime they allowed the handcuffed Azouri to see Hava and he covered her with a blanket and closed her eyes, which they had forgotten to do, and one of the policemen said to him angrily, who do you think you are, her father? Dirty Arab! And the judge before whom they brought Azouri said, all the evidence shows that the accused is not guilty, the state of health of the departed, the way her body was lying and the speedometer. The policemen tried to prove that it was impossible for Azouri not to be guilty, and then the judge said quietly, but Azouri heard him, I'm ashamed to be a judge in a country where people like you are policemen, and a sergeant standing outside said, with judges like that no wonder there are so many terrorists, these bleeding hearts are killing us, and another policeman said, let me get my hands on that Arab and I'll get you proof that he killed his mother too! No one could understand how Hava's face was untouched, how the glass hadn't cut her, as if, said Franz, she had planned her death so it would leave no marks, she didn't take into account how much suffering she would cause Azouri, or perhaps that was her intention. Franz would never have said such a thing but for the terrible pain he felt after seeing the truth through all the accursed cobwebs which Käthe had brought with her and kept in her suitcase ever since they arrived in Haifa in 1936.

Afterwards I said to Azouri, my mother wanted to kill her mother's love, but she didn't succeed and she paid the price. The accident didn't kill her, she died a few seconds before the car overturned, this was proved beyond any doubt by the inquest. A few years later I wanted to take him to court, and he said, go ahead, but by then it was too late, and he sat and listened quietly to me repeating my accusations one after another and he said to me, you really are a cruel child, Yosef. I burst into tears and said that I knew that Hava had died before the accident, that she had borrowed Käthe's death and made it hers, and that was how she had been able to disappear and betray me and let me grow up without her. She couldn't face what she imagined her life would be in the country which Käthe did not want to live in but which she had insisted on coming to.

Franz always tells me that Hava was drunk, that she loved Azouri too much to have planned the whole thing in advance. He says, all the evidence shows that she played with the wheel, took pills, drank wine, she was a sick woman, there was nothing Azouri could do. But she didn't even know what she was doing. And then he adds, my poor daughter, she could have gone on living for years, why did she have to inherit her mother's hostility to life?

But I wanted to blame Azouri. Somehow he was guilty, if he had been a better driver, if he had driven more carefully, the accident wouldn't have happened, if he had made my mother happier she wouldn't have died. And that was how I could say to him, you sat there in Koloniya and you shot her Azouri, you killed her, and he said nothing, somewhere inside him he believed that he was guilty of the death of the only woman he ever really loved.

19

Franz once said to me, when I was already living with him and Azouri would come and visit us twice a week, I see death before my eyes five times a day. I've lost everything but for you and Azouri, why must you trouble the slow dripping of my grief?

I knew it wasn't fair but it helped, every night before I fell asleep I thought of Azouri, Azouri whom I loved, my father on my mother Hava's side, I imagined him as an executioner and I pitied him, and myself, and my mother, and Franz, and Käthe, but the thought wouldn't go away. Perhaps it helped me to betray him, to take, as Bunim with his penchant for biblical phrases would say, 'an eye for an eye'.

If you want to belong you have to pay a price. Käthe wanted to save Franz and Hava so she insisted on coming to Palestine, but even when she was still well she hated it, she said, I don't want to live in this country! And so she didn't stay in it even after she died, she had herself scattered to the winds, whereas I went over to the other side, to Bunim. Bunim provided some kind of answer to Franz's nightmares, to the ruined lives surrounding us, the wounds of those who had no moral yardstick by which to measure the suffering of Azouri and his brothers. After all they had been through, after what had been done to them – the pain of the Arabs who had twenty-two other states to go to seemed too insignificant to count. I was forced to choose at an early age, perhaps it was after my mother's death, and I chose to be for Franz and therefore against Azouri.

172

Azouri didn't put any pressure on me, he didn't oppose my decision, which wasn't taken in a day or formally announced but which took shape gradually until it became a reality. He understood that I had to choose. He even told me later on that when he had urged Hava to return to Israel from Paris he had taken this possibility into account, and he had gone to get reparation money for Hava from Germany for the same reason – perhaps it was the cunning of a clever Arab, between restriction orders and house arrests, police harassment and humiliation, to bring up a Jewish son as a kind of shield against the daily round of persecution and discrimination which an Arab in Israel is supposed not only to accept, but even to excuse.

Actually, it was probably less a conscious choice than the result of circumstances, understandable and not always pleasant. For a time I went on staying with Azouri, who returned to the flat in Tel Aviv and spent a lot of time with Franz. Gertrude spent the whole day sweeping and cleaning the house, and she got rid of Yona the maid. Franz paid Yona severance pay and Yona muttered curses to herself, for years she had served Käthe faithfully, and now another woman would live among the cobwebs the disintegrating queen had left behind her. Gertrude wanted Franz to herself, her dreams were painted in technicolour, her huge nose twitched eagerly. Gradually I began spending more and more time there. Azouri published his new book about the history of the Arab national movement, which was greeted with abuse and hostility in some quarters but with acclaim in others, it was translated into several languages and Azouri was in great demand, he travelled to give lectures and participate in seminars in Paris, New York and London. While he was away I stayed with Franz, and the arrangement gradually became permanent. Franz wanted me with him, I was all he had left in his empty house. He went to work in another, bigger hospital, they began calling him 'the Professor', he gave lectures at international congresses, he

173

taught at the medical school, for a while he was the dean. I went to school, the other kids weren't interested in who my parents were, I didn't talk about being Azouri's son and he kept away from the school. When my teachers wanted to see my father, my grandfather came, but the mothers knew, they heard it on the gutter grapevine. I would go to visit some girl and her mother would hint that it was time to go home now, Yosef, nothing was ever said straight out, there was always room for another interpretation. I was a child, I wanted to see myself as part of the community that I was living in. I tried not to think about Azouri and Acre, about the blood that was flowing in my veins, tricking me and driving me mad with dreams that come straight from the famous sword of abu-al-Misk ibn Kafur Sherara, whom I had never known. I had one recurrent dream about a big house on a mountain, about a marvellous garden planted on the hillside. I told it to Franz and he told me about the garden of abu-al-Misk Kafur. Franz's words lacked the vivid power of the dream, he turned the garden into an exquisite tapestry which three times a day merged into a symphony of smells, but in my dream the garden was a sword I waved to defend myself against nameless enemies. I fell in love with Dina at the age of twelve, she was in the class below me, I saw her in the playground, I never tried to approach her, I waited, she stared at me and ran away, perhaps she wanted me to chase her. I was afraid, I was alarmed by the lust that made me want to hold her naked in my arms, I thought that maybe it was the Arab in me that wanted her like this. Whenever I came to visit my friend Giora, whose father Nachie was a big fighter against the Military government in the Arab sector, he welcomed me and took me aside for friendly chats, during the course of which he told me how I was the heir to two great cultures, and once he even said that I was the truest Jew he knew. When I turned thirteen I forced Franz to give me a bar-mitzvah. Friends and a few relatives came to the bar-mitzvah

174

and Azouri stood at the back of the synagogue and listened to me read my portion of the Law. Looking back it seems somewhat superfluous, but inevitable. The rabbi taught me *mishnayoth* and *Haftara*, he didn't know anything about me, in those days the Ministry of the Interior didn't pass around black lists, the rabbi didn't know that my father was an Arab, and even if he had known he couldn't have refused to take me, from the point of view of Jewish law I was a Jew because my mother was Jewish. Nachie would say to me, you're a minority in your own country, you're a Jew and also the Jew of the Jews. It was from Nachie that I learned the phrase I was later to mutter to myself in silent and resentful fury when he threw me out of his house in an anger that he himself did not understand when I came to condole with him on the occasion of the death of his son. Giora and I went to demonstrations with Giora's father. We went as Jews, and Azouri laughed and said, you're demonstrating for me, Yosef, but I wasn't demonstrating for Azouri, I was demonstrating for Giora and Nachie, I wasn't even sure that the Arabs weren't dangerous, a potential fifth column, or that it was such a good idea to dismantle the military government with all its restrictions, and the bitterness and gall that Azouri swallowed in silence was full of despairing longings for Hava, as he searched for a way of reaching me, of touching the son who was growing further and further away from him.

It was clear to me that Israel was a necessary, if impossible, answer to the holocaust. I was surrounded by kids whose parents had come from there, and the tales of suffering affected me much more strongly than my friends, who wanted to be normal Israelis and not to think about *aktions* and about skeletons sent by Eichmann to the Institute of Racial Research. I read everything I could lay my hands on about the holocaust, I felt total identification. Parents of friends talked about the cruelty of the Arabs in the '48 war, about massacres and tortures. One of them, whose son was later wounded in the

June war, told a story about Jewish heads stuck up on poles. Azouri tried from time to time to tell his side of the story, but without too much passion or conviction, about the expulsions and expropriations, the way the Jews had encouraged the Arabs to leave, the massacre at Deir Yassin, the arrests and the beatings and the tortures, but I couldn't feel complete identification with him. I understood that he was speaking of pain, but the real pain was the pain from which Hava had escaped, my mother on Franz's side, the humiliation and degradation, the despair of finding yourself in a world of locked doors where everyone shuts their eyes and allows you to die in a slaughterhouse. I read Anne Frank's diaries. I wrote an essay about her, I drew her, I fell in love with her, I tried to dream about her at night. Giora spoke about the Macabbees and the Palmach, I was proud of them, I was seduced by the myth, Azouri knew that he was losing me but it was part of the risk he took. He realised that I needed an identity and the one he had to give me wasn't strong enough, at least not then. The great and terrible justice was still on my side. Nachie demonstrated, Azouri was put under house arrest and beaten, but I said to myself, nobody's putting him into a gas chamber, the world's doors aren't closed to him, the world is full of Arabs, full of Arab states, he's a member of the great Arab nation, he has somewhere to go, and Nachie has nowhere. I identified with Nachie, I didn't think about the absurdity of my position, I wanted Dina but I was afraid and Giora and I dreamt about girls, we looked at pictures of naked women, and one day Giora met the female cousin of a friend of his who lived in Jerusalem. Franz arranged for us to stay with a friend of his and we went up to Jerusalem. It was the summer vacation when we were fourteen. His friend's cousin had a party, boys and girls, I don't remember much about it. There was a girl there called Nina, she had big tits spilling out of her dress, I watched her dancing in her mini dress, she must have been about eighteen and I could see that she fancied me. She came up to me and asked me in a foreign accent if I wanted to dance. I said, no, I want to fuck, which was funny because I was really shy but Giora and I had rehearsed it all the way to Jerusalem, we had decided that if some dame asked us if we wanted to dance we would say, no, I want to fuck. We wanted to be professionals, we thought that real men went straight to the point, and it worked, it really turned her on, she measured me with her eyes as if I were a horse, not my teeth maybe but all the rest of me. Giora still looked like a baby then but I looked seventeen at least, I told her I was eighteen and she believed me. I told her fearsome tales about a secret society I belonged to, a group that went out on dangerous missions across the border. This was the time of the reprisal raids when stories about the famous 101 special commando unit were making the rounds. I had to put on an act and play the part of a man who went out at night to kill himself a few Arab terrorists across the border, and it really turned her on. We went to Independence Park, it was a warm evening, I embraced her, I was mad with excitement and she said, what's the matter, honey? Haven't you had any practice with girls? But she was no less excited than I was and I had an agreement with Giora that I would go back to the room first and switch off the light and he would come in afterwards. Before we went out we hung an empty grenade Nachie had given him on the wall, and thus with the memory of the battle I invented on the spur of the moment, I undressed her, and suddenly I saw a girl's body. She was as white and soft as piles of fresh sand on the sea side. We struggled for a while, panting and heaving, and then I entered her, and she let me go all the way in, and suddenly I realised that it wasn't going to work, but it was too late, I was already inside her. I shut my eyes and summoned Dina to my aid, and she came and sat in the pupils of my eyes, as if she'd been there all the time without my knowing it. I thought that perhaps I was in love with Dina but I didn't want to think about her and suddenly when I should have been in the seventh heaven of delight all I wanted was to run away, because it wasn't Dina. I convinced myself that Nina was Dina and everything was okay. Afterwards Giora came back, full of smiles. He too had found himself a girl, she hadn't let him go all the way like Nina had let me, but almost. He was in love with her, her name was Rina, and he was going to write to her and she was going to come and visit him in Tel Aviv. I wanted Dina. Giora wanted to stay on in Jerusalem, I arranged to take Nina to the movies but at the last moment I ran away to Tel Aviv. I spent days lurking outside Dina's house but I didn't go up, I phoned her, her mother answered and I banged the phone down. Franz thought that I was sick and he phoned Azouri and Azouri came and looked at me and said, he's lovesick, and Franz laughed, in his eyes Azouri was an expert in this strange disease.

After that on the school excursion to Acre my romance with Dina began and it was something else entirely, as if we had been born together, we felt no shame or distance. Her parents came to see Franz, they wanted to go and complain to the headmaster, but somehow their opposition was overcome, Dina was a girl with a lot of will power and they were forced to give in. Their sadness touched me, I realised that I hadn't arrived yet, I was still an outsider, the pain they had brought with them from where they came couldn't include me, and this began to burn me up and then at the end of my penultimate year everyone got their call-up papers for the draft and I waited and waited but nothing came for me.

20

Somewhere in my mind I was the child of holocaust survivors. I had fantasies about it. For most of my contemporaries joining the army was a sign of rebellion against everything that had happened 'there'. But for me it was a continuation, not a rebellion. I wanted to be a soldier for the sake of what had happened there. I didn't dream of a military career, I wanted to be an artist, I went to art classes in the evenings. But I was strong, I had a firm, lean body, I was tall for my age. My average grade in school was ninety, I majored in science, I knew a number of languages perfectly, Hebrew, Arabic, and French, I could read and speak English and my German was quite good too. I read the evidence in the Eichmann trial in the original, this was during the period when my desire to be Jewish was so strong that I invented a past for myself, Azouri was effaced, I called him 'Uncle Azouri' and I stopped going to Acre. Then the call-up papers came and none came for me. Giora said there must be some mistake and I would get them soon. I felt uneasy, humiliated. Dina came and sat with me, once I cried and she was appalled, my tears were as big as Azouri's, afterwards she said that all Arabs cried enormous tears. Then Dina went home and Franz came out of the room where he was sitting listening to music and asked me what the matter was and I told him, he asked me how much time had passed and I said two months. He took his hat and went out. I was alone in the house, Gertrude had gone home, she wasn't actually living in the house yet, and we were often alone, Franz and I. There was a picture of Käthe holding Hava in her arms on the wall. I switched on the radio and listened to Arabic music, an announcer told stupid jokes about politics, he got on my nerves with his cuteness, I sat stuck to the radio and about an hour later Franz came back and said, I've spoken to Nachie, tomorrow we're going to make inquiries. I wanted to ask what Nachie had said, but Franz didn't want to talk about it, we sat in the room which had once been Käthe's, outside the moon was shining and Franz told me about the day he heard that Hava had been wounded, and how he had gone to see her in the hospital, and tears welled up in his eyes, and suddenly she was my mother, not on anyone's side, not on Franz's side, not on Azouri's side, but on my own side. I asked him if she loved me and he hugged me and said, she only loved two people in her life, you and Azouri, perhaps she died because she loved you too much. I looked at the old man and I envied him his suffering, the dignity and endurance with which he bore it, and the fact that he seemed worthy of it. The next morning we picked Nachie up in Franz's new car, a big blue Ford. We arrived at a camp near Tel Aviv, I didn't know exactly where we were, Nachie showed them his papers, he was an officer in the reserves, they showed us into a room with a sergeant sitting in it and Nachie said, I have to go and see about something else, I'll see you later. The sergeant opened a file and stared at us and told me to go in. Franz wanted to go with me but the sergeant said, you stay where you are, mister, and Franz sat on the wooden bench, perhaps he thought of the benches he was forbidden to sit on in Berlin, and I went in and the door closed behind me. I saw Franz's dejected face, the air of defeat in his eyes, his slightly twisted smile, his noble white head, as if he were waiting for Azouri to come and sew the yellow star on his jacket again.

After that interview I thought I would never be the same again, but looking back from my present perspective, as I sit and write these confessions, I know that the refusal to let me paint the desert red and the arbitrary meanness of that nature-loving ex-officer was far more significant for me. Me as I am today, that is.

I sat there facing three officers, one of them was chewing a pencil and he tried to smile at me. For some reason he looked familiar. Now I know that he reminded me of Rammy, but I didn't know Rammy then of course – but even then all those Rammys I so longed to resemble were to deprive me of what was mine by right. One of the officers asked with barely concealed irritation, perhaps you could tell us what we're doing here and why you had to drag Nachie into it? Nobody asked you to come here, what exactly do you want? I was taken aback by the simple logic of these words and searched for a dignified reply, I needed time to think, this was a crucial moment for me, the person I had constructed out of my broken pieces was now on trial. I felt sorry for Franz, I thought of my mother, this time the enemy was Azouri. There was a kitschy picture of a Mirage on the wall. I said nothing and the three men exchanged a glance, and then one of them said, you're not liable for the draft and you're not being drafted, so what's all the fuss about? Why make waves? I said that I was a Jew and therefore I had to be drafted. He said, are you trying to tell me that you know better than me what you have to do? Maybe the army knows better than you do who has to be drafted and who doesn't? He was tired, he wanted to get the whole thing over as quickly as possible. The officer with the pencil in his mouth said, if you're not up for the draft you won't be drafted and that's all there is to it!

I looked at them and I said, my mother was a Jewess, I was born in this country and my grandfather is a holocaust survivor (stretching the facts a little), the draft laws apply to me and you have to draft me!

The officer sitting on the right, the one who had been trying

181

to catch a glimpse of Franz before the door shut behind me, said in a voice which sounded indifferent but was hard and determined at the same time, as if he were reflecting on some profound philosophical problem while swatting a fly, your father is an Arab called Azouri! He's been under house arrest four times, a member of an anti-Zionist party, he's published books that have caused great damage to the state of Israel. I'm not blaming you, it's not your fault that he's your father, but those are the facts. Azouri has family in Jordan, on the West Bank and in Lebanon. I said, okay, but I have another side too, my mother's side, and you certainly don't suspect my grand-father of anything, and Azouri hasn't been accused of any crime either as far as I know and even if he has what's it got to do with me, I'm Yosef Rosenzweig, I'm an Israeli, I went to an Israeli school, I live here, what gives you the right to deprive me of the duty...The officer shouted 'the privilege!' and I repeated, 'the duty', it's my duty to serve in the army, the Germans could have made me into soap if Azouri hadn't saved my grandparents, but that's not relevant and it's none of your business anyway, what matters is that I'm fit to serve in the army and I want to serve in the army, I have no problems with my conscience, my father hasn't got any objections, it's my duty as a citizen of this country to serve in the army and you won't stop me. The officer said, you can volunteer and then we'll think about it. I said, I won't volunteer, there's a draft law in this country and that law applies to me, why should I have to ask for favours and then be turned down? How can you disqualify me unless you've got something personal against me? If I've broken any laws I want to know what they are, I'll get myself a lawyer and I'll take you to court and I'll fight you, I've got rights here too! The officer chewing the pencil lost patience at this point and he said, there are some Arabs (he almost said 'good Arabs' but he caught himself in time) serving in the army but they serve in it *as Arabs*, and you're not exactly

182

one of them. Do you want to go and serve in the Border Police with a lot of Druse or be a Bedouin scout perhaps? What exactly do you want? What do you need it for? We don't want to see happen here what happened to your parents and grand-parents in the First World War when they found themselves fighting on opposite sides, brother against brother, father against son. I told him that that was my affair and the decision had to be mine. I said, if you called me and I didn't want to go I could have appealed to the draft board, but why do you have to appeal for me, what gives you the right?

One of them said, what gives me the right is that I'm a Jew fighting for his country, which is my right and my privilege. And me? I asked. He said with a hidden sneer in his voice, you? You? What are you, exactly?

I felt sick and stunned, as if the disguise I had been wearing for years was falling away, as if under those contemptuous eyes I was turning into the embodiment of all the stereotypes of the cruel primitive Arab with a dagger between his teeth who wanted to throw all these charming officers into the sea. I was furious and desperate, but all I said was, It's my choice not yours. And then the pencil-chewer took the pencil out of his mouth and said in a voice which was quieter than anything I have ever heard, slowly and almost gently, Don't you under-stand that you're not wanted, Yosef? It's nothing personal, it's a matter of principle. Why must you insist on pushing in where you're not wanted?

Then I lost control of myself and I screamed, don't you talk to me like that! My mother was as Jewish as you are, I'm a Jew, I wanted to be one, I learnt to be one, what do you mean 'you're not wanted'? And then he said in words that hardly touched each other, what did your mother have to marry an Arab for? And after a moment he added, Can't you understand that it's for your own good? Your mother's already made you pay enough, now you'll have an opportunity to go and study, to get ahead, it's a free country, can't you understand that it's to your advantage not to go to the army? Can't you understand that we have to be careful? Why must you be so stubborn?

I was on the point of tears but I didn't let them see my tears. I want to serve in the army, I said, I'll fight you, you're not being fair, you've got no real strength or understanding. The pencil-chewer yelled, I came here from Europe, boy, I went through it, I walked between corpses and took shit out of dead men's backsides, you won't teach me what understanding and compassion are! I don't want Arabs in my army, I'm in charge of drafting soldiers here and you won't fight anyone, you'll put your tail between your legs and slink away like the Arab you are, maybe you'll take a pot shot at me in the dark, I know your kind. And he stood up, gave me a look of cold contempt, and left the room. The other two tried to pretend that nothing had happened, they said, You'll be able to get ahead, you'll be three years ahead of all your friends, by the time they're out of the army you'll be finished at the university and you'll have your pick of all the good jobs. What do you want? In the last analysis we're not trying to do you any harm, it's for your own good!

One of them looked at me and I could see he was really sorry. He said, how could you stand and point a gun at your own family? Even if it's only half your family. Your mother's dead, your grandfather's an old man already. You've got an Arab father with a big family in the region, it's against them you'll have to fight, how will you be able to kill them? Believe me, boy, it's a hard thing to kill a man, and killing a member of your own family is even harder, even if you don't know him... it's not necessary!

It is necessary, I said, weakly by now, but maybe you don't trust me? You can interpret it that way if you like, said the other officer impatiently, and he added, that's it. You'll get your exemption in the post, at Azouri's address in Acre. I said, you know I live in Tel Aviv, I've been living in Tel Aviv with Franz

Rosenzweig for years, you've got it in your files, why are you trying to make me into an enemy by force?

Because that way maybe you'll understand who you really are and stop driving everyone crazy, said the officer drily. The certificate will be sent. You're exempt from army service. I have just one request – you have friends who are getting their call-up papers now. In less than a year they'll be soldiers, it would be better if you didn't ask them too many questions about where they're serving and what they're doing. Friendly meetings are alright, but you realise that every army has its secrets and civilians don't have to know about them. Try to mind your own business, okay? I started to shout and the pencil-chewer came back and said, if the situation were reversed and your Arabs had won the war you wouldn't be standing here shouting, you'd be hanging upside down from a tree while they cut off your balls, slowly. A piece of friendly advice, he added, don't ask any questions, and if you've got any friends who fancy the idea of marrying an Arab, tell them that every fuck has its price. And then he yelled, who's next?

I sat at home and refused to go out, I didn't even go to Dina's. She came to the house but I wouldn't open the door. Franz sat locked up in his room. Gertrude said, look what you've done to him, and I yelled at her and she ran away and cried. Later Franz phoned the Minister of the Interior whom he knew from Berlin and pleaded and insisted and pulled strings until he was given an appointment with the Chief of Staff, and I went with him. The whole thing was a bloody farce, but I didn't care, I felt as if they'd shoved Azouri down my throat and pulled him out through my backside. Poor Franz put on his German officer's uniform from the First World War with all his medals and decorations, and went to see the Chief of Staff. When we got there he spoke in a dry, stiff voice that was as full of pain as if he were giving birth to me right there in the office. He saluted. Franz was ill-suited to play the part of a buffoon, but he was like a man with a devil on his back, enveloped in a fog of pain so thick that even I, for all my humiliation, could not imagine its intensity. An old scarecrow of a man in an ancient uniform with obsolete decorations, he stood facing the Chief of Staff who had once sent him a bunch of flowers and a thank-you note for operating on his father, and he talked. The Chief of Staff was a busy man, he had wars on his mind, he would never have agreed to meet Franz but for the pressure of various people to whom the Minister of the Interior had passed the buck, and now he was trapped. Franz said, Yosef could have adopted his father's identity, but he didn't, he entered into our history with all his heart and soul, in details that even I don't know. He could have joined the terrorists, but he didn't. He is my grandson, Hava's son. Hava who fought with you outside Jerusalem. He is also, there is no need to deny it, the son of his father, who is a loyal citizen of this country. What gives you the right to deny Yosef the duty of serving his motherland? I know how he feels – most of my friends didn't join the army and fight in the war but I said, it's a war, I'm a German, and I enlisted. Nobody stopped me from doing my duty because I was a Jew, and the Germans are not exactly our greatest admirers, as you know. Some of my officers may not have understood my motives but none of them said, none of them dared to say what Jewish officers – after everything this nation has been through – said to Yosef. True, there is a war on between his country and his father's people, but my family in Germany had relations in Russia and we fought each other, it was hard, perhaps it was inhuman, but it was understood. We were patriots and we wanted to be good citizens. Did anyone try to deprive us of that right? You are lending your hand to something that could be a dangerous turning point in the Zionist idea, that will turn it into a nationalist adventure, bolstered by narrow religious prejudices, you're releasing Jewish devils, self-righteous devils who can see only themselves and no one else, who judge only others and never themselves, full of paranoia, destroying everything we dreamt of here, you're making a mistake, sir, a very grave mistake! The Chief of Staff tried to calm him down but Franz didn't even hear him. He was in the grip of a vision, he said to himself, I'm saying what has to be said, I'm standing guard, and to the Chief of Staff he said, Yosef is a Jew because he feels Jewish, but you want him to be an Arab, you want to turn him into his own enemy. Can't you understand what a terrible thing you're doing to him?

The Chief of Staff lost patience. He had important things to do. I could see him thinking, the complexes of a German Jew, a good surgeon but a fool. He didn't stop his daughter from ruining her life and now he wants me to clean up the mess. Aloud he said, we make our own beds, Mr Rosenzweig, and we must lie on them.

For three days Franz did not leave his room. I sat and kept guard over him. Dina came and I let her in. Gertrude came and Franz refused to let her into his room.

And then I began stealing from my friends. I borrowed money and I didn't give it back. I planned revenge. Millions of vengeful thoughts raced through my brain, I even went to bed with Dina as if I were revenging myself on them. Franz tried to cheer me up, to explain what he himself found inexplicable, even Azouri tried to console me. There was something new I had to learn now. Every playground conversation turned into a conspiracy in my eyes, an attempt by my friends to exclude me from their secrets. And the truth is that they really were confused. The fact that I was, in the last resort, an Arab, had been brought home to them with an official stamp on it, they were really afraid to talk about their preparations for enlistment in front of me. And then we left school and they joined the army, and when they came home on leave they took care to meet me only in public, at discotheques or the movies, and they were careful not to talk about their daily lives in the army in my presence. Even my friendship with Giora began to disintegrate. He was a good friend, he was truly fond of me, I was always welcome in their house, his father was really sorry for what had happened to me, but now he had a son in the army, he was worried about him, there were rumours of an impending war, Eshkol made a speech in the Galilee warning the Arabs that we were keeping accounts, seven Syrian Migs were shot down on Passover night, and then the waiting period began. I went to people's houses and I felt that they didn't want me there, I wanted to talk to Franz but he was busy, the pain had passed or dulled, he was busy getting the hospital ready for the wounded. The alert was on, the fist clenched. Azouri went into hiding with a friend because he didn't want to be arrested by the security agencies who came looking for him on the first day of the alert. He knew they would come for him, by the end of the war most of his friends were in house arrest or administrative detention, without a trial of course, nobody told them what crime they were accused of. And Azouri, who had been through it all before, phoned me up and said, I'm in hiding with a colleague from the university, a Jew from South America, a Party member and a friend, yesterday he was called up and I'm sitting here with his wife and his baby daughter and praying, what should I pray for Yosef? I said to him, pray for the Arabs to win! Pray for them to finish these self-righteous bastards off once and for all! He laughed and said, no, I don't know what to pray for, I hope there won't be a war, I'm afraid for my friends, for the husband of this nice woman, and on the other hand I've got a family in Jordan, I've got a brother in Lebanon, I'm torn Yosef, perhaps they were right not to let you join the army. I'm torn, I'm looking after my friend's wife, helping her with the little girl, she doesn't know where her husband is, he's against the war that's going to break out but he went with everyone else, it's not easy, hang in there, Yosef. I said to him, I want you to win, and Azouri asked me, Yosef, who exactly do you mean by 'you'?

21

Until the moment the war broke out I had been looking forward to a Jewish defeat, fanning the flames of my hatred with the dreams of revenge that were consuming me but when the war was over at first I was proud of the crushing defeat inflicted on the Arabs, swept up by the general euphoria. But not for long. The first trip I took to the West Bank was a shock. The Arabs I saw there were different from the ones I had known up to now. I saw the refugee camps, I saw the wounded eyes. I met Azouri's brother, he sat facing me over a cup of coffee, he looked at me sadly and asked me to use my 'influence with the authorities' (as an Israeli Arab!) to get them to allow him to return to his shop in Amman. Everyone was in a trance. After Nachie threw me out of his house when I came to console him for Giora's death I felt the full extent of my isolation.

I said to myself, I'll fix all you bastards, but I didn't know what to do with myself and the more I thought about it the more apathetic I became. I was dazed and confused, helpless and hopeless, uncomfortable with the three 'Noes' of the Arab summit at Khartoum, wanting revenge but not getting any satisfaction even from the first acts of Arab terror. I knew that something terrible had happened and was about to happen, that nothing would ever be the same again. I knew that I would have to choose and I wasn't ready to choose yet. I wanted to find a good place in the middle where I could hate both sides with the same just hatred. I painted furiously, I received a grant from the Israel-American cultural foundation, I was sent to Florence for two months and I took Dina with me. It was terrific. We forgot everything, we slept in the woods, I painted. I didn't paint well and I didn't paint badly. Dina said that I was too intellectual to be an artist. Everything was against me and I was against everything too. When I stole from my friends and took money from them I felt a kind of relief. But I stole from Dina too, and Franz, and Azouri. I felt trapped, they were against me, I was against them, when Bunim arrived on the scene he was like a rope thrown to a drowning man. Through him I could revenge myself on everyone. I said to Franz, who had long ceased looking for potsherds and came home weary and defeated from the hospital, you're not an old-fashioned German officer acting the hero in the Chief of Staff's office any more, you're an ageing refugee. When you came here you didn't know you were coming to dispossess Azouri, you didn't know that in a tragedy there isn't one justice but two. And he looked at me, my grandfather who loved me with a heavy, steadfast loyalty, already a little subdued, worn out by the years of struggle, and took my hands in the sensitive hands which had won him an international reputation and through the trembling of his hands I sensed the weight of his sadness and desolation, how much he longed for Käthe and Hava, and all he had left were Azouri and me. At a time when the whole country was playing at being a great empire, running from one end of Greater Israel to the other, speaking in a new voice, loud, threatening, discordant, drunk with the victory which marked the greatest defeat in a history which I no longer had any part in but which was still mine – he felt the crushing weight of everything he had lost.

When Dina married Rammy it finished me off. I remember how I went to Haifa and knocked at Laila's door late one night. I was on the point of giving up when she suddenly opened the door. I heard footsteps in the other room, the room which had been her sister Silwa's before she went to America. The footsteps stopped, Laila said, you look tired Yosef. I said, I'm desperate Laila. Who's hiding in Silwa's room? She put her arms around me and embraced me, she had so much love and tenderness to give someone who would be worthy of her and she of him, but there was no one. The footsteps in the other room belonged to Kassem, they were working on a new play together and he was sleeping over at her place, he didn't want to come out because he was afraid I would be jealous. I put my arms around her and told Kassem to come out and then I told them about Rammy and Dina and Laila prepared an excellent salad which I ate and then Kassem went to bed.

Laila sat and looked at me through weary eyes. She said, everything is harder because the devils haven't got any horns, the horrors are disguised as something almost human. Someone told me that the Syrians buried twenty-five thousand people alive in concrete – who cares? The Jews are playing the good guys on dangerous turf. New voices are emerging on the other side of the Jewish night and shouting that their blood is white as snow, people are returning from the oblivion of history with a dark, deadly racism, the catastrophe is waiting in the wings, in the centre of the stage the violence is sporadic, there's no one really to fight against, Fatah doesn't play according to my rules but I can't close my eyes to their anger, they've got justice on their side too, they're murderers but they murder so that I can hold my head up.... Yosef, how are you going to survive?

I slept with her that night. It was so sweet to kiss her, so sad to see how she yearned for love and how she was wilting away because she had no one to give her marvellous body to, her firm breasts, she would be wasted on the clumsy attempts to create a dialogue between the deaf and the dumb, she would look for other Yosefs, she would find them in her bed ready for everything except an acceptance of the simple truths which she knew but could not find the words to describe. She would have liked to place her body, which I was holding, in the hands of an enemy with horns, an enemy she could fight with no holds barred. She hated Hava's son but I had a lot of Azouri in me too and Azouri was a man she respected, the most attractive man around, Dina called him, and who could fail to admire Azouri's sweet, cruel honesty? But Laila was in bed with a pale copy of Azouri, and what did we have to give each other? She made me wish I were someone with simple slogans to hang onto, black and white, absolute good and absolute evil, anything to save myself from the fate of being the Jews' Arab.

I told her she fucked like a high-class whore, and she said, what do you know about high-class whores? I said, Laila, this isn't Arab work. She laughed, perhaps she cried, and I realised how degraded I felt by the Arab labourers filling the towns, from Gaza, from the West Bank, doing all the dirty work, eager for any job offered them, providing the cheap labour the Jews were only too happy to take advantage of, humiliating me with their downtrodden looks, poor downtrodden Arabs for their Jewish lords and masters to patronise and exploit. Laila had gone to Nablus, to Jenin, to Hebron, she had seen what was going on there, she had met passionate people she had nothing in common with, she had gone to a congress in Moscow, met Arabs from all over the world who threatened her, who called her a Jews' Arab, the Syrians abused her, the Iraqis looked barbaric to her, the comrades from the West Bank were foreign to her, what could she do? She dreamt of an Arab Zionism, of a beautiful Joseph in a coat of many colours. I wanted to sketch her naked in the night, as I had once sketched Dina in Acre, she sat up, I sketched her, and then she said, You should be a lawyer, Yosef, a writer, a doctor, not a painter, you haven't got the nature of an adventurer, you're full of tenderness, Yosef. I was angry, I didn't want to be full of tenderness, Dina knew how much tenderness I had to give, but I didn't want to

192

give it. In the morning we sat there, Laila and Kassem and I, we drank coffee, there was a melancholy light over the bay, violet clouds over Acre on the other side of the bay, the air was misty, the water was dark blue, almost purple, birds flew in elegant formation back to their countries of origin. We sat above the tears Haifa was weeping into the bay, tears for the smashed garden of abu-al-Misk Kafur, what could we do, where could we go? We could work for the Party, submit to its discipline and find a place for ourselves, in the last analysis everyone plays with his hands tied, but deep in our hearts each of us knew that we had been betrayed and we had betrayed ourselves and the war between the Jews and the Arabs was over, they had won, they had wanted all or nothing, we had aroused their devils and their devils had turned into kings, they were the masters now and all our poor friends with their beautiful poems, their stirring slogans about the freedom and brotherhood had about as much chance as a fly in a snowstorm.

What good was the co-existence of a handful of intellectuals in a progressive club in Tel Aviv to us? As long as they were Zionists, as long as we were Zionists, as long as they, we, wanted a Jewish State, the Arabs, they, we, would have to fight, and the war was over, the Jews had taken the lot, we, the Arabs that is, could win a few more battles and then the Jews would rule over us like the whites in South Africa, they wouldn't be popular, so what, when had the Jews ever been popular? Nobody loved them, us, even when they didn't have conquered territories and Arab subjects they locked up in their shops at night so they could wash the dishes in the morning in the restaurants of Haifa and Tel Aviv and build houses for the Zionists on the West Bank, which with the suppressed longings of two thousand years they had begun to call Judea and Samaria...

It was a sad and moving morning. We knew that we were lost and we sat there holding hands. I said to Laila, if I could really

193

love you, without any conditions, and you me, we would be saved, but I have Dina, only she belongs to Rammy now, you're afraid of me, you couldn't live with Hava's son, it would be too much for you, a sure sign of your defeat. You'll be left alone, I'll be alone, Kassem will be alone, what will become of us? And Laila said, we have to learn to build a bridge, and I said, I can't even build one between Yosef and Yussuf, between myself and myself, the son of Hava on Franz's side and the son of Hava on Azouri's side. The only ones who knew how to do it were Hava and Azouri, and what happened to them? They didn't get a medal for bravery, they didn't even get reparations, pensions, the compensation any soldier wounded in a war gets. They remained alone. She died to save herself any more suffering and Azouri sits in the local council of Acre under a picture of Lenin whom he believes in as much as I believe in the divinity of the bottle of Coca Cola in your fridge. Look at Haifa bay, it's mine, it's yours, it belongs to all the people who've been fighting here for four thousand years, and the country never gives in, she bows her head and then she butts her conquerors into the sea, and they disappear and new ones come. Only the people of the land remain, and you're the people of the land, Laila, once you were a Phoenicean, once you were a Roman, once you were a Greek, once you were a Christian Arab, and once you were the concubine of Yosef ibn Azouri, and you loved him and he loved you, and both of us loved Rammy and Dina and they us, they won the war but they're as defeated as we are, as you are, we're defeated, they're defeated. Once when I was in high school we were in the military cadet corps, they took us to the sea of Galilee, I was with my friend Giora, who died three years ago, his father was a hero of the peace movement, he fought against the military government and for the return of Arab refugees to their villages, and he threw me out of his house! I came to console him for the death of his son and suddenly I was a dirty Arab, whose parents should have

194

been exterminated in order to get rid of the 'means of production' once and for all, in the immortal words of the Jewish conquerors of Deir Yassin.

We were camping next to Tiberias, there was some sabotage activity in the area, they must have forgotten that I was half Arab, they took me with them to search the buses, I was a Jewish policeman with a band on my sleeve. There was an Arab there from Bak'a el Garabiyeh, he looked at me, he tried to read my expressionless face, I searched his pockets with all the Jewish passengers watching and I felt good, Laila, it was good suddenly to be powerful and search people's pockets. He had some olives and figs in his pockets and I felt the blade of a knife, I didn't take it out, I looked at him, he looked at me, I didn't say a word, I had power, I could have had him arrested, I wanted to call out to the officer who was walking up and down shouting, boys, have you found anything? You have to learn where to look for the weapons on these shits, but I didn't say a word, I couldn't, not even to go on enjoying that feeling of power for a little longer. I got off the bus and I saw him looking down at me from the window. You want to know how he looked at me? With contempt. He wanted me to know that he was stronger than I was, that miserable Arab peasant who could have sat in jail, been beaten up for a lousy knife that might not have been good for anything but stealing a bunch of grapes – he looked at me with contempt for not turning him in. I looked back at him and then I crossed the road, and with the sun beating down on my head I spewed my guts.

22

Laila said, I'm tired, I'm not active in anything any more, I do what I have to do, I live without knowing why, everything will pass in the end. I went back to Tel Aviv. Rammy and Dina phoned and I banged the phone down. Franz took me to a concert and I cried when they played Bach. My tears were for Laila the night before.

After I decided to escape and Bunim realised that I was looking for a way out of the country he did nothing to stop me. Suddenly he lost interest in me. As if his long war was over at last. I went to Dina to ask her to help me and she was embarrassed and didn't know what to say, Rammy was on reserve duty, I insulted her and ran away. In the end I managed to get out of the country, there were cops at the airport but they didn't even know whom they were looking for. Bunim wasn't programmed any more, perhaps he was trying to tell me that I was burnt anyway and it was no skin off his nose if I left the country, he had given up on me and was willing to give the other side a chance to trap me. I arrived in Rome and from there I flew to Zurich, where I met Nabil who said to me, we heard about you and what you did, why don't you come and work for us? I said, I haven't done anything, and he said, look, you worked for the Mossad and it's an open secret that you worked for them, now it's your turn to pay. I waited for the bullet in my back, but someone had evidently decided that there was more profit in keeping me alive. After all, I knew things that nobody else knew, I was half theirs, my mother was

Hava the heroine of Koloniya, it was worth their while to keep me alive for the time being, or so I thought. Nabil asked me to go with him to Beirut and I agreed. My uncle, Azouri's elder brother, was living there.

The plane was already flying over Cyprus when Nabil, who had had too much whisky, told me a few things from which I understood that Bunim had decided to keep me guessing to the end. Perhaps, and I say this with caution and in the light of what I think today, waiting for my fateful meeting in Paris and writing these confessions for the third time, perhaps he wanted to protect me. Perhaps the fact that we had all passed through his hands, my mother, my grandmother and now me, the fact that he had arrested Franz on his way to Acre, that he had been the officer in charge of Haifa port in 1936 when Franz and Käthe arrived in the country, perhaps all this made him hold his tongue, write *burnt* across my file but not bring the match too close. All Nabil really knew was what he had read in the Israeli press, and that wasn't much, or to be more precise it was far from accurate.

As soon as I had left the country details were leaked to the press and reporters began sniffing round Kassit and other places. Hedva and Nissan sang their heads off and they talked so much rubbish that I wanted to cry. But Rammy kept quiet. Dina too said nothing. Laila said something very strange, they came to her house and she said, Yosef is confused, he lacks political backbone, a direct, pragmatic approach to the Palestinian problem, he's a romantic and a half, his involvement with the Mossad was against himself more than it was against the Arabs. Kassem said he knew that I hadn't given anything away and the only reason why I collaborated in the first place was that an Arab had once tried to kill my mother. Kassem had a highly developed sense of drama which he knew how to exploit for all the wrong ends. The poems he published in Hebrew translations were grieving poems, with a hypnotic lyrical

197

power, only his plays were cheap entertainment for yawning commissars. In any case, they didn't succeed in getting much out of Kassem, apart from a few stupid stories about me and Laila. Laila wrote an angry letter to *Al-Ittihad* protesting about the way my name was being dragged through the mud and *Ha-Olam Ha-ze* translated it into Hebrew. Azouri and Franz were taken in for questioning. That was Bunim's cruel game. He knew that neither of them had anything to say, but he wanted to sit opposite each of them separately and suck their blood with the enjoyment of an ageing sadist. He was jealous of their love for me. Bunim had a dead son, he was a hard, lonely man, he should have been Japanese, committing hara-kiri for him would have been as easy as eating ice-cream, he had faced death so many times that it was like a chess game for him – you plan your moves, you kill a king and then you have a cup of tea and go to bed and sleep like a dog. A dead dog.

Bunim sat and enjoyed the deliberate, disillusioned loathing he felt for Azouri, whom in the depths of his heart he may perhaps have admired for his patience and strength. Perhaps Bunim and Azouri together could have provided the foundations for the new state, the dream of a Jewish state after the holocaust, a state which would be a refuge for people who knew what locked doors meant, and perhaps the dream was already lost, not only for Azouri who had had his balls burnt because of it, but also for Bunim. A new spirit was already raging in the Jewish streets, Bunim was already obsolete, the voice of reason and moderation, the new religious nationalism left him far behind. He wasn't even competing any more. He sat opposite Azouri and went through the motions of trying to milk him, but Azouri knew that he was trying to hear his own mouth saying the things he should have said to others and didn't dare. He questioned Franz as if they were not only fellow conspirators but partners in some crime. Franz was offended, but he realised what Bunim's game was and he played along according to Bunim's rules. All this was trickled to the press and I read it. No one said exactly what I had done in the Mossad, no one told the reporters that I brought the rain to Kassit. No, that's not true, Nissan and Hedva mentioned it but nobody took them seriously. The more serious sources said nothing about it. It seemed to me that I wasn't being burnt so much as kept on ice. Nabil himself didn't know exactly what I had done for them, he thought that I translated material for them from Arabic to Hebrew, read the Arabic press and helped in the graphics department, which doesn't sound like anything to write home about or burn an agent for – but that's what he'd been told and that's apparently what he believed. I felt quite relieved. I didn't mind being considered a traitor in the eyes of those who read the Israeli papers, my life was finished anyway, I had nowhere to go and nothing to hope for, but I didn't want them to know about the rain I brought to Kassit. I didn't want people to know how I had gone to Kassit looking for love and sympathy. In my fantasies at the time Rammy and Dina were having babies like dogs on heat and it wasn't a pleasant sight. Franz was growing old, Käthe and Hava were dead, Azouri was waiting for me outside Kassit, I was trying to avoid him, there were times when I couldn't stand my double life any more and then Azouri would wait for me with the patience of an Arab peasant. In the end I would go to him, we would fall on each other's necks, we were always putting on these repeat performances of the return of the prodigal son, we would sit and talk for hours, sometimes whole nights at a time. He understood, he realised that I had to pin the blame on someone and he was the most convenient target. When he stood opposite Kassit and I refused to look at him he could afford to wait, go back to Acre, teach at Haifa university, and give me as much rope as I needed to hang myself on when I came to cry to him afterwards. He waited for my tears like a peasant waits for rain. We would sit at Abu Cristo's or on the beach, drinking chilled wine and looking out at the bay. One evening, when the sun was about to set, I was sitting next to the sea throwing stones into the ripples when a child approached me and asked in Arabic, what are you wishing for? I said, what? And he said, from the water, and I said, what water? and he said, you're throwing stones into the water and when a person throws stones into the water they wish for something. Azouri came up and heard the last part of this conversation and he said, he's wishing for Haifa to be on Acre's side of the bay and Acre to be on Haifa's side and I laughed because that was exactly what I would have asked for if there had been anyone to ask. But both of us were tired now, with all the years of stubborn struggle behind us, during the course of which I had brought enormous tears to his eyes more than once, the days of Kassit were over and gone, Rammy and Dina were living together in my flat, I spent my time with Azouri and Franz. They knew that I was planning to get away, they realised that what I was doing for what I called the 'government' was not exactly painting the desert red or anything else, they realised that like them I was trapped, I was defeated and they weren't surprised when in the end I ran away. I had money, both of them had deposited money in Swiss banks for me years before and there was a tidy sum waiting for me there. I'm a rich man, I could have given Nabil more than the duty-free whisky I brought from the German stewardess who was surprised to hear my elegant German. I spoke a German that nobody spoke in Germany any more, she didn't know that it was the German of Schiller and Heine, Karl Kraus and Goethe, her German was post-Nazi, mine was antediluvian. She would have sat on my knee if she wasn't too scared to, she probably thought all Arabs were hot-blooded rapists, she knew what they did to the German girls in Beirut. I laughed and said in pigeon German, Me Arab, my blood hot! She laughed but her eyes didn't laugh. They were blank and cold.

I arrived in Beirut exactly two years ago. Since then so many things have happened there. I went with Nabil to a small hotel that stank of whisky and hashish. The rooms were full of the mistresses of officers in the Organisations and their children swarmed in the corridors. These were the leaders Laila tries to believe are saints. I took a taxi and drove to my uncle's house. It was five o'clock in the afternoon, the town looked like a huge bazaar, cars flew in all directions with manic speed. Armed soldiers cut the town in quarters, shooting indifferently at anyone unfamiliar with the complexities of the system. Every group had its private army. In the middle of it all bored Syrians patrolled like police. I arrived at my uncle George's house. He looked at me with the calm, almost fatalistic, surprise which I learnt to recognise on the faces of the Christians in Beirut where every knock on the door could mean sudden fortune or sudden death. When I told him who I was the house came to life, my aunt came and kissed me, my pretty cousin presented her cheek daintily for me to kiss and we had a magnificent supper; the maid heaped dish after dish on the table, the night was torn with shots and distant cannon fire. Nobody seemed to know who was shooting whom, or to particularly care. My uncle was waiting for the Israelis to come and save him, he was living in Beirut as a Maronite Christian. My aunt was exquisitely polite, she and her husband both worked at the American University. Their daughter sat cold and reserved, staring at a handsome painting on the wall, above the piano. I asked who the artist was and my uncle said, that is a painting by your cousin Annette, I said that it was a beautiful painting and my uncle said, she studied at the Beaux Arts in Paris. We talked about Israel and Lebanon and Azouri. The conversation was awkward because they were waiting for the Israelis and I was escaping from them. The rules of etiquette prevented them from asking me what my business was there, they couldn't have guessed that I was there to help their enemies.

They didn't know much about their so-called friends either. They didn't know Bunim.

My uncle leant over me with longings so old they were almost mouldy. He remembered me as a baby of one in Paris. We began to talk French, we drank more wine, outside we could hear Arab music from across the way, next door someone was practising a Tchaikovsky concerto on the violin. My uncle said, would you like to see your cousin? I asked if he meant the artist, and he said yes. He and his wife took me into their bedroom. It was a large room, above the bed was a closed window and underneath the window a small crucifix. The other walls were bare but for a huge photograph hanging opposite the bed with its shiny yellow counterpane. My uncle switched on the light which almost blinded me. I looked at the photograph. In five boxes standing next to each other lay the dismembered body of a young girl. Her face was slashed, her eyes had been gouged out, the gouged-out eyes lay in the box which held her face. My uncle said, meet your cousin. This is how we found her. They tortured her before they killed her, but they gouged out her eyes after she was dead. My aunt said, I took the photograph. All I could find to say was, how big is it? And she replied, one metre by one twenty. I tried to imagine the nights when they lay there opposite their daughter, and I felt a terrible revulsion. I wanted to run away but they took me back into the salon and their other daughter played the *Moonlight Sonata* on the piano.

My uncle was a kind of desiccated Azouri, dripping with a murky poison, hating with restrained passion, speaking through his nose and waiting for any form of aristocratic death which offered itself. His wife was in command of a private army of five armed boys who were waiting outside next to a new Mercedes. My cousin said, tell us about yourself, we know so little. All night, with the ghastly photograph slicing through my brain, I sat and told them about Azouri and Hava, about myself and our lives. I found myself delivering a speech which might almost have been written by Bunim. I felt disgusted with myself. My hatred seemed unreal, my anger insignificant, what seemed to me cruel looked to them like a chivalrous game. I sensed that the distance separating us from Acre where Azouri was sitting was not fifty or sixty kilometres, but a hundred years.

When we sat down to a midnight supper, my aunt said, try the salad, we'll fix those Palestinians, we'll cut off their balls, we'll gouge out their eyes, try the shrimps. I couldn't eat. I asked my uncle, and you, aren't you a Palestinian? He said, me? I left Acre forty years ago, I'm a Lebanese Christian. When I left there were no Palestinians, it was the Jews in their stupidity who created a homeland for Azouri. When I left there was a British mandate and a pan-Arab dream of Greater Syria. Now we're all dancing to the Syrian tune, everyone is killing in the name of Allah and the holy conquered land. Here they are all corrupt, rotten to the core, there are no soldiers here, only the hired assassins of Arab frustration. No, I am not a Palestinian. And you, Yosef? Are you a Palestinian? I said that I didn't know any more what I was, my mother was a Jewess, my father was Azouri, and what was Azouri? My uncle said, Azouri, what a beautiful boy he was...

23

Nabil came to the hotel and took me to headquarters. On the way we paid a visit to the Palestinian library. I met a doctor from Acre with an aristocratic air who knew Azouri. We had coffee. He didn't say much, and he looked at me with longings which seemed sad and weary. He looked at me and tried to see the Jazzar mosque through me, he spoke desolately about the bay and Haifa. I was taken to a poet whom we had all revered in Haifa. He sat opposite me sunk in gloom, at eleven o'clock in the morning he was already drinking straight from the whisky bottle. The window was open, we could see the Beirut port bathed in sunshine. I had once met him, very briefly, in Haifa when I was still in high school and Azouri had taken me with him to a meeting of Jewish and Arab writers at the Party club in the German Colony of Haifa. He said nothing about his flight and about what had happened to him since he left. Perhaps he was sorry for me, perhaps his hatred was too bitter for words, he was different from most of the people I met in Beirut, he knew I was an enemy not because I had worked for the Mossad but because for him I was a Jew, a painful wound which he sensed like a man sensing his own shadow, for here he too was a Jew. Perhaps he was frightened by the mirror-image we reflected to each other. After a few minutes we began to talk in Hebrew, as if the language had a concrete reality of its own, as if we were touching something that existed outside the walls of this room, our own homesickness, the shoulder of a beloved brother, Haifa – which he knew how to hate in the poems he wrote but which he never ceased to yearn for. We exchanged enigmatic sentences, perhaps he was trying to warn me. I told him about the meeting between Franz and Azouri in the garden of abu-al-Misk Kafur and he looked at me with glazed eyes as if he were trying through me to return to Haifa in order to mourn his dead and count their graves.

I met a number of the heads of the Organisations who tried to milk me for information but the whole thing was a farce. All I could give them was words, I couldn't give them what I had come here to give. I suddenly felt so heartsick at my flight that I offered them only meaningless information, trivial details, and I concealed my gift from them. I couldn't bring myself to give them anything that I imagined might harm Franz, or even Laila and Azouri. The absurdity of the situation became crystal-clear to me during a conversation with quite a high-up commander who, I was told, was considered a moderate. He was a tough customer with haunted eyes, he did his best to get information out of me, but his military expertise was zero. Compared to Bunim he was a total amateur, and Rammy could have made mincemeat of him with one hand tied behind his back. He was an ideologue who thought he was a freedom fighter, but he was sophisticated enough to realise that he was playing a part in a cruel farce. I felt as sorry for him as I did for myself. That night Nabil took me to a luxurious night club where drunk fighters rushed at their naked mistresses with desperate battle cries and bayonets on their guns. Nabil wanted me to see the night-life of the freedom fighters, or perhaps it was the ghost of abu-al-Misk ibn Kafur Sherara who wanted to present me with my heritage, the ruins of his dreams of glory in all their sordid, brutal decadence. I could not get the picture of my cousin's dismembered body out of my mind. My uncle tried to get in touch with me but Nabil told me it would be unwise for me to be seen in the company of a traitor like him. Late one night I sat in my hotel room, a woman Nabil had sent to the room sat waiting in an armchair, drinking whisky and talking to me, for some reason, in English. She said, the life here very sad. My boyfriend dead, he was officer, dynamite, boom! I belong to Organisations. And you? I told her I was an investigator into the insect life of Kiryat Haim and Kiryat Bialik, married to a fat woman disguised as a sand dune and that my mother was a woman called Gertrude who collected old men to marry before they died. I was drunk and I lay down next to her and she tried to undress me. Someone had paid her but I didn't want a woman, I wanted to hear the rattle in her throat, I wanted to smell the stink of an ideological whore. I told her to lay off, I shut my eyes and tried to remember something just beneath the surface of my consciousness and suddenly it came to me – Dina. Dina in her uniform standing at the gate of the army camp. It was Independence Day and a lot of demonstrations had been organised throughout the country against the expropriation of Arab land. I drove down to visit Dina in Azouri's Volvo. On the way I was stopped and searched. They shoved me, they hit me, they abused me and mocked me. I told them I was going to visit my girlfriend and they said, and what about the land then, bloody little Arab, what about the raped Arab land, the holy Arab land? I said, the only good Arab is a dead Arab, and they said, you said it, not us, and one of them, Druse in the Border Police whose poet brother I had met in my Haifa days, pushed the handle of his gun into my stomach and I said to him, what are you doing with them? And he looked at his Jewish officer standing a few yards away and said, they like to see us putting on a performance for them, and I wanted to cry but I didn't cry. They kept me there for an hour, tormenting me and slapping me around, they had nothing against me personally but I was the only Arab who had turned up at their roadblock and they had to make the best of me. Afterwards they let me go, with the warning not to show my face at any of the demonstrations.

Before I drove off a man in civvies came up to me and said, what are you looking so sulky for? It's war, isn't it? And I said, yes, it's war, and you're a big hero. He pointed at me and said to his friend, you see this monkey here? This is the kind of monkey who waits for a red light to cross the road. You'll never make human beings of them.

I arrived at the camp, parked the car and went to the gate where Dina was standing, holding an Uzi. I stood opposite her and she saw that I had been beaten up. I asked her if she thought she was capable of shooting me and she said, I hate guns, they made me take the Uzi, but it isn't loaded. All around us it was one big picnic, fathers and mothers had brought cakes and sweets for their daughters, they were boiling water for coffee on campfires. Dina's parents would come later, they didn't want to come with me, her mother said, you go ahead, Yosef, we'll get a ride later with someone else, but I knew that they were going to take a cab and it hurt me that they didn't want to drive down with me. I looked at the enormous picnic, laughing mothers, enthusiastic fathers taking snapshots of their soldier daughters striking military poses next to old tanks, young soldiers dancing attention on their soldier girl friends. We stood apart in an awkward silence. I felt sad and I said, here's some chocolate for you, and I gave it to her. She ate it greedily. I took the unloaded Uzi from her and pointed it at myself and in a dramatic voice which wouldn't have shamed Kassem I said, What are Yosef's last words? It's good to die for our country!*

And I pressed the trigger. Dina shrieked and I said, but the magazine's empty, isn't it? and she said, but there's always the danger of a bullet in the barrel!

I said to the woman in bed with me, there's always the

---

*A reference to the famous last words of Yosef Trumpeldor, an early Zionist pioneer killed by the Arabs.

danger of a bullet in the barrel! And she said, give me fuck, anyhow they pay me, you smell good. In the end I let her rape me and her orgasm was an expert work of automatic art, she knew exactly the right moment to moan, maybe she did it in accordance with the instructions of the Organisation, as if how to kill Jews and how to moan in an orgasm came from the same instruction manual.

I was interrogated by officers who had given up hope of getting anything significant out of me. I didn't even talk about Bunim. He can burn me if he likes but I won't burn him, I said to myself. I felt full of disgust, all I had seen up to now was a lot of self-pity, cheap money, and blood shed in vain. I belonged neither to them nor to Bunim, but at least Bunim felt close to me, he fought me with my mother's hands, he enjoyed seeing his own tired loathing, his own sacred rage reflected on my face. They were indifferent to pain, they didn't give a damn about me, and the way they carried on about their holy land reminded me of the Jewish rabbis who had broken out of the rotten eggs of a Jewish fanaticism which had been trying to restrain itself for so many years and was now competing with Khomeinism. One night when I was sitting with Nabil I said to him, I feel like a stranger here, and he said, listen, Yosef, the name of the game is the game itself and you're right in the middle of it, burnt from both sides.

I stayed in Beirut for three months. I was a failure and the people at the top were beginning to show signs of impatience. The propaganda value I had brought with me was fading fast, the Israeli press had forgotten me. They wanted blood and I had blood to give them and they knew it, they smelt that I was hiding something, holding something back. They tried to bully me, to threaten me, even to dope me. I thought of how I once said to Bunim, I'll do what you tell me, I'll bring the rain to Kassit for you, but I'll never inform on my friends or people I know. And he said, that's okay, for the rest I've got better rats

208

than you. And I kept my word, I saved the lost honour of those superior rats, and I did the same thing in Beirut too, except that there I didn't even bring the rain to Kassit. I had my own code of honour, I was the heir to the Salomon family of Germany and abu-al-Misk ibn Kafur Sherara, I wasn't afraid of death, perhaps I even wanted someone to shoot me. I was afraid of the harm I might do to Franz and Azouri, both of them were in the same boat now. One day I phoned my uncle and told him to come to the Hotel Commodore with money. He arrived dressed up as a Phalangist, in a uniform that looked ridiculous on his old body. I said to him, I have to get out of here and you have to help me. He didn't ask any questions, I knew that I was being followed and we drove down sidestreets until we reached Junia. My uncle hid me with a young officer who didn't ask any questions either, he gave me cigarettes and a very young girl, almost a child, and he gave me Turkish coffee, the best I've ever tasted, to drink. That night they put me on a boat to Cyprus and before we sailed my uncle said, phone Azouri and tell him to give me back my daughter, and then he left. It was a short trip but I spent the whole of it in a panic in case I was discovered. I lay in my cabin with the lights out, grinning like an idiot and breathing in the smell of the stormy sea I could see through the porthole. I sent regards with the fish to Acre. I felt as close to Acre as it was possible to be, in a certain sense I realised that I would never be so close to Acre again.

At Cyprus I was taken to the airport. I was told that people were looking for me. Nabil had sworn to be revenged on me, his men were after me, but I got away from them. When the plane took off I breathed a sight of relief but I still didn't know if I was safe. We flew to Copenhagen and there I was followed by the Volkswagen Transit, by this stage I wasn't taking anything too seriously, their ineptitude made me laugh, I got away to Zurich, at five o'clock in the afternoon I checked in at a hotel and fell asleep in the clothes my uncle had given me and I slept until the following morning. I stood in a public telephone box with a handful of Swiss francs and I phoned Azouri and said, I'm okay, Azouri, don't worry about me, I'll phone again in a few days' time, give my regards to Dina and Franz, and the next morning I took some of my money out of the bank and I flew to Paris.

Before I left Israel I took Franz to have coffee in a Tel Aviv cafe. Gertrude already had him completely under her thumb, her fat daughters smiled at me from every corner of the house. I couldn't stand Gertrude's house, I kept searching for Käthe there. Franz had grown old. At the age of seventy-eight he looked like a desiccated butterfly. He wore a summer suit and sipped his iced coffee slowly. His refined face was etched with elusive lines, he looked as if he had lived his whole life in a no-man's land, untouched by the bombs exploding on either side. There was no sign of the catastrophes he had suffered on his face. Reality seemed little more than a nuisance to him. He no longer performed operations, from time to time he went to the hospital to talk to the young doctors who regarded him as a relic of the ancient past. He stirred his coffee fastidiously, with the air of one who belonged to another age, with the delicate movements, the smooth and smiling face of a world long gone.

Sitting there in the glare of the Tel Aviv sun Franz's eyes were full of a cold and dignified despair. He grew old indifferently, his eyes were fixed on a crystalline memory which compensated him to some extent for what life had done to him. Like Dina, Franz did not believe that I was cut out to be an artist, my paintings frightened him. The truth is that I no longer paint, in Beirut I did not illustrate the articles and stories I wrote for the Organisation papers. The men at the top said, do you really think he worked for the Mossad in the graphics department? Perhaps he was far more important than we imagine and they sent him here as if he were burnt to make us fall into a trap? They suspected me of being an impostor and they were right. I deceived everyone, I stole from everyone, love, friendship, money, war souvenirs, but I never deceived myself. Dina knew how to stand between me and myself, and I never succeeded in deceiving her. As for Franz and Azouri, they were the last innocents of the century, the last aristocrats, they really believed that they were building a bridge with their love. They didn't know the extent of the abyss yawning between them, they didn't know it in 1917 when they met in the garden of abu-al-Misk Kafur, and they still didn't know it when everything was over.

The Organisations tried to catch up with me. After I escaped from Beirut they discovered that I had worked for the Mossad in a very different capacity from what they had imagined, and that I had brought the rain to Kassit. Today too I can close my eyes and see things that will happen tomorrow or the next day, but I hardly ever do it any more. I don't expect anything good to happen and I have no desire to know about the bad things before they happen. I try to hold onto the image of Franz at our last meeting. He was baffled by the mathematical logic of the incomprehensible tragedy of his life. Life seemed to him like an intricate and terrifying maze from which he had extricated himself only by the sacrifice of everything dear to him. All that remained to him was an ancient memory of Azouri and a grandson who was about to leave him forever. Artists play forbidden games with violence, he said to me, you should take up research, a scientific investigation of the situation of the Jews, the Israeli, the Arab, what happened here. We left the cafe. The street was full of people. We reached the old house surrounded by tall leafy trees. We went into Franz's room. There were pictures of Käthe and Hava on the wall. He switched on the radio and we listened to a Haydn symphony. I had always understood his fear of me, he was afraid that my art would try to express what had happened to us and that would be a catastrophe, a story that it was forbidden to tell, dangerous to both sides....

211

If this book is ever published Franz will never read it. He died a month ago, Gertrude had him to herself for two years of stolen happiness but she too, said Azouri on the phone, has no intention of outliving him for long. The insect investigator of Kiryat Bialik has escaped the net, laughed Azouri, meaning that the infant prodigy had abandoned Gertrude's fat daughter for a Rumanian who wanted him to be her entrance ticket to Germany.

I know the sick side of things, I've operated on thousands of diseased lungs, Franz said to me after we had listened to the Haydn symphony together. Beware of sickness, Yosef. I told the Chief of Staff what I had to tell him, he said, but after 1942 I know that if a Jewish state had existed here then two million Jews would still be alive. And now the Jewish state has built a kind of prison where a million of the Jews who died wouldn't have been able to be buried here because their blood wasn't pure enough for our new breed of rabbis. Your blood isn't pure enough for them either, Yosef, and you'll be buried outside their fences too even if your mother was a Jewess, my daughter Hava, the loveliest daughter a man ever had. Franz was growing sentimental in his old age, I kissed him and left him with the soup Gertrude had made for him. The eternal beauty of music saved him. As long as we still have Haydn all is not lost, he said to me. Dead flies no longer float in Franz's soup bowl, the huge cypress trees are already so tall they touch his balcony, but Franz is no longer there to see them, or the sea through them. But he was there to see his grandson flee, his honour wounded. Azouri sewed the yellow star onto my jacket, he said and Gertrude said, eat, Franz, and Franz said, you remember that Chief of Staff, what lack of taste, his office was full of kitsch, all those awful pictures of tanks and aeroplanes in pastel colours, coffee table albums about wars on his shelves, and that secretary with her creased skirt, chewing gum. No aesthetic sense at all, he said, they could learn a thing or two from Azouri.

24

Parting from Azouri was very hard. He was afraid for me and I said, why did Käthe want her ashes scattered over Acre when she hated living in this country so much? And he said, you know the answers yourself, Yosef, or do you think you know them anyway. Put it out of your mind and forget. Look after yourself, Yosef.

And now I'm in Paris. A big, beautiful city in which I am a stranger. Every now and then I take a trip to Switzerland, to Italy or Belgium, I phone all the people I love, I stand for hours in public telephone boxes with fistfuls of foreign coins in my hands and I make phone calls. I talk to Azouri and to Gertrude who told me all about Franz's funeral, about the memorial evening they held for him at the hospital, about the article Moshe's son, whose father was already dead too, wrote about him in the newspaper, such a beautiful article, said Gertrude with astonishing sweetness for her, as if after Franz's death she needed to draw me closer to her. I talk to Dina, she is living alone now, she tells me that Rammy went to Europe to look for me and came back empty-handed. I know that Bunim knows where I am. I think about my peculiar relationship with Bunim, how it went so deep that in the end that battle-scarred old warhorse passed beyond his loathing of me and reached the point at which he had once lost his only son. He was no liberal like Nachie, who went to demonstrations and fought for co-existence and threw me out of his house in a rage when I came to console him for the loss of his son. Bunim doesn't give way to impulses, he's a man who calculates his every move. I know today that he never burnt me completely, he wanted me to come back and if I ever do go back he might even help me. But I won't go back, I'm not prepared to pay the price, because deep in my heart I don't believe that I committed a crime by going to Beirut, or anything else. But the law isn't interested in justice and injustice. The struggle continues and the end is not in sight. Azouri and Franz will go on killing each other for many years to come. Laila and Dina will be like guns with bayonets fixed, pointed at each other.

Dina is on her way to me now, this is the meeting I have hinted at, the meeting I am waiting for. She came to Europe on a trip, she looked for me and she managed to get on my track. She made contact and I told her to go to Geneva and wait. She's sitting in a hotel in Geneva now and waiting for me to arrive, or for me to tell her to come to me. She wants to see me, she wants to begin again and I don't know, I said to her on the phone, what do you want of me, Dina, and she said, I want the love you left behind in me. I said to her, I'm a dirty Arab, and she said, and I'm a bloody Jew. I said to her, the only good Arab is a dead Arab and she said, I need you, Yosef, I need your venom. My poems are dead inside me. Laila came to see me and we cried for you. I lay next to her in bed, her skin is so soft and prickly, we wanted to touch one another, not with passion, in the repose of the battle-weary, we lay and stroked one another the whole night long, and you were between us, Yosef, you were mine, and hers, and Azouri's, and Franz's and Hava's, and Laila said, for a Jewess you smell good, you belong to Yosef and he belongs to you, his real home is me but he wants to live in a hotel and the hotel is you.

My longings for them were terrible then, especially for Dina, my beloved, capricious Dina. Now I sit with my hand on the phone, my confession is over, Bunim is waiting for me, wondering what I'm going to say about him. If I go back they'll pretend they have never heard of me. Dina is sitting in a hotel, devils are climbing up the balcony walls. I yearn for her and her sad eyes. I'm thirty-two years old already, Dina is thirty. We're not children any more, I said to her over the phone. Should I phone her now? Should I take a plane and fly to Geneva and surprise her in the morning? And Bunim? Is he really waiting for me to come back? Will I ever go back? Nabil's bullet or Bunim's, which will get me first? Am I really so important to them? Perhaps it's all one big joke and I'm nothing but a historical mistake, a freak programmed for self-destruction, not even worth wasting the price of a single bullet on. And that's all there is to it. I was born divided and I'll die divided, and all that remains of the bridge Hava my mother on Azouri's side and Azouri my father on Hava's side tried to build is the scar left on Franz's heart when he was crucified by a mob of over-enthusiastic students fifty years ago in Berlin while the dean stood by helpless and was forced to dismiss him from his post.